Rosanafalls

Erica Rogulski

ISBN:979-8-218-78451-5

TO MY HOPELESS ROMANTICS:

DON'T SETTLE FOR ANYTHING LESS THAN THE WILDEST
FANTASIES YOUR HEART DESIRES.

Content Warning

To my hopeless romantics,

Your mental health matters. I ask that you read this novel cautiously regarding potential triggers. This novel contains sexually explicit scenes, sexual assault, violence, and mature language. This story may not be a fit for all readers.

Your Author,

Erica Rogulski

PLAYLIST

"Somone to stay"- Vancouver sleep clinic
"Dandelions"- Ruth B.
"Ocean Eyes"-Billie Eilish
"Tag, your it"-Melanie Martinez
"Wolves"-Selena Gomez, Marshmellow
"Into the Unknown"-Aurora
"Meet me in the woods"-Lord Huron
"RunRunRun"-Dutch Melrose
"Again-Noah Cyrus"- XXXTentacion
"Match Made in Hell"- Dutch Melrose, Benny Mayne
"Down the Rabbit Hole"-Kendra Dantes, Mystic Femmes
"Hoax"-Taylor Swift-Hoax (Zach's betrayal)
"Woman's World"- Little Mix
"Medusa"-Kailee Morgue
"Flowers in My Hair"-Wes Reeve
"Monster"-Willyecho
"Wolves"-Sam Tinnesz, Silverberg
"Petals and Thorns"-Austin Giorgio
"Princesses Don't Cry"-CARYS
"Love and War"-Fleurie
"Sunshine and Roses"-EllaHarp

CHAPTER ONE

A faint growl of thunder rattled the glass of the windows as streaks of lighting scattered across the sky. Erin enjoyed the sense of calm and clarity it brought. Her thoughts grew silent as she focused on how the lightning illuminated the darkness to reveal a violet sky. Each flash of lightning lit parts of her room. Then a loud thud smacked against the glass, along with a shudder of thunder that caused her muscles to tense as she rose from her bed.

She walked toward her sheer white curtains that clung against the window and brushed them aside, then examined the glass for damage. Water trickled down like veins as she observed a clear path toward the woods with zero evidence of anything lurking beneath the trees. Her heart rate slowed to its normal pace as she tiptoed back to her bed. Then a tapping noise resonated against the glass, echoing through the room. Feeling frustrated, she ran toward it and pulled it open. Before she could say anything, cold hands wrapped around her wrists.

In front of her stood a man with bright blond hair, an olive complexion, and muscles that revealed themselves through his soaked white shirt. His light blue eyes reminded her of the clear Bahama waters. "Zach!"

"I could have been someone dangerous," he warned while pulling his wet shirt off.

Erin forced her eyes up to the ceiling before he caught her staring. Then she realized she was only in a shirt and underwear and quickly grabbed soft pajama shorts from her drawers.

"If they're that dedicated to climbing up to my bedroom, then they are more than welcome to come right in."

"Don't say that!" he snapped. "I will admit, for someone who loves being scared, you do scare easily." He laughed, taking a step closer.

"Scary movies, stories, and Halloween events do pique my interest, yet I am vulnerable to fear," she said. She fell back as he closed in her space. He placed his hand on her cheek, causing warmth to surface through.

He locked eyes with hers. "I can't promise not to scare you, but I will never let anyone hurt you."

Her shoulders dropped. "I am glad that you're here. My parents aren't home, so I could use the company." He wrapped his arms around her while pulling her into him. The truth was she loved it when he came to see her because it cleared her mind of inside stressors. She remembered the first time they met, in a space filled with her favorite things—books.

#

The library became her hideout where she lost herself in the fantasy of stories. She remembered sipping on a hot chocolate while enjoying the hint of peppermint flavoring as she read a vampire romance. Zach walked over and sat down on the brown leather chair next to her and laughed at the cover. "Expectations are dangerous. They can cause a hunger for something that does not exist."

"Fantasy can be whatever it wants to be."

"Or you could recreate some of those fantasies." He winked.

She rolled her eyes. "Too bad Vampires and Werewolves don't exist."

"So, you read fantasy but couldn't imagine the possibility?" He smiled while tossing a bookmark onto her lap. It had wolves engraved on it with a silver moon and a stormy dark blue background.

Erin's face lit up, and she smiled. "I love wolves."

"Keep it," he said while remaining eye contact.

She noticed him showing up whenever she went to the library. As their conversations continued, they became close friends, and Erin began to open herself up to him. That was when her crush began, and after that, he never left her side.

#

He knew how to distract her from the loneliness that kept her awake each night. As they let go of each other, there was a moment when their eyes connected. Erin wanted to reveal her feelings because she had held them back for some time.

"Zach." He looked at her, and then both jumped as thunder rumbled, and lightning flashed through the curtains. The lights cut out, and darkness wrapped around their bodies like a blanket. "Let me go find some candles."

Using the walls to steady herself, she was careful not to hit her toes on any foreign objects. She reached for her eucalyptus candle and lighter beside her bed on the nightstand. Then she dragged her finger across the tip of the lighter and pressed down while hovering over the wick until it grew into a warming orange glow. She could already feel herself unwinding as the stress relief candle filled the room with mint, honey, and citrus.

Zach disappeared as she picked her phone up to reveal her flashlight. She pulled her small wolf throw from her bed and wrapped it around her body. The house was silent as she walked into the dark living room that lit up briefly from the flashes of lightning.

"Zach, where did you go?" she whispered. She walked through her kitchen while shining her light as her phone buzzed to reveal a low battery signal. "I thought I charged you?" The light turned off, and she stood in the darkness alone. The scene reminded her of a scary movie as she pictured a monster crawling towards her from the darkest parts of the room.

"This is how it ends," she chuckled.

A roar of thunder pounded through the house, causing her to shriek. Strong arms wrapped around her waist and lifted her from the floor. She immediately began to squirm and yell while Zach threw her onto the couch. "You're just too easy to scare," he teased, tickling her side.

"You're just a pain in the ass." She laughed. They both grew silent for a moment as she felt the warmth fill her body, thankful Zach couldn't see her red face.

"Erin," Zach said as the electricity jolted back on.

She wanted to know what he was about to say, but once the lights turned on, the mood between them shifted. She then realized he wasn't wet anymore, but instead, wore a loose grey shirt, and black sweatpants.

"Let me place your clothes in the dryer," she insisted.

He blocked her from moving with his hand. "I can manage that," he said while disappearing.

To bide time, she turned on the television to search for a horror film. Might as well have a fun night. Not like we're going to sleep anytime soon.

As he walked back into the room, he brought popcorn and drinks, as if he already knew the routine. She extended her legs onto his lap and covered them with a throw. They watched one of her favorite older classic movies, *A Nightmare on Elm Street*, which featured nightmares and claws. She felt at peace in his presence, like being next to a warm kindle of fire.

Her legs laid across his lap as he used his thumb to brush against her skin. Warmth filled her cheeks. She couldn't help but wonder if he noticed how much she wanted him to move his fingers closer to her thigh. If only he could read her mind, then she wouldn't be stuck in this internal loop of never moving forward from friends. Although each fiber in her body awakened just from his touch, it led to nothing further.

CHAPTER TWO

Erin's ears filled with the sound of flowing water. Upon opening her eyes, she realized she was standing on the edge of a waterfall. A rock slipped from underneath her feet, and she watched it tumble and splash into the deep blue pool below. A breeze carried in an earthy grass smell, along with the sweet perfume of honeysuckle. Despite her fear of heights, she felt unafraid as she lost her balance and then began to fall. She braced herself to hold her breath and accept the impact.

#

She jolted upright and gasped for air as her lungs reminded her to breathe. Pulling the covers off, she realized she was back in her room. Beside her bed was a rose gold watch and a note with the words Happy Birthday written on it. Sweet maple syrup and bacon filled her senses, escaping from underneath the cracks of her door. After grabbing some clothes, she tiptoed to the bathroom and indulged in a steamy shower.

Her long brown hair looked a mess as she brushed through it, inhaling the notes of a vanilla and almond mixture from her conditioner. While mindlessly working on her hair she thought of Zach. She had remembered last night and how he hadn't made a move on her, yet his eyes would tell a different story. After graduation for her eighteenth birthday dinner, she had worn a loose-fitted red dress that had stopped at her knees while pairing it with her favorite thigh-high boots to claim his attention. It worked in her favor as his eyes seemed to trail down her body while noticing her revealing cleavage. She was proud of her bra size; it was a bit over average as it filled into dresses.

But then he became overprotective instantly and wrapped his jacket over her arms to cover them up. "Let's not advertise to the perverts," he whispered. With that she rolled her eyes and obeyed. "The only perv is you." She wouldn't admit that his comment had hurt her feelings.

Snapping out of the memory she pulled a black dress over her head. It had soft cotton sleeves that flowed down her arms and cuffed against her wrists, the neckline curved just above her breasts, while the length was an inch above the knees.

In the mirror, she observed her blue-green eyes. They were calm blue and stood out with silver eyeshadow and black mascara. She held the small button down to turn her new watch on and smiled as she wrapped it around her wrist. When she entered the kitchen Zack was there dancing with headphones in his ears and swishing a skillet in one hand.

She tiptoed behind him and tapped lightly on his shoulder. He jumped and pulled out his headphones. "You can't be creeping up on the cook like that."

She raised her eyebrows and smiled, "Don't let the music distract you."

Zach smirked and shrugged his shoulders and turned back around to place the pan on the stovetop. He served her favorite blueberry pancakes along with a side of bacon.

She caught a glimpse of his baby blues as heat flushed through her body. "Thanks."

He nodded while chewing on a piece of bacon as he sat down in front of her.

His brows furrowed.

"Where are your parents this time?"

Her chest caved as her shoulders dropped. "I don't know. It doesn't feel like I know them at all; they haven't been around." She felt a sharp pain in her chest, but when she noticed Zack's sad eyes, it hurt her more. Once she finished her plate, she stood up and walked to the kitchen window to brush the curtains to the side and allow sunlight to fill their space.

She wanted to tell him the truth, that she never felt connected to her family. At times she fantasized about being a child who was loved by her parents. She could imagine everyone gathering for holidays and adventuring on family vacations. The isolating feeling of being alone caused her house to never feel like home. It gnawed at her when her friends complained about family nights. She couldn't remember the last time her family had even watched a movie together.

Then there was a fear of hidden truths in her home. She couldn't remember much of her memories and Zach filled most of them. She had been afraid to bring it up to her father. Although even if she had wanted to, he was never home. And when he was it would only be brief to replenish what she had used, such as toiletry, food, and soaps. He left her a credit card for necessities and provided her with a driver. He provided her with means to survive, but that wasn't enough.

She fought back the tears that wanted to escape from her eyes and directed her focus onto Zach. His gentle gaze conveyed empathy. She felt lost at sea from the comfort of his deep blue eyes. She enjoyed staring back at them, as they made her feel safe.

"I'll be okay. This happens often."

His eyes quickly changed from empathetic to anger. Then they darkened.

He pushed himself from his chair and stood up. "I will be right back."

Then he disappeared out the front door while causing her tears to fall. Inhaling a gasp of air, she sank to the floor. She could not imagine why he was frustrated. He knew her situation, and there was no way of changing it.

Time passed until she heard a car door slam as she lifted back onto her feet. Looking outside the window there was a shiny black sports car in the driveway. It appeared to be an older model Mustang. The dark windows were tinted while making it harder to see inside.

As she stepped outside, she felt the whip of a cold breeze along with light raindrops that brushed against her skin. She wrapped her arms around herself to calm her shivers.

Is it a friend of my parents?

She stepped onto the sharp pavement, jumped over a puddle and found her way towards the car. There was a loud shuffle from behind, and before she could turn around in time, someone forced her mouth shut with a hand, and she was pulled back into a firm surface. She tried to bite the hand and wiggle free, but dizziness and fear caused her to pass out.

#

Her nostrils filled with a mixture of metal and oil, reminding her of a car garage. The cement was hard and cold, and her body felt bruised from the pain of lying on it for what felt like hours. She attempted to move until she quickly became aware of the chains that bound her wrists and legs. A lump formed in her throat. She wanted to scream yet was unsure if that would help or hurt.

The sounds of footsteps alerted her senses as she tried to stay calm.

"Erin," whispered a voice. She felt calmer knowing it was Zach's.

"Over here!"

There was a pull on the chains and then a sound of metal snapping apart.

"You came prepared." She teased while fully knowing it truly wasn't the time for jokes.

"You better stay quiet before we are unable to escape," he whispered.

She directed her eyes at the phone light flashing down at her and could see Zach's flushed face. He wiped the beads of sweat from his forehead. She hugged him tightly as tears poured from her eyes.

"How did you find me?"

He brushed his hand through his hair, "Remember that watch I gifted you?"

She glanced down at her electrical watch, which had a rotation of diamonds around the center.

"It's connected to my phone so that I would know your location for emergency purposes." He looked a bit embarrassed as he shifted his gaze from her.

Irritation arose as she realized that he had invaded her privacy. She couldn't be upset about his overprotectiveness as it just saved her life. "We're going to have to talk about that later, but for now let's get out of this place."

He nodded in agreement and grabbed her hand as she observed the room she had been captured in.

Computer equipment was set up along a marbled countertop, accompanied by multiple towers with blue and green lights. The remaining space was filled with car equipment, tools and an assortment of knives hanging on the walls. As they approached the door, Zack touched the door handle but hesitated at the sound of footsteps. "We need to hide!" With limited options, they improvised and hid behind a motorcycle stashed in the corner.

A door slammed shut as fluorescent white lights brightened the room. A man with a black hood over his face and a wide build entered. His eyes were dark, with a shadow of a beard surrounding his face. Reasons for why this man wanted to kidnap her replayed in her mind. She wanted to stray away from the reality that it was related to sex trafficking.

She had watched the news and television shows of girls being kidnapped from their homes, or when walking alone. She couldn't imagine being held from creating new memories with Zach or finding out more about herself.

Her captor turned on the computers as Erin witnessed a surveillance camera in the top corner of the room. It pointed directly at her location. Her fear amplified at the realization of being caught.

You might as well come out," he said.

Erin began to shake uncontrollably. She had never been in this predicament before as she hid behind Zach.

He leaned down next to her ear, "Everything will be alright, just follow my lead." He stood up tall and stretched his arms out to block her body from the man.

"Just let us go and nobody gets hurt."

The guy smirked as the dimples on his cheeks appeared. "I just need the girl, and you can be on your way."

Erin's body tensed as she felt a rush of panic.

"That's not happening!"

Zack turned around, grabbed Erin's hand and attempted to rush her out the nearest door.

"You would find it smart to listen, kid," The man growled. He puffed out his chest and groaned in aggravation. Then he began to stomp his way towards the two.

Anger flushed through Erin's body as she felt pure hatred towards this man. She never had seen his face before, and she wanted to know his reasoning behind the kidnapping.

"What do you want from me?

He stopped and forced his hands out to the side, "You do not belong here."

She furrowed her brows in confusion as the anger settled, and the fear kicked back in. "What do you mean?"

Before the man could say another word, Zack swung his arm while punching him in the face and pushing him onto the ground.

Zach turned back to her, "Run!"

Her stomach twisted into knots as the man jumped back up while slamming his fist into Zach's stomach.

"No!" she screamed. She looked around for a weapon and found an old tire axle, then proceeded toward the man. While swinging her arm back, she slammed it into the back of his legs. He grunted from the pain and turned around quickly while shoving her down.

He straddled her with his legs while forcing her arms above her head so that she couldn't move. "Let. Me. Go!" she screamed.

"I need you to listen to me and stop struggling," he said while inching close to her face. The lights shut off as she gained an advantage while pushing the man from her body and rolling over. She pushed herself up off the floor while backing into a warm surface, and then an arm pulled her back.

"Let's get out of here," Zach whispered.

She knew that they had a small window of time as she allowed Zach to pull her in the direction towards freedom. Her heart felt like it was beating out of her chest as a tightening pain wrapped around the middle of her sternum. She repeatedly chanted to herself, "It will be okay, I will be okay, we will fight our way through this." I will not be trapped.

She didn't waste time finding out as she continued to run past the grey halls and black doors. A rush of relief spread over her body as they approached a door with light that escaped from underneath the cracks.

Zach burst out of it and pulled her through to the other side. Cold wet raindrops landed on their faces as they splashed through a mixture of water and mud puddles. Erin couldn't feel her legs or even the grip of Zach's hand, but she could feel every beat of her heart.

CHAPTER THREE

The moisture in the air thickened while the sky darkened. As Erin and Zach slowed down to catch their breath, they leaned against the trees for support. Erin felt nauseous as she slid to the ground and wrapped her arms around her knees.

Zach sat down next to her while placing his arm around her shoulders and pulled her into his chest, "Are you okay?"

She nodded while holding back more tears from the chaotic events they just endured.

She wanted to rewind time, but she knew time went backward in memories alone. A slight chill from the air brushed upon her skin, causing her to shiver. There was an echo of wolves howling through the woods and insects chirping. She felt overstimulated by the loud thoughts in her head that she could not calm down.

"So, what's our next move?"

"I suppose we rest and find our way out of the woods in the morning."

"What if that man—"

"I won't allow him to harm you."

Too exhausted to argue, she helped him gather branches together as he began a small fire. As she lay on his chest, he pulled an arm around her and gently rubbed his fingers across her back. She dozed off to the soft pounding of his heart.

#

The mist of a cool breeze jolted Erin awake as she opened her eyes to the sight of smoke from the burned-out fire. She lifted herself on her elbows and realized that Zach was gone. She screamed his name, but all she heard was the echo of her voice fading through the woods. Now what am I going to do? she thought, trying to control her rising fear.

Walking ahead, she increased her pace as she searched for a path out of the woods. The forest used to be a means of escape, as she would go on walks, taking in the scent of pine and exploring the mushrooms that grew all around. It was one of her favorite places to explore when she was younger.

She didn't realize that there would come a time when she would feel trapped here. Her calves began to sting with pain from walking as she finally spotted a stream of water. There was a path downward that led to a mound of stone walls revealing a cave. Its dark gaping hole caused her skin to crawl as she imagined the creatures living inside. But there was also a sense of mystery of the unknown that tugged on her curious mind.

She entered the cave, and the light grew dimmer the farther she walked. As the atmosphere began to change, she hugged herself from the chill in the air. She continued to walk through as she heard sounds of running water and spotted visible light. Placing her hands underneath the falling water, she stepped closer. The fall was not too high as she spotted the plunge pool a few feet below.

She thought about turning around to find Zach. She knew that he may head back to the spot they had been. But she wanted to know what was on the other side of the cave. She desired to explore the waterfall.

She decided not to think too much about it. Holding her breath, she jumped into the frosty water. Her feet dived straight down as the world grew silent, and she slipped underneath the barrier. The pressure forced her back up to the surface as she wiped her eyes clear. She embraced the beautiful waterfall in front of her and floated on her back, enjoying how weightless she felt. It reminded her of days at the beach, relaxing in the calm waters of the ocean. She could swim there forever when the currents and waves were calm.

What a lucky day to come across this beauty, she thought while staring at the water trickling down the rocks.

"You're breathtaking," someone said from across the way.

She looked up and noticed a man on top of the rock on higher level ground. It startled her as she sank into the water while slowly kicking her feet and swaying her arms toward the wall. He was around her age and was alarmingly handsome, unlike anything she had ever seen. He seemed familiar.

His hair was dark and slightly messy as if he had tossed a hand through it, and his eyes reminded her of a sunset on a desert. He wore a black leather jacket with white underneath and black pants to match. The word dangerous rolled off the tip of her mind as she observed him. She knew he could see the fear in her eyes as he knelt and extended his arm. "Let me help you out of there."

I should not trust him. But why does it feel like I can? She swam up closer to him and placed her hand into his. As he assisted her out of the water, she could see the freckles that spread across his cheeks and nose. He smelled like eucalyptus, fresh mint leaves, and a hint of lemon. "Sin," he said while captivating her with his eyes.

"Huh?" she said.

He smiled, revealing the cutest smirk as his eyes darkened. "My name."

She had never known a man with that name. His gaze did not falter, and he stared down at her as if he had known her for years. "I feel like I know you from somewhere," Sin said with a look of confusion in his eyes.

"I would certainly remember you if we had met before," she blurted out.

He giggled at the comment as his eyes lit up, and she swore she could see them sparkle. "My name is Erin, and we have certainly not met." She stretched her hand out to him.

"Right," he said. She could tell that he was not convinced. He grasped her hand and began to pull her away from the waterfall and towards a trail path. "Let's get you some clean clothing and something to eat."

"I can't. I need to find my friend." She stopped and pulled her hand from his.

"It is dangerous to be out here alone." "You will run out of energy and could catch a cold if you don't rest."

He wasn't wrong, but could she trust this stranger? "Fine, you win, but I better not find out you're some psycho."

"Afraid to trust the big bad wolf?" he said while grasping her arms and pulling her toward him.

"I know nothing about you, of course I am." She jerked herself from his hold.

She needed a plan. She was not being as cautious as she should, but she did not want to find out what could be lurking in the forest when the sun set. She needed to be smart about her motives and right now basic survival needs were a priority. She followed behind his footsteps through the trail while trying not to imagine the worst possibilities. Of course, I am the girl to find my way into a dangerous situation when I finally venture out alone. Genius plan, Erin.

The sky was dull gray as if it were going to rain, and the trees surrounding them were dark and twisted. She could feel a storm brewing. The air felt moist, and the earth fell silent.

I wonder if Zach's, okay?

She started to miss his presence and realized how much she had depended on him.

Although, she learned at an early age that she could only count on herself. Never let someone else become your crutch, words she lived by without realizing that love would change them someday.

"Welcome home," Sin said with his arms stretched out at the large mansion before them. She locked her eyes on two wolf statues on both sides of the threatening twelve-foot gate. Thick green thorns wrapped around the iron poles as they contorted their stems around it like it was their life source.

He pressed the gates open and then walked through them while she stood there in awe. Uneasiness swept into her stomach, but she felt that she would stick to her decision in following him.

CHAPTER FOUR

Erin's gaze shifted toward a three-tier fountain. At the top stood a large silver wolf as another wolf descended, their paws in the water of each tier. The water was clear, and at the foot of the fountain were red roses and vines wrapped around the support system. Sin flexed his arm out and insisted on walking her up the stairs. She hesitated but decided to place her hand into his.

He pulled the door open, and she took the first step inside. The lights were bright, unlike the dark twisting appearance from outside. A warm and safe feeling embraced her as she inhaled the smell of cranberry spice in the air. The room was large and surrounded by antique paintings on the walls along with statues of wolves on the sides of the stairs.

Beneath her feet was a cherry-red oak floor that was sleek and shined as though dirt had never touched it. "Let me show you to the master restroom," Sin said and tugged at her hand. Erin nodded as she walked down the hallway and observed the gold-painted walls with abstract artwork of mythological creatures placed upon them.

He opened the door that led to an extravagant restroom. It had marble floors, a counter that wrapped around the room on each side of the sinks, white vintage leather sofas, and a huge bath filled with water as steam rolled from the surface. The light above them illuminated the room with a warm glow, and the mirrors were equipped with LED lights. Erin turned to look at Sin as he smiled brightly back at her. "Take this." He handed her a long black button-up shirt that was long enough to wear as a dress.

"I'll wash your clothes, but I don't have any women's clothing. You can find everything you need in the drawers. After you're finished, a meal will be set up in your room just across from here," he said and pointed. "I'll meet you in the morning, and we can discuss what comes next." He spoke calmly and carefully, as though he were trying not to scare away a vulnerable rabbit.

"Okay, thank you," she said as she grabbed the shirt from him. He nodded and slowly shut the doors behind him. She walked over to the beige counters and searched through the drawers, finding all the supplies she needed for her shower and oral care.

If she relaxed in the bath, she might fall asleep, and the thought of Sin walking in on her caused her cheeks to flush. The warmth from the shower enveloped her skin as she massaged minty shampoo into her hair and scalp. Despite this, she wasn't going to overstay her welcome and planned to leave in the morning. She was unsettled by Sin's comment about "what comes next."

After she finished her shower, she noticed that her clothes and shoes were missing, and a pair of black slippers had been left in their place. He better not have been peeking at me. When she put on his shirt, it fell like a dress and smelled of sandalwood and clean cotton. She put on the slippers, wondering how he knew her size, and then ran outside the bathroom.

Then she bumped into a hard surface and looked up. Sin's mouth twisted into a smile.

She locked onto his eyes, "Were you watching me?"

He stood up straight, seeming surprised. "I sent one of my female maids in to gather your clothes to be washed. I'm sorry if I startled you."

Her cheeks flushed.

"Now run along to your room, I know you must be exhausted," he said while pushing her lightly toward the door.

As she walked into her room, she kicked her slippers off to feel the soft fur of the red-carpet. In the middle of the room, there lay a king-sized mattress with gold, red, and cream-colored pillows, and a matching comforter set. The room smelled of floral perfume, and the walls were painted with roses all around. Just like the rest of the house, artwork covered the wall, some featuring blue and red birds, and others depicting humans and creatures. Erin turned off the lights and slid under the covers, knowing it wouldn't be long before she fell into a deep sleep.

#

Erin awoke to the sounds of a blue, sharp-beaked bird whistling from her bedroom window. It observed the room and chirped beautifully as though it had a message for her alone. She was intrigued by the unique patterns that were collaged on its back, like a shining diamond with reflective colors as the light hit it from different angles.

Pulling the soft comforter off her body, she got out of bed and then noticed her clothes beside her on the nightstand. As she put them on, she decided to wear Sin's shirt over the dress in case it was cold.

A knock at the door alerted her. "Come in," she said. The door slowly opened as Sin appeared before her wearing a dark-green silky button-down shirt and black pants. His hair was styled with a slightly messy look, and his eyes appeared darker than before, which made her knees feel weak.

"My shirt looks good on you. Keep it." He winked.

"Okay, sure," she said nervously.

Sin walked toward her, then gently took a hold of her right hand and kissed it. "My pleasure." The warmth from his lips sent a shock straight through her body as she reclaimed her hand. "Now meet me in the dining room for breakfast, and we shall discuss finding your friend."

Erin nodded as she quickly left the room and went to the bathroom across the way. She looked at herself in the mirror and took a deep breath. Everything will be just fine. You will find Zach, and life will go back to normal. Now that she was able to live on her own, she would need to go to college and find a job. It wouldn't be any different from how she was already living. Just before she left the bathroom, she noticed an old stuffed wolf that was black with glossy emerald eyes.

As she picked it up, she felt a slight attachment to the object. Then her brain revealed a flashback.

"If you're ever feeling scared, just hug on tight. It has helped me through some tough times," said a little boy with tousled dark hair and sunset-colored eyes. He resembled Sin.

I've never had this memory before. The animal felt like something she had missed for so long that she almost didn't want to set it back down.

It felt like a security blanket, and she decided to hold on to it and ask Sin about it. She swung the door open, and he appeared.

"I was getting a little worried. Just checking on you."

Erin felt wary that he was at the bathroom door just as she walked out. His attention focused on the wolf she held.

"Oh, you found my old wolf."

"Can I hold onto it?"

There was a softness in his eyes. "Yes, he's all yours."

She smiled and pressed it safely against her chest. Once in the dining room, Erin's eyes grew wide while taking in the large wooden table with all kinds of food decoratively laid out for them to feast on. "You eat like this every day?"

"Only when I have company to impress."

After breakfast she was ready to leave and search for Zach. An alarming amount of time had passed, and she began to feel guilty.

"I am grateful for your hospitality, but I need to find my friend." As she stood, she noticed a twitch in his jawline and a flicker of irritation in his eyes.

"Don't worry, guards are looking for your friend. I don't want you to further entangle yourself into those woods." She understood his caution, but she almost felt as though he didn't want her to leave. A scary thought trickled through her mind: What if I can't escape?

She didn't just trust that Zach would be found; she wanted to go look for him herself. But if she said she wanted to leave again, he might complicate things. She heard footsteps from behind her as a handsome man with long black hair appeared. He looked to be in his early twenties, wearing white pants and a navy-blue button-down shirt. His eyes were a mustard color, like golden halos, and his skin a darker shade of tan. His features were delicate and softer than

Sin's. His face lit up, and his lips curved into a smile as he noticed Erin's eyes on him.

"This is Sylvian, my close friend."

"Nice to meet you. I'm Erin." She glanced at Sin and noticed he was smirking.

"What brings you to this side of town?"

"Honestly, I'm lost and need to find my friend so we can return home and report the person who kidnapped me."

Her heart sank to the floor. She felt like an idiot for revealing so much information.

Sin immediately looked at Sylvian with a worried expression, like he was sending silent signals. Good luck leaving now.

"I would advise that you stay here with us," Sin said while pushing himself from the table to match Erin's stance.

"Well, I'm going to go to the ladies' room, and maybe we can find him together." She walked the other way without waiting for an answer.

Instead of the bathroom, she snuck into her room while remembering the bird on the open windowsill. Luckily, the drop was not far down, and if this was the only way then so be it.

CHAPTER FIVE

"Time to escape," Erin whispered to herself. She walked over to the window in her room and pulled back the dark-red curtains. She looked out the window and observed the glow of the sun upon the dandelions and soft-green grass. Luckily, she was on the first floor and would only have to jump a few feet. She unlatched the lock on the window and lifted it open.

Slowly, she put one leg over the ledge and balanced her body while throwing the other leg over. She looked down with a little pit in her stomach for the fear of heights while concentrating on landing on her feet.

She pushed her bottom off the ledge and fell, immediately crashing and rolling into the dandelions. Laughing at herself, she picked one and blew its petals into the air along with a wish. Then she felt eyes burning onto her back as she peered up at the window and witnessed Sin staring directly down at her.

Dammit, she thought as she ran through the grass and into the woods. She had to be careful not to roll her ankle as she ventured into the forest. Then, like before, a memory surfaced.

#

"Alright, it's time to bunker down and fire when I say so," Erin said, directing her team of girls. At age ten, Mary, Jenny, and Sam were ready and prepared to win against the boys on the other side of the fort. They all giggled as they grabbed a pile of pinecones while laughing at poor little Sam who could hold only a few. Erin noticed a little piece of white cloth waving in the air on the other side of their fort.

"Wait, hold your fire. It looks like the boys might have given up already."

Hmm, I don't know. Not sure if I trust them.

It was too late as Sam ran out as soon as she had spotted the cloth. "No!" She tried to grab her shirt, but she escaped too soon. "Ha-ha, you boys knew you were no competition for us." Sam laughed.

Then, behind the fort, there was loud laughter from eleven-year-old Zack. "Fire," Zack yelled as they threw their pinecones. Erin quickly ran in front of

Sam while taking on the damage from the attack.

"Sam, run back to the site," Erin said. Sam listened to her as Erin began after her toward the base. Before she could continue, someone grabbed her by the waist and pulled her back. Erin struggled but was no match for his strength. "Hey, get off me. Put me down," she yelled.

The boys looked at Zack like he was a madman at first until they realized why he did it. "Good job. They're nothing without their leader." Larry high-fived Zach.

"Cheater," Erin yelled, pushing him to the ground as they started to fight. When they stopped, Erin pushed herself from the ground, but Zach held her and leaned toward her ear. "You're not hurt, are you?"

Erin rolled her eyes and pushed him from her. "Just my ego. I'll be fine."

#

Erin forced herself to reality as her energy waned. She leaned against a tree for support and slowed down her breathing. Wait, why are these memories suddenly appearing? It was strange, as she had no recollection of these memories before. She wondered if she should retrace her steps back to the waterfall she had come through just the other day.

She walked through the forest while noticing the contorted and twisted oak trees. Bright green leaves wrapped around them as white mushrooms grew from the side.

She yelled out, "Zach."

Only the forest answered her as the wind blew the leaves on the trees through the air. It was a calming sound, the brush of leaves falling from the trees as each footstep crunched them into tiny pieces. Locating a stream of water, she sped up the pace to follow it.

The sound of trickling water rolled gracefully from the rocks. A floral rose smell flooded through the air with its sweet aroma as rose petals fell into the pool of water. She felt as if she belonged there and had been to this place in her dreams. While running toward the fall, she felt a thorn bush catch her by the leg and tear through her skin. "Ouch," she yelled.

She slipped her legs into the water to wash the blood away. The water was a shocking cold as the wound burned for a couple of seconds and then the pain lifted. Once she pulled her legs out of the water, she noticed that the cut had disappeared.

How did that happen? Then she became dizzy as the aroma of floral perfume grew stronger, and she fell headfirst toward the water and into a deep sleep.

#

The warmth from the forest integrated through the air with trails of smoke. Screams echoed through the trees. It was as though she were watching a movie before her eyes. A woman appeared in distress running towards Erin. The woman tripped over a stump while attempting to place her hands and arms in front of her to catch her fall as she slid across the leaves and dirt. In front of her body lay a leather brown book. Erin observed her curly dark-brown hair, dark-brown skin, and long white gown.

She studied the woman's appearance while noticing a slash of crimson blood covering the front of her dress. The woman slowly crawled toward the book and flipped it open. She repeated unrecognizable words. Then she grew silent as her eyes fixed on the waterfall. Her jaw dropped as her body collapsed onto the ground.

Erin gasped, "She's dead.

"Galena." A voice trailed from behind.

Erin turned around to catch the same dark green eyes from the woman that had just fallen to her death seconds ago. Her world grew fuzzy with darkness as it began to fade.

#

Erin awoke and found Sin hovering over her body. She tried to push herself up, but he placed a hand on her chest before she could move. "Why do you want to run from me, little jackrabbit?" he asked.

Erin caught herself lost in his eyes once again, adoring how his skin seemed to glow and illuminate his dark eyes. "For starters, I am not an animal," she said while pushing him back.

"You crawled into my home while needing to be taken care of. You are my little jackrabbit." Sin smiled. "It would be nice if you treated me with the same kindness."

"I am not your anything. You offered to help me. I wasn't signing over my life."

"Whether you like it or not, you are mine, and you will not escape me this time." He lunged toward her, but she dodged his arms and began to run as fast as she could.

"I will not become his pet. I am certainly not going to be contained and told that I am his property to own." "This little jackrabbit as he calls me will slip through the openings because I need to be free"

She hid behind a tree as crunching leaves sounded through the air. Then she spotted a squirrel scurrying up a tree as it snatched an acorn. She smiled at the creature's mindlessness. Unfortunately, she saw all too well how many birds claimed it as prey. Was that what she was right now? Prey being stalked and hunted? She lifted her feet from the ground once again, but this time was yanked back by the collar of Sin's shirt she had still worn.

She attempted to pull forward as her wrists were locked behind her back from Sylvian's grip. "Just let me go," she pleaded, but he tightened his hold and pulled her back into him.

"I'm sorry, Erin. Just following orders."

There was a sharp stab on her shoulder. "Ouch." A wave of dizziness crashed over her as she collapsed into Sylvian's arms.

CHAPTER SIX

The sounds of crackling firewood and the smell of smoke filled the air. Erin realized she was back in the king-sized bed at Sin's mansion, and that her wrists and ankles were bound to it. She felt stupid for trusting Sin. Of course he would trap her, especially knowing someone else was after her. He probably does not want me to figure that out.

The door flung open, and Sin paced in with closed fists and furrowed brows. Why is he doing this? She drew in a steady breath, but her body continued to shake uncontrollably. "What do you want from me? He slowly walked toward her, then grabbed underneath her chin, forcing her to look up at him.

His jaw twitched as he locked eyes with her. Her pulse fluttered like the wings of a hummingbird. "It's you that I want, and if you ever pull a move like that again, I will never allow even the rays of the sun to touch you.

She stiffened and then moved her chin away. "Please let me go. You don't want me!"

He flashed his eyes away from her for a brief second. "Sleep tight," he whispered in her ear while throwing a blanket on top of her. Her body relaxed in defeat, and she flinched as he left her alone with her thoughts.

Damn. This was the second time she had been kidnapped and tied up. She had never thought something like this could happen to her. She blamed herself for not being strong enough. This is ridiculous, she thought while trying to figure a way out of the contraption.

Then she noticed that the fabric locked around her ankles was shiny and soft like a ribbon. Ribbon can be pulled apart, tethered, or burned. She then decided to roll from the bed and next to the fire. It wouldn't be an easy task, but she had to try something. Please let this work. She wrapped herself securely around the blanket and rolled from the bed, hoping the noise wouldn't alert anyone.

Once she had rolled her body close enough to the fire, she positioned her back toward it while pushing her wrists slightly back. Before she thrust her arms into the fire, she noticed an iron fire poker hanging down on a hook next to the fireplace. *I like the odds of that idea better.*

Then she scooted closer. Luckily, it was low enough for her to sit up and place it between the ribbon on her wrists. She carefully pulled her wrists down against the hook until the ribbon tore.

Feeling relieved, she pulled the ribbon off her ankles and stood up. Sin hadn't tied her up too tightly, but she could still feel a slight pressure from where the ribbon lay taunt against her skin. She tiptoed to the window and realized it was bolted shut, so there was no way she was getting out that way. Then she remembered the bird. "I wish I were on the other side of the window with you, little friend." she whispered.

Noticing a closet next to the fireplace, she opened the door. It was dark as she felt around the walls for a light switch. "Ouch," she said as she hit her knee on a hard surface and caught her balance before falling. *What is this?* She knelt to examine the object.

Running her hand across the top of the leather surface, she felt for a latch to open it. It pulled open as bright lights spilled out and revealed what was inside. It was cluttered with clothing and paper, but a dagger caught her eye. She gazed at its beauty. The handle contained a wooden material that was olive green and three dimensional. It looked as though it was wrapped with vines to create a sturdy grip.

The tip of the blade was a burgundy color that faded into silver. Underneath it was a leather holder that contained a strap with a belt buckle. She carefully placed the weapon in the holder and wrapped it around her leg, as the dress she wore covered it.

Looking around the room, she realized that it was empty—just a dead end. She straightened her spine. *This time instead of running and hiding, I fight.* She turned back around to the doorknob and slowly pulled it open while looking around the corner. Shaking her head from side to side and rolling her eyes, "Bolt the window shut, yet not lock the door?"

The hallway was dark, and she wondered if she would run into his staff if not careful. Sneaking around brought back memories of childhood when she would stay up late watching her favorite shows. Her stomach twisted in knots as she felt a rush of excitement from disobeying Sin.

The sound of footsteps from the hall alerted her as she shifted toward a spiral staircase and began to walk down them. The stairs narrowed toward the end and led to a cellar-like room. She pulled the dagger out its case, then jammed it into the side of the door while shifting it up and down.

A hand grasped the back of her neck and pulled her back. "My naughty little jackrabbit, always on the run," Sin whispered. He held her up against him firmly as she tried to wiggle free. She tightened the hold on the dagger and shifted her body to attack.

A crash and loud thud distracted Sin. She took the opportunity to jam the dagger into his leg while pulling it out as he dropped his hold on her. "Shit," he wailed.

Turning around, she stared at him in panic, his blood dripping from the dagger in her hand. "I am not yours to keep. I decide that for myself!"

He chuckled while placing a hand onto his wound. Sweat began to bead on the top of his forehead as the warm glow from his brown eyes captured her attention.

"I will never let you go. You are mine."

She struggled to move from her position. His words made her feel. Wanted.

He grabbed both of her wrists while thrusting her up against the cold metal door as the dagger fell to the floor.

One thing she didn't anticipate was how wet she felt, how turned on and playful. She tried to contain her smile, but it twisted upward without hesitation. She could tell that he had seen right through her act, the one that wasn't fooling anyone. She yearned for this, but she feared this feeling and decided to abandon it. He slowly grasped her throat and smiled.

"I've waited patiently for you, wondering if you would ever return. I never imagined that I would find you floating underneath the falls while looking like an Angel. All I could think about was taking you right there," he whispered while thrusting her head against the wall.

"But you didn't remember me, and that stung a little, and I figured it would take some time to refresh your memory."

What is he rambling about? As he loosened his grip on her and pulled back, the warmth she felt turned cold, and her body began to miss it. "What do you mean?"

He grasped her face and gently fell forward against her body. "I've known you since we were kids." Her eyes widened because she never recalled those memories, yet she remembered the wolf.

CHAPTER SEVEN

Erin gasped as a force ripped Sin from her vision. She raised her head and found her best friend standing in front of her and Sin lying on the ground next to him. Zach's deep baby-blue eyes flashed with anger, but then he lifted his shirt to wipe the sweat from his forehead. She felt paralyzed as he held her gaze.

"Tell me, did he touch you?"

She was pissed, but she did not want to cause trouble. "No, let's just go."

He raised a brow at her. "Maybe you didn't need saving." He laughed while grabbing the weapon from the floor and wiping the blood onto his pants.

"Wait, how did you know I was here?"

"Oh, you know, just had a hunch." He softened his stance and scratched the back of his neck, a nervous tick of his.

"Nice to see you, brother," Sin said, trying to stand. Zach's body stiffened but he remained silent as he took hold of Erin's hand and led her up the staircase.

"Wait, you poisoned me," he cried.

Erin turned her head back at Sin as her eyebrows pinched together. "How?"

He collapsed onto the ground as guilt worked its way through her stomach into a bald knot. I didn't mean to poison him. Was it the dagger? She examined the bright green color on the tip of the blade. It had been burgundy, why is it this color? She felt a pull, like a pulse of energy within herself as she desired to help him. Sylvian stood at the top of the stairs with his arms folded, blocking their path.

"Erin, if you leave, then he will die. I can't allow that to happen, as much of a pain in the ass he can be," Sylvian said.

Zach stepped up towards Sylvian while glaring at him. He straightened his body and pushed his chest out. "Don't worry about him. I can get past this pretty boy."

Sin was quiet, and she instantly knew what she had to do. He was covered in sweat, becoming pale, and her heart couldn't allow him to die there.

She turned away from Zach and knelt in front of Sin. "Why couldn't you have just left me alone?"

His eyes sparked like the red cherries from a flame, "I will not lose you again."

She closed her eyes and tried to connect with the vibrations inside of her body. It was a feeling she had never felt before—power. She turned to Sylvian who was now sitting on his knees beside her. "What should I do?"

"You have to extract the poison from his system."

She remembered learning about first kisses from one of her friends. "It's not something you learn. You instinctively know how to do it as you open yourself up to the other person." Closing her eyes, she leaned down and placed her lips on Sin's, imagining the toxins transferring from his body and into her own. She had to mix her saliva with his so that her healing properties would work.

Luckily, he had enough energy to kiss her back, rolling his tongue around with hers. Feeling nauseous and weak, she lay her head on Sin's chest and drifted into a deep sleep.

#

Erin awoke to the sounds of voices bickering. "You're such an idiot. If you hadn't pulled that stunt, she wouldn't have been in this situation to begin with," Zach yelled.

She wiped her eyes and observed Zach and Sin arguing in another room.

Sin's arms flared out to the side as he motioned his palms upward when speaking.

Zach leaned against a counter with his arms crossed.

Sin's tone was sharp and accusatory.

"I found her playing in the water by the fall while alone. I saved her from danger." "Where were you?"

Zach's shoulders rounded forward as he dropped his head down.

"I wouldn't have let anything happen to her."

"How can you be sure of that?" Sin asked.

Zach's eyes flashed upwards as he straightened his stance. "Her protection should not concern you, Sin. "I need you to stay the fuck away from her. She's already been here long enough."

What are they talking about? Her mouth felt cotton dry as she lifted her body from the leather couch. Once her dizziness calmed, she gravitated toward the voices.

Her movement was interrupted by a dark shadow. Sylvain stepped in the way as his long dark-brown hair hid part of his yellow eyes. He smelled like bergamot and citrus. "Are you prepared to be ripped apart like the end of a frayed ribbon?"

Erin took a step back and watched as his expression revealed his seriousness.

"Is that a threat?"

He pushed off from the wall and closed into her space, then stopped at her shoulder. "Just a warning. Those two men are beasts who lack control, and you are nothing but a beautiful temptation. Your innocence will be shattered if you are not careful."

Erin grasped his shoulder before he could walk past her. "You're quick to judge the outer shell of someone's appearance before cracking the code behind what's inside. I am not the delicate butterfly you picture me to be. I have been through quite a lot, and I can hold my own."

With those words he backed off while flashing a smile.

CHAPTER EIGHT

Zach stood over the stovetop whisking a skillet in one hand and turning his head briefly towards Sin while conversating. The thought of these two growing up together tickled her insides as she giggled. It made her a little sad, thinking about why he never shared the fact that he had a brother. They stopped talking as their attention gravitated toward her.

"I need some answers," she demanded.

Zach led her to a chair. "Sit here, and I will bring something to you."

Zach brought over a glass of ice water and orange juice and placed it in front of her, as well as a plate of eggs, toast, and mixed fruit. He had taken care of her despite her parents never being around.

"Thanks, Zach."

He grasped her chin and raised her head upward toward him. "Listen, don't ever do that to me again."

She felt just like a kid, in trouble, but instead of her parents, it was the man that stroke a pin in the deepest parts of her chest.

He applied slight pressure. "Promise." She nodded up and down as her cheeks burned with fury and Sin cleared his throat.

Once satisfied, Zach let go of her face and walked over to Sin. Sylvian appeared around the corner while peering towards Zach, "I expect you to clean up this mess when you're finished."

Zach jerked his head up in Sylvians direction with cutthroat direct eye contact. He sighed while shifting his stance and flipping his hands up. "Yes, I'm not a toddler."

Sylvian held Zach's gaze, "You sure act like one." "You know this is my kitchen."

Erin giggled, then silenced when she noticed the pull from Sin's dark eyes.

As she ran hot water across her dish, warm air brushed against her ear. It felt like each nerve fiber had been awakened. She clenched her abdomen and sucked in her breath as hands slid on each of her hips.

"Thank you for saving me," Sin whispered.

She spun out of his grip while turning towards him. She pursed her lips as her hands gripped her waist. "Keep your hands off me, Sin! I saved you because it was the right thing to do, not that you deserved it," she said and brushed past. He grabbed her arm before she could walk farther.

His eyes softened and his smile faded into a serious expression, "I am sorry, Erin."

She rolled back her shoulders while loosening the tension in them. "Sin, I forgive you, but don't ever try anything stupid like that again." She reclaimed her arm and sped from him.

She chose to save him, although she couldn't help but wonder why her heart pressured her into it. Zach and Sylvian watched as Sin followed Erin's trail. Zach's expression hardened toward Sin.

Erin met with the deep depths of blue ocean eyes from Zach as she thought about the events that transpired. I need answers, why would Zach hide his past from me? This world and his brother? What else has he hidden from me? She would need to speak with him alone.

With his eyes settled on her she asked, "Is there a nearby town?"

"It has been a while since I have been here, but I think I know one," he answered.

"I can take you," Sin said from behind.

She sighed in annoyance while meeting Sin's golden gaze. I need space.

She forced her palm towards Sin to distance herself from him. "No. just leave me alone, please." She turned around and left the room while finding her way to the bathroom. She didn't want to witness the sadness in his eyes. Why do I even care if I hurt his feelings?

#

Leaving the bathroom and running toward where Zach had been, Erin mindlessly bumped into Sin. "What is with you popping up around every corner?"

"I need you prepared for anything that could happen," Sin said while twirling a strand of her wet hair around his finger. She rolled her eyes and pushed past him. Turning around, she ran to the doorway where Zach stood and watched him toss Sin a death glare.

"Blood won't keep me from killing you. Just keep that in mind," he growled. Zach grabbed Erin's hand and pulled her toward him.

Erin's heart fluttered, only able to focus on his warm hand in hers. She knew he would be overprotective. "Looks like he pushes your buttons as well." She smirked.

#

Walking along the paved dirt road, they passed the fountain. Erin looked at Zach and realized she had a lot of questions. This would be the perfect time.

"Wait for me," yelled Sin from behind.

"Shit!" they both said together.

"Come on, let's run," Erin said as she held Zach's hand and pulled him. "Hurry, before he catches up to us!"

As she took off, she missed a stump sticking out from the ground and tripped, which sent them both tumbling down. She could feel the warmth of Zach's body, and as they were laughing, she could feel her heart beating faster as she looked up at him. His blond hair glowed from the sun while reminding her of the colors of soft raw silk.

His eyes softened as he leaned in close enough to caress his lips against her own, but Sin pulled him from her.

"Running from me is impossible, jackrabbit," Sin said as he pulled Erin back up onto her feet. Feeling the burn on the back of her arms, she flinched.

"Are you alright?" he asked as he began to dust her off and examine her.

She backed up from him. "Yes, I'm okay, just some scratches."

He nodded and wrapped his arm around her.

"I'm holding onto you, so you don't fall. It's this or I carry you."

She was frustrated that she couldn't have a moment alone with Zach. She focused on the way the weather felt instead, reminding herself that she could only control her own actions. There was a slight chill in the air as the sun shed its warmth on her body. The leaves were brown on the trees, and she felt a sense of happiness. She loved this time of year. It was always her favorite, especially when Halloween rolled around.

#

"What are you going to do, turn me into a toad?" said a young boy wearing a bloody mask with ragged jeans and a torn blood-stained shirt. He shoved her down onto the road as three other boys laughed.

"Why yes, I shall make you a toad and put you right in the middle of traffic. How does that sound?" Her eyes pierced into his dark browns.

"Too bad you're just an ordinary sad lonely girl." He laughed.

She jumped up and dived into his chest while knocking him off guard, but then he grabbed her wrists and pushed her back to the ground.

"Let go of me, Benny," she yelled while struggling to get free from his grip. Then he was pushed off her. Zach had his hand fisted around the fabric of Benny's shirt. Benny's friends pulled Zach from him while holding him back from throwing punches. Shoot, he wouldn't be in this mess if it weren't for me. She started to run toward them but was pulled back by the collar of her shirt.

"Where do you think you're going?" Benny asked. She did what any girl would do—

kicked him low as he knelt in pain. But she knew that it wouldn't help matters because Zach was still being held back by Benny's friends. "Let him go," she demanded.

"Benny," yelled a man from down the street, "get your ass over here." When he finally stood back up Erin imagined the flames in his eyes creating smoke effects blow out of his ears.

"You will pay for that," he rumbled. He nodded to his friends to break from their holds on Zach and then followed the direction of the voice that called for him.

Zach yelled out, "You better stay away from her!"

As the bullies left Zach ran towards Erin while placing his arms around her. "Are you alright?"

She dusted herself off and nodded, "Yes."

"Your costume fits you," she giggles while tapping the top of his brown sheriff hat.

His shoulders dropped as he bent over to adjust her black and purple witch hat. "I could say the same for a girl that knows how to conjure love spells."

What does he mean?

Kids run past them in a direction toward red lights flashing from a distance. Erin tugged on Zach's sleeve, "Let's go see what they're up to."

#

As they observed the old farmhouse that was decorated with spider webs, ghouls and splattered blood on the doors both Erin and Zach shivered. Gray smoke rolled through the cracks of the doors as a green light flashed from inside. Red glow sticks were tossed around the ground, and a dark forest heightened the spooky appearance. Screams, cries and high-pitched clown-like laughs trailed from the farmhouse. When Erin turned to Zach she noticed his body trembling.

A wave of cold air wrapped around her skin as she stepped closer into Zach for his warmth. His shaking calmed down and he straightened.

"Let's get this over with," he seethed while pushing through the barn doors.

Green and white lasered lights flashed while illuminating a path for them to follow. Erin tightened her grip on Zach's arm. "Come play with us," whispered two little girls who wore crimson-colored dresses. In each dark corner monsters tiptoed around them while creating disturbing chuckles, wails and screams.

Then the sound of a chainsaw set off right behind them causing fear to set and both to run. All the lights shut off, and it became dark. Realizing she had lost Zach's hand, she started to worry. "Zach," she whispered.

Something pulled her arm, and she was shoved down. Too afraid to move, she felt alone, lost, and scared, much like when her guardians would abandon her for days.

"Boo!" whispered a familiar voice from behind her ear. When the lights flashed back on, she recognized her attacker. Benny.

"What do you want?" she shrieked.

His smile twisted into a malicious grin as the sharp canines stuck out like arrow heads. He wore a dark cape with white paint on his face and a drool of fake blood running down his chin. "To get even," he spoke.

Her nostrils flared out as she shoved him aside to escape. Bumping into something hard, she looked up. It was one of his friends who was dressed in a white-and-black skeleton costume. Benny's minion seized her arms tightly and held her back, "Got you." He whispered.

#

Erin blinked out of her flashback as they arrived in a cottage town. Originally her motive was to speak with Zach about his secrets. But since Sin invited himself on their journey, she would need another reason. She glanced down and remembered she was still wearing Sin's button-down black shirt like a dress. *I need to find woman clothing.*

She could hear the rushing sound of water and a large waterfall with a large wooden wheel. There was a fountain with layers folded out into the shape of a rose in front of a purple vintage building. Water spouted from each layer while falling into the fountain—its appearance was majestic. Closing her eyes, she listened to the sounds of rushing water and breathed in the sweet smell of fresh roses.

"You are so damn beautiful."

As she opened her eyes and saw Zach, her cheeks flushed, and she turned away.

"Why would you say that out of nowhere?"

Zach placed his hand in hers and bent down to kiss her cheek. "Because it's true," he whispered in her ear. Her heart fluttered, and she felt a desire to reach up and kiss him, but before she could get the thought out, a girl yelled out.

Running up toward them was a woman who appeared to be in her early twenties. She had honey-colored curls and light-brown skin. She wore a white long-sleeved ruffled blouse with cross stitches on the front and a black skirt that hung to her knees in feathers with black stockings and brown knee-high boots.

"Zach, I haven't seen you in forever," she said. Then she directed her attention toward Erin. Her face lit up, and Erin realized that she must have been an important piece of the past life she had forgotten.

"My name is Flora." She smiled brightly.

CHAPTER NINE

"Memories connect us to the past. Without them, there isn't one."

Erin wondered if Flora had been a friend from her childhood. Then her memory of the forest in flames and the women who had fallen to the ground resurfaced. She noticed there was a resemblance between the woman in the forest and Flora, as they shared the same dark jade-green eyes, light brown skin, and curls. She had felt a connection, like she had known the woman and yet couldn't rely completely on her memory.

Flora nodded in the direction of a cottage-like brick home. It had lilac-colored shutters, and lavender grew all around it. "Come on in, and we will find something for you."

The warmth of an arm snaked around Erin's shoulders, "Need my assistance?" Sin asked.

"Get lost." Flora waved her hands.

Zach placed a firm hand on Sin's shoulder. "Let's allow them space."

"Fine, I will be here when you come out," he kissed Erin's cheek and released her from his hold.

Zach sighed from annoyance while yanking Sin's arm in another direction.

Pressing gently on the stained-glass violet door, Erin noticed an aroma of sweet jasmine with notes of subtle pear. The floors were white marble with black swirl designs. Green vines and white lights surrounded the walls, reminding Erin of a fairy room. The room had a calm ambiance, and amethyst crystals hung from a large chandelier above.

"Is purple your favorite color?" Erin asked.

"It's been an important part of my culture; it represents a spiritual awareness and contributes to mental growth. To me it's more of a comfort color, like how blue is calming for some. I don't believe in a favorite color because all colors are unique and can be represented in multiple ways."

"I've never thought of it that way." Erin admitted.

Flora smiled while directing Erin towards a set of marbled stairs.

"Time to show you my little creations."

Erin's eyes widened as she followed Flora up the staircase. There were mannequins featuring different clothing designs, sewing machines, and walls full of all kinds of fabric. It was a designer's dream world, and she could tell it was Flora's passion.

"Expression is freeing and rewarding," Flora said proudly.

Erin ran her fingers through the silk threads of the dresses that hung on a rack. "I'm impressed."

She found a silver dress with glimmers of sparkles as light touched its surface. The sleeves were lightweight with a slit from the forearm to the wrist and cross stitches of silver bows. It hung in layers on the chest and had white sheer fabric that fell from the hip line and down just above the knees. Erin immediately felt a connection with it and a desire to try it on.

"Inspiration from an old friend," Flora said. She pulled the dress from the rack and placed it against Erin's body. "Try it on."

Erin didn't want to refuse her, so she grasped the dress, blushing. She had never spent time with girls back home and found it difficult to find female friends, and she didn't have a sister. This moment felt like one she had been missing for some time. Old fashion girl time.

As she pulled the dress over her head, her eyes widened. She was in love with how the fabric clung to her body and couldn't contain her smile. Her head spun in circles as she remembered since she had arrived in this new world that dreams have been resurfacing. She had also felt a connection with this place and the people. Why does it feel like this is where I belong? I hope that time will reveal the truth.

Erin quickly snapped out of her internal thoughts while sharing her joy twirling around to reveal the dress. "I absolutely love it, thank you."

Flora's face brightened. "This dress suits you."

"I believe tonight deserves to be celebrated!" Flora walked towards a cabinet while pulling out two bottles of wine.

Erin was not much of a drinker. I am not refusing a woman that just handed me a dress for no cost. Besides I could you a little wind down time.

"Sounds good to me." Erin smiled as she picked out clothes, shoes, and garments, then walked outside to find the guys chatting by the fountain. Their gazes centered towards Erin, and both their jaws dropped.

Now this feels awkward. "Come on, Flora. Let's go back to Sin's house and party." She laughed, grabbing her hand and leading her back down the path they came from.

"You remind me of my old friend."

Erin paused, unsure how to answer. "Maybe we are soulmates," she teased as they laughed and skipped toward the mansion.

#

As they continued towards the mansion down the dirt path Erin noticed

Flora's demeaner had shifted. Her head was down as she avoided eye contact; slumped shoulders and her eyes lacked the sparkle she had back at her cottage.

She reached out for her arm. "Are you feeling alright?" she asked.

Flora turned to Erin and sighed, "It must be obvious."

"I have many memories of being here as a child, but when I lost my friend." She paused. "I honestly didn't think I'd ever feel like myself again."

Erin remembered how difficult it was when she lost her grandmother. She thought of the days they walked along the shoreside searching for sand dollars and how safe she felt in her presence. Now the beach reminded her of those days—bittersweet, but also full of love. She couldn't forget how warm and happy those memories made her feel, and sometimes that was what she needed to get through the tough days.

"Tell me about your friend," Erin asked.

Flora's face softened. "She protected the people she loved, anyone she met would describe her as kind and caring. Although she struggled to stand up for herself and was stubborn, her perspective changed my life. That's why I create clothing for women who need them, at no cost—to make them feel beautiful and confident. I felt that my actions could change someone else's life, and in return create a domino effect."

"You are an amazing person and friend, Flora."

"Thanks, I guess I owe it to my friend."

Erin felt a warm hand on her shoulder as she turned her head around to see Zach smiling at her. "I'm going to have to keep my eye on you, miss lightweight."

"Yeah, okay, Mr. 'I can only handle two beers and I'm out like a light.'" She laughed.

"Well, then you will just have to talk to me when he's passed out, wifey," Sin teased while grabbing her waist.

She slipped away from his grasp. "Nope, I would rather drown in a pool of water."

"Ouch." Sin folded his arms.

Once they were all inside, Flora brought out the wine. "Pick your poison."

Erin poured herself a glass of red wine and took a sip. A taste of sweetness and tart rolled onto her tongue as she enjoyed the flavors. As the night sky sheltered the earth with its shadows Erin was on her second glass of wine. My kidnapper could be hiding in the woods as I sit inside of a mansion while drinking alcohol. I must have lost my mind because this is not one of my best ideas. Erin finds Sin's eyes on her as she glances up at him. At least if he does come looking for me then he will have an obsessed man to go through.

"What kind of movies do you have?" She asks him as if they are the only two in the room.

"I have collected multiple ones over the years, any favorites?"

"She likes horror films," Zach answers as he opens the built-in cabinet set in the wall.

"Pick whatever while I grab snacks," Erin offers while heading to the kitchen.

She walked over to the wooden cabinets in search of a box of popcorn. Next to it was a drawer filled with assorted candy.

"What are you doing?"

The voice caused her to drop the box of candy she had in her hand. She knew who it was as she sighed while remembering their last conversation. He smelled of sweet peppermint and wore black jeans, and he was shirtless, revealing muscles she would never have noticed otherwise. She could feel her cheeks turn red as she glanced back up at his face.

"I was just gathering snacks for the movie. Want to join?" she asked while bending over to pick them back up. He bent down to help her.

"I believe that I owe you an apology for my words earlier."

As she straightened her back, she leaned against the marbled counter that spiked cold claws into her skin.

He closed into her space while setting the candy box beside her. "My intention was to warn you."

A rush of nerves sent chaotic thoughts into her mind as his body was close enough to brush against hers. Why is he so close.

She leaned in closer to whisper, "Is there something I should know?"

"Have you two become friends?" Sin asked while walking toward them.

Her eyes widened. "Sin," her voice trembled.

Sylvian had already walked out of the kitchen while leaving her alone.

Sin reached his arms around her while grasping the counter. "Perhaps you should stay close to me because I can't contain my jealousy when seeing you so close to another man."

The alcohol had her emotions shaken like a slushie. He wore sandalwood mixed with musk that she could drown in. She peered up at his soft brown sunset eyes then down to his pink sultry lips. The temptation was pulling her in his direction. But she remembered what he had done. I absolutely cannot fall for him.

#

Zach sat next to her and draped a soft lavender blanket across her body. Flora took over the lazy boy chair in the corner, and Sin sat on the other side of Erin. "Okay now, I can't be stuck in the middle like this," she said.

"Trade sides with me," Zach said while squeezing in between her and Sin.

She claimed the corner of the couch, her comfort zone. All the lights were off, and the movie was set to begin.

Her stomach twisted and turned during the scary scenes. She felt a warm arm slide around her waist to find Zach had already passed out. Then she heard snoring from across the room and saw Flora with her legs kicked back.

"Someone can't handle their alcohol," Sin joked. The movie finally ended, and Sin and Erin were the only two awake. Erin slid up from the couch and covered Zach with the blanket. Peaceful, she thought while he cuddled up to the blanket.

"Erin, I will be right back," Sin whispered.

She nodded and walked outside. The night air had a chilly breeze, and the sky was dark with white flickering lights from above. The moon was a crescent, and she smiled as she listened to the creatures of the night communicating through the woods.

As a child the mystery of the woods allured her curious mind. This time instead of staying out of danger she was compelled to investigate. This could be a bad idea, but I need answers. I should hurry before Sin scolds me for being outside alone. She disappeared into the woods while traveling down a path she hoped would lead to answers.

CHAPTER TEN

Erin watched the water gracefully slip from the rocks while splashing into the large plunge pool. Thoughts of Sylvian's words filled her mind. Just what were Zach and Sin hiding? She felt lost and directionless. Zach's past—along with her own—was a mystery she'd work to unravel. She thought of the events that recently occurred such as learning that she had the ability to heal and extract venom from a victim.

She bent down and grabbed the dagger that she had used on Sin while twirling it around and admiring its beauty. It fit perfectly in her hand, and it felt like it belonged to her. As she ran her finger across the cold metal, she strung her finger along the top of the sharpest point.

"I can't leave you alone for one second," shouted a voice, causing her to jump and slice the edge of her pointer finger.

"Shit!" Her heart felt like it stopped for a moment as she looked up at Sin walking toward her.

"You know it's not safe to be out here alone."

Erin bent down and let the water wash the blood from her hand. Sin grabbed her hand while applying slight pressure on it with his sleeve. "You need to be careful. A young beautiful woman like you could get swept away."

"Hmm, by someone like you." Sin's eyes were inviting, dark, and dangerous, yet she couldn't resist becoming lost in them. There was a magnetic pull towards him and when her trust normally faltered, for him there was no resistance. Sure, he was annoying, but it also felt comforting to have him around. *Am I falling for this man?*

She noticed slight creases next to his lips when he smiled. The wind carried his cologne while filling her space with deep sensual smells of sandalwood and musk. She couldn't stop thinking about how romantic it was by the waterfall, amid the flowers and underneath the night sky. The cool breeze and mist from the water embraced them with cold kisses.

"You know I have loved you since we were young," Sin said and drew closer. She was fitting the pieces together slowly—that she had a past here, but for some reason, her memories had vanished. *Where have my memories gone?*

She wanted those memories back, especially because that would reveal the deeper meaning behind her relationship with Sin. "I wish I could remember," she said softly.

"Let me remind you." He held her hands and leaned in.

She thought of the kiss they shared when she was saving his life. It felt like she was high in the clouds, consumed by the feeling radiating throughout her body and the touch of his lips.

Cold chills ran down the back of her neck and along her arms just at the thought.

It was exciting, and something she could become lost in. She'd hoped Zach would become her first kiss one day, but instead, it was Sin. What am I doing? This is insane. I don't even know him. She pulled back and stood up, rubbing off the bits of grass that clung to her dress.

He stood up and tried to lean in again, but she knew she couldn't take the risk, so she placed a hand on his chest to stop him. As she stepped back, she lost her balance. Sin began to reach for her but was too late. Her body fell backward, and she felt the bitter pierce shock of the icy water touch her skin. Immediately something wrapped around her legs tightly before she could pull herself up for air. Before she knew it, darkness crowded her mind.

#

A whooshing noise filled her ears as she coughed up water and gasped for the air. She was submerged in a shallow pool of water. As she pushed herself up from the ground, she discovered she was in a cave. A sliver of light shined through the cracks above as water dripped from the waterfall. "What the hell was that?" she yelled out.

Walking around the corner, she observed bright red rubies scattered across the cave walls like a mosaic art piece shaped into creatures with wings. There in front of her stood two double doors with wings that matched together by the seam. The double doors were painted bright red and had a vertical key insert. She applied pressure on the door, but it did not budge, so she grabbed her dagger and shoved it into the spot. Then she turned it to the right as if it were a key, heard a click, and pushed the doors open.

The room was set up like a miniature living space, as there was a kitchen with white cabinets and an island counter. The island had a sink placed in the middle and a wooden glossed tabletop. There was a living area with a black leather couch and bright fluorescent lights from the ceiling. A lemon and citrus smell circulated through the room, and the place seemed untouched.

The master room had a bathroom in the corner and a king-sized bed with a pink bedspread that was covered with white lilies. She picked up a doll that was lying on the mattress and studied its appearance. The doll's black hair was twisted in a bun and tied with a red ribbon. Its face was painted white with silver eyes, and it wore a deep red dress that had a bow tied to the back, cotton socks, and black shoes.

It had a piece of jewelry tied to its neck with twine—a gold band with a ruby in the shape of a rose in the center. She slipped it on her finger and realized it was a perfect fit. The doll felt as though it had something in it, but when she turned it around, she couldn't find anything. She pushed on the doll and realized it must be underneath the dress, so she removed it to reveal a key strapped to the back.

As she placed the key on the twine and tied it to her wrist, she realized the room was filled with books built into the surrounding walls. She gently dragged her finger across the spines while reading the titles and authors. Then she stopped at a thick dark-green book with gold-plated writing. Pulling it out, she realized the title was not written on the spine itself. It was heavy as she opened it, revealing a storage container.

It contained a silver chain necklace with a wolf-shaped figure, a letter, a map, and a picture of a couple with a child. In the picture, she saw herself, a young man, and a woman. I am in this picture but who are these people? She moved on from the picture and walked over to the bed and sat down to read the letter.

Galena,

I never wished for any of this to happen and only wanted to protect you. This is a safe place for you to go to when you're in trouble. It's protected by a barrier, and only you can cross it, along with your dagger. Tread carefully around people. You hold desirable power that could be abused.

I'd advise you to be on guard. I know that you will do what is right in your heart. Therefore, do not go looking for me; I will find you. Soon enough, you will learn the answers to your past. For now, protect yourself, and don't trust anyone.

Amaryllis

"Galena?" Her eyes filled with tears, and she felt like she couldn't take in enough air to calm down. Her instincts told her that things weren't right at home, but she just chose to ignore those feelings. Picking up the silver wolf-shaped necklace, she rubbed her fingers across the rough, rocky surface. She remembered how, at night, she'd listen to the wolves howling in the wind, and it brought peace to her soul.

None of this makes any sense. If this letter is from my actual mother, then who was I living with just recently? She would find answers, even if her mother recommended that she stay away. If her memories could be taken, then maybe she could get them back.

CHAPTER ELEVEN

Erin grabbed the paper map that was sketched out with a pencil on a sheet of paper. They must have been skilled artists, judging by the detailed drawings of landmarks and buildings. She was determined to remember her parents and find the missing pieces of her past self, and then maybe her heart would feel more whole. Her memory was blocked, and she needed to figure out how to unlock the truth.

The first question was whether they were still alive. She had hoped that much to be true. Erin looked back down at the map and noticed that the waterfall was placed on it. It had the cave underneath, and the safe place made for her, which felt like something she'd come across in a video game.

It included the first waterfall she crossed with the word "Portal" written on it. "That's strange," she said. She noticed towns and mansions beside waterfalls, each surrounded by the forest. There was one mansion that caught her eye—it was labeled "Home."

She smiled brightly because that was her first clue that she'd find this place and her family, learn about her memories and her past. As she folded the map and placed it with her items, she knew what her next move was.

Ready to leave, she searched for dry clothes to wear. She found a vintage black dress with red roses stitched into it. It was strapless with a sweetheart neckline, and the bottom was white and flared out with ruffles that fell to her knees. Erin dropped the dress she had on and slipped the new one over her head.

She spotted a red leather bag on the floor and picked it up. There was a rope, flashlight, matches, and a homemade wooden water bottle. She placed the doll and all her other belongings in it, then stashed a couple of random books inside the bag.

Once she pulled her dagger from the keyhole, she glanced back at the door as it closed and locked. She had a flashlight in her hand as she placed the dagger in her bag. The cave was cold and damp. She grimaced at the thought of insects hiding in the walls.

She noticed a light shining from above her and a set of stairs leading toward it. Slowly, she walked up the rugged steps while careful not to slip and fall. She climbed to the top and realized she was at the highest point of the waterfall. The view was breathtaking, and the sun was just rising, gracing its rays of light upon the earth. It felt like home.

She could see a whole town up ahead and the tip of the mansion Zach and Sin lived in. Roses sprouted from the ground, and some of the petals had fallen off, gracefully floating in the stream below. As exhaustion crept in, she sat down on the grass and closed her eyes. The sun warmed her skin like one of her favorite blankets.

#

"Galena, what are you doing, sweet girl?" A young Erin looked up at a woman with reddish-brown hair pulled back in a bun with a red rose planted in the center. She wore a bright red dress paired with red gloves.

"Momma, I tried picking a rose for you, but it attacked me." She had messy hair and seemed to be about six. Blood trickled down her fingers as she held them up to her mother.

"Roses are so beautiful. Therefore, they are vulnerable to the world and must protect themselves with thorns." She grabbed a cloth and held it against Erin's injured fingers, then wrapped each one up with white bandages. "They're not so different from us. We possess the same skillful tactics to keep harm away."

"Mommy, I hope nobody ever tries to hurt you, or else they will have to deal with me!"

The mother smiled, a softness in her eyes as she ran her fingers through Erin's hair. "You know I'll protect you, Galena. You don't ever have to put yourself in danger for me."

#

Crackling noises filled the room as Erin awoke. Looking down, she realized she was wrapped inside of silk white sheets and a crimson-colored comforter. She was back in the room Sin had set up for her previously. How did I find my way back to Sin's mansion? She slowly cracked the door open to see if anyone was out in the hallway. The coast was clear as she tiptoed to the bathroom where she could take a bath to clear her mind. She brushed her teeth and figured she would wear her dress since it wasn't that dirty.

She eased herself into the heated water and sunk into the tub. A loud slam caused her to snap her head up. Zach was shirtless, and she could see the lines that shaped his muscled figure, his loose-fitting gym shorts barely hanging on his waist.

"I have been worried sick about you. I'm never letting you out of my sight again." There was a shadow beneath his eyes from lack of sleep and stress.

A tinge of guilt shocked her system. "Zach, there's so much we need to talk about."

"I know I have a lot to tell you. I just hope that you can forgive me."

"Erin!" Another voice trailed around the corner as Sin walked into the bathroom looking down at her in the tub. She watched as Sin's eyes grew hungry with desire. "Alright, peep show is over. Both of you, get the hell out of here!"

Zach turned around and shoved Sin out the door while locking it behind him. She could hear them arguing outside the door as they walked away.

She let out a sigh and giggled as she fell back into the hot steaming water. Her brain felt hazy as she remembered Sin going in for that kiss right before she had fallen. Then she thought of Zach and what he meant about her forgiving him. It was just too much to handle, and she needed to focus on priorities.

There was also the crushing realization that she needed to share her feelings for Zach, but what about Sin? She remembered him kidnapping her, putting her on lockdown—then quickly shivered that thought away. "Nah." She smiled. It'd be insane to have feelings for a man who lied to her and forced her to stay. She couldn't imagine losing her freedom. But she couldn't forget that kiss, how alive she felt around him.

After washing up, she placed her dress over her body, then brushed her long brown hair carefully to unravel the knots. Looking in the mirror, she noticed how the dress complimented her beige skin. She felt beautiful in it as she twirled around while smiling. Then she opened the door and walked into the hallway, enjoying the silence for a change.

The flames flickered inside the black-and-orange lanterns that hung on the walls. She almost felt as though her existence was defined by hiding in the shadows from deceptive strangers. On top of that, she'd learned new information about her life and realized that her young adult years had been altered. "I did say I wanted to visit new places." She smiled, trying to be optimistic.

"You seem to be lost in thought," Sin said as he approached. He reminded her of those vampires in her romance books—seductive and inviting, ready to tear your throat out at the chance. But that wouldn't be her fate.

"You are captivating," he said, and she could feel the heat from her cheeks flare up as she nervously looked down.

Compliments made her so uncomfortable. Whenever someone gave her that look, she felt nervous and just wanted to hide. As she walked away, she felt the warmth of his hand as he grasped hers. He pulled her into his chest, and her pulse quickened. He was mesmerizing, dangerous, and annoying.

She pushed him away. "Sin you better stop doing that, or else."

"I think I would take the punishment." Sin gave a crooked smile.

"She can't even leave the bathroom in peace." Zach grimaced as he walked up toward them, then shoved Sin against the wall and pushed his elbow into his neck. "Leave her alone."

Erin laughed while walking away from them. "You two are so cute when you're fighting." She continued, "Zach, after I get a bite to eat, I need to talk to you alone."

Zach softened his grip on Sin, and a hint of worry crossed his eyes. "Okay, we will go for a walk together."

Erin nodded and went around the corner in search of the kitchen as her stomach growled. Once she arrived in the kitchen, she saw a plate on the dining room table along with a glass of water. There was also chicken, potatoes, and green beans along with a roll placed on a plate. As she breathed it in, it reminded her of lazy Sundays when she would just relax and watch a football game with Zach.

Sylvian walked in, wearing black slacks and a white button-down shirt. "It's going to get cold if you wait too long," he said, pulling the chair out for her.

"Thank you, Sylvian, you didn't have to," she said, sitting down to eat. It even tasted like home cooking; she was amazed at how well he could cook.

He slid over a red notebook that had a rose printed on the outside of it along with a black pen attached to it. She felt the smooth velvet finish of the outer layer with her fingers. "It seems to match that dagger of yours." "I found it while searching through that closet in your room after I noticed the dagger. I remembered my father crafting one just like it for the royal family."

Her eyebrows pinched inward at the new information. She wanted to mention what she had found underneath the waterfall but didn't know if she wanted to go into that until she spoke with Zach. "Sylvian, can I ask you a question?"

"Yes."

"Why do you stay here and serve Sin?"

"Let's just say I owe a debt to him that I'm not sure I'll pay off anytime soon." He looked down at the table.

She stood up with the plate in her hand and put her other hand on his shoulder. "Maybe we can change that for you." Then she walked over to the sink to wash the dishes. Over her shoulder, she said, "Selling yourself to pay a debt is no way to live. I have a feeling there's something else you're meant to do in this life."

When she turned around, he was right in front of her. "You would say something like that." He gave her a tight hug.

A bit taken aback; she wrapped her arms around him. Although she had just met him, she knew when someone needed a change. While he completed his daily duties, he always seemed as though his eyes were lost in thought.

"Erin, if you ever need me, let me know. I will always be here." He unlatched his arms from her body.

"Same goes for you." She grabbed her book and smiled at him just before leaving the kitchen. At least he seemed to come around more, instead of trying to send her away. She almost felt like he was a protective brother in a way. Perhaps she should tread lightly. She had to earn trust first and that would take some time.

CHAPTER TWELVE

Erin pulled open the door and walked out of her room as she spotted Zach. He was wearing just a towel wrapped around his waist. His hair appeared a warmer color while combed back as she imagined tossing her fingers through it. His muscles glistened from the way the light shined on the water that clung to his skin. She froze in place while witnessing a pink flush display across his cheeks.

"Come here," he waved.

He interlaced his fingers through hers while pulling her in the direction of a door and inside a room. Her senses were overwhelmed with honey, cinnamon, and spice while reminding her of fall. As he unraveled his towel, she turned around to allow him privacy. *Don't you dare let those muscles distract you, remember you need answers.* Even if you have been in love with this man for years.

His fingers brushed the back of her arm as heat rolled through her body while awakening senses she wanted to bury.

"Let me start with the truth."

Erin wished she could return to when there were no lies between them. The comfort of just spending time with Zach was something she never wanted to lose. Her life was changing whether she liked it or not, just like the destruction that occurs within a hurricane's path. We can't change the inevitable.

Zach led her to the bed and sat next to her. He wore a long-sleeved white button-down shirt with light gray dress pants. He proceeded to roll his sleeves up slowly while resting one hand on the bed and the other close to her leg. Her body tensed, yet she tried to remain calm, straightening her back and grounding her feet against the soft carpeted floor.

"I was ordered to stay by your side and keep you from finding out about your past. When we were kids, my father saw how protective I was of you, and he decided that I'd be the one to guard you. He told me that if I didn't, then something bad would happen, and I could never forgive myself if it had."

He paused to take a breath and grasped her hands. "Erin, you are the sun to my moon. I am lost in the shadows without your light. He leans in to brush the softest kiss against her lips. "I love you. I always have and will."

Erin's eyes watered, and her heart ached because this was not how she wanted to hear his confession. She had felt the same way for years and yearned to be with him. But she could not imagine telling him that right after finding out about the lies, the ones that explained her existence.

Water edged in the corners of her eyes as she broke free from his hold. "Zach, how can you lie to someone you love?" Each fiber in her body pushed her to escape her emotions, she had too many surfacing. Not waiting long enough to hear his response, she bolted for the door and into her room. She was unsure who to trust and would take caution with her choices moving forward.

It occurred to her that she may have to do this on her own, as much as she wanted to include the others. Maybe I can convince Sylvian to help me. She would need to get him alone to speak to him about it.

There was a knock at the door. I hope it isn't Zach. I can't face him right now.

Erin walked over to the door, then slowly opened it and saw Sylvian standing there.

"Hey, are you alright? I saw you run into the room in a rush." His eyes revealed his concern.

Erin grabbed his sleeve and pulled him into her room. "I have a proposition for you."

His expression grew curious. "Keep talking."

"I need your help to search for answers about my past."

"I found a safe house left for me and tools to find my way home." She maintained eye contact with her arms relaxed by her sides. She leaned in towards his space. "I may not know much about your intentions, but you have proved to be concerned about my safety since we've met. Except for when he helped Sin kidnap me.

I am placing my trust in you because you're the first person who came to me and warned me about secrets. Will you help me?"

Sylvian placed a hand on his chin, "This could be risky, Erin. Those guys might just have my head if I betray them."

"Sylvian, I must do this. If you don't help me, then I'll be forced to do it alone, which could be worse. A woman all alone in the woods, at night. She remembered her rose dagger while reaching for her bag to show him it. I also have a weapon and power that could help us," she said.

He walked towards her and dropped his gaze to the wolf pendant that hung from her neck. "I remember this. It was created by a type of rock called Galena—a dangerous but rare stone. I wanted to know who it was created for as I watched my father carefully working on it. His eyes widened as he studied her for a moment with a sudden hint of realization behind his bright sunflower eyes. "I learned that it was for the princess of Rosanafalls when it was handed to the Queen at the time."

"Galena," Erin said while remembering the letter and whom it was addressed to.

"It's an honor to be in a princess's presence." He bowed in front of her.

She took a step back. "I'm not a princess."

"I understand it's hard to take in, but it's the truth." He smiled as he raised his head.

"I can't accept that, but if it's true, then let me bargain with you."

"Alright, but I'll let you know what my price is when I figure out what I truly desire."

She nodded. "I need to plan this out. Please pack food and drinks while I map out our journey."

"Now go before someone sees you leaving my room and gets the wrong idea."

She pushed him toward the door. She knew it was too much to ask, but she didn't have a choice. If she involved the other two, they would forbid it, and it was not their decision. Hiding her past from her was selfish. Just how long did Zach plan to keep this secret?

Her chest ached again as she remembered Zach's confession. He was her best friend, and it hurt that he betrayed her trust. She reminisced on laughing at scary movies, playing hide and seek, and making up games together. Never let someone become your crutch.

She began to write a letter in hopes that he would accept the reason behind her leaving. Right now, she needed space. "Please, just understand," she whispered.

Zach,

Although you withheld information, I'll never regret the memories we shared together. You were my distraction from myself, my parents, and the cruelties of circumstances. I could tell you anything, count on never feeling alone with you by my side. I felt like something had been missing, but I could never understand why.

I've recently learned that part of my past has been kept from me. I need to know more about my family, where I came from, and who I am supposed to be. Please understand that I made this decision because I know you must follow orders that don't align with my own. I promise I'll be safe; you have nothing to worry about.

PS: Tell Sin to behave himself and not to follow me either.
Sincerely,
E.S.

It felt good to express her emotions on paper. Space would clear her mind and help her focus on the task at hand. She folded the paper up and put Zach's name on it, then placed it onto her pillow.

Then she wrote out plans for her journey while redirecting her focus toward the map and its landmarks. She would begin in the direction of the main palace marked as "Home."

She placed a lighter into her bag along with her dagger and notebook. Soon, she would have to find Sylvian to figure out sleeping arrangements and how they would slip out into the night. Her stomach was in knots, but she'd have to maintain a poker face tonight. She'd leave the letter, along with the watch Zach had given her.

A paper slid under the doorway, and she ran up to pick it up. Meet me in the kitchen when everyone is asleep. I have everything prepared.

Great, she thought as the door swung open, alarming her.

Sin stood there in the doorway as she quickly balled the paper up.

"Are you alright?" he asked.

"Yes, I'll manage," she said quietly while she walked over to her bed. He followed and sat next to her as she slid the note underneath the pillow slowly. She figured she had better tell him something to keep him from finding out about her plan.

"I can't even piece my memories together to make sense of my past. I know Zach had to do what he was ordered, but there comes a time when you have a choice, and he made his."

Sin gave her a sincere look and covered her hand with his. "That's tough. I can only imagine how you feel. I wish I could rewind time and change this all for you. I would have chosen to protect you but not keep you from your family."

"Did you know?" she asked, genuinely curious.

He placed his hand on her cheek. "If it were my choice, you would have been here with me under my protection. Zach had disappeared from my life, and I was only told that he ran away because your family left, and he was upset." He smiled. "As children, we played together, and Zach and I were both in love with you, but of course, you didn't know that. You involved us in your fantasy games while pretending to be anywhere but Earth. To me, you were intriguing and full of adventure and fantasy. I pretended there would be a place solely for us."

Erin glanced down at the floor. "I wish I could remember those days."

As she found her way back to his eyes they were soft and warm as he listened patiently. An overwhelming feeling, like a tingling sensation, came over her body. It felt as though her comfort around him was slowly mending. But now she felt as though her heart might be pulling toward Sin, and this terrified her. She felt that he knew it too.

Then he pulled her into him while laying a hand on the back of her neck, sending warm tingles throughout her body. His mouth crashed into hers as she allowed him to break her lips apart. As he sucked on the bottom of her lip and massaged the back of her neck, she let out a little moan.

A sudden knock at the door broke their kiss as they pulled from each other painfully.

The door pushed open as Zach darted toward Sin. "I told you to keep your damn distance," he yelled, his fists raised.

"She isn't your prize! She has a choice," Sin shouted.

Erin's heart raced, feeling panicked by all the chaos. She slammed the door shut and found Sylvian behind her with a key. He locked the door as she yelled, "Work it out! You two are family, and nothing should come between that—not even me."

CHAPTER THIRTEEN

Sylvian tossed her a bag, and she placed it onto her shoulders and followed him out the door. She felt a slight pinch of hesitation and guilt, but she needed to find her parents and learn about her past. Zach wouldn't allow that, and Sin wouldn't let her out of his sight. Then there was that kiss. She blushed just at the thought of it, how she almost lost complete control.

Sylvian followed her lead as she guided them with the map. Luckily, the sky was clear, the temperature warm with the hint of a chilly breeze. Once fatigued, they decided to rest, although her mind wouldn't calm down from the mixed emotions.

Sylvian placed his hand on her shoulder. "You're going to be alright. Try not to let it all get to you." She offered him a simple smile. "Of course, and we're on the direction to find my parents."

Sylvian started a fire as the night air grew colder. Erin glanced up at the gleaming stars, each a bundle of gas that mysteriously existed in space. "It's insane to think about how big the universe truly is. It reminds me of how small we are at times."

"There's a lot to think of when it comes to space and science, but if you ask me, the uncertainty is interesting." His long hair fell past his shoulders as he sat with his legs crossed. His eyes were the color of plated gold, and she could smell a bit of mint still lingering from his hair. He was a mystery. I want to understand him. What better way than to ask personal questions.

"Have you ever been in love?"

Sylvian cocked his head back to laugh. "If we're talking love, then I want a drink." He pulled out a flask that smelled of an oak and sweet vanilla. "I have had some lovers in my lifetime, but there was one that had slipped through the cracks of my fingers."

Erin leaned towards him with eager eyes as she held a hand underneath her chin and pulled her legs against her chest.

"Before I met Sin, there were flings to cure the boredom. Until the day that

I met her," he whispered while looking down at the ground. "Falling in love is the most powerful spell."

He was silent as she grew impatient, "What happened?"

He took another sip and let out a sigh. "It was too late. She had already been in an arranged marriage, one that promised her a comfortable life. Who was I to take that away?" He held sadness in his eyes. "She loved me, but she had to do the right thing for her family.

"From my experience woman who weren't given power had to find their own from another source. It was her responsibility to take care of her family and doing so meant to marry a man that had money and a high status. This would ensure that her family along with herself would be taken care of. I came from a family of skill. They worked hard to become successful without magic."

She crawled next to him while resting her head on his shoulder. "I am sorry that you lost her because of the way the world was, it's not fair. Whether you find someone who can match your heart or not, just know I will be here if you need help mending it back together."

"Ah, thanks, bestie. Better watch out—I may just keep you all to myself." He winked while placing an arm around her waist.

"Good luck getting past Zach and Sin," she teased.

"Yeah, they can cause headaches, but I can tell you that Sin is loyal, and he has been dealt some shitty cards—not that it's an excuse for his behavior. Zach, on the other hand, is one to watch out for—just be careful with him."

Erin nodded, contemplating what he said. She was impressed by how fast he assembled everything; she had not given a lot of thought to Sylvian and his background.

"My father would say, 'Learning is like an infinite ladder. The more you climb, the higher you grow.'" Sylvian grinned.

He stepped into her direction, "In the morning, I want to take you somewhere."

She nodded, although she didn't want to waste too much time. "Alright, I trust it will help with the journey."

"Yes, it will benefit you, I believe."

She shifted her stance. I want to know more about him.

"Sylvian, why are you in debt to Sin?" She didn't want to change the subject, yet it had been tugging on her mind for some time.

"He saved my life. It's as simple as that." She didn't pressure him to elaborate. I will allow him time to tell me what he needs to.

He straightened his back and turned to her. "My turn to ask you some questions."

They both gravitated towards the fire and sat next to each other.

Her body stiffened at his words, but she was prepared to reveal a bit of truth about herself.

"Does your heart lie with Sin or Zach?"

She grasped the flask from him and tossed back the drink which warmed her insides.

"I thought I knew the answer to that question, but it seems that I need to explore my feelings. Zach was my first crush. We had been best friends for some time, and I fell for him. I wanted to further our relationship until I ended up here."

She pulled her knees to her chest and hid her head in them. She didn't realize how uncomfortable she would feel talking about her love life. There is no time to worry about boys when I must relearn my past.

"Don't stress—you don't need to marry anyone. For all you know, it's neither of the two."

She softened her posture, "I can't argue with that reasoning, life has a funny way of revealing a new path that may have not been visible until the right time."

Sylvian glanced at her and raised his eyebrows, "Exactly."

Then he stood up while stretching his arms out and presenting a yawn, "I think it's time we get some rest and prepare for the road ahead. It won't be an easy one." He stretched his arm out as she took his hand.

"You're such a gentleman," she said.

"For you of course," he admitted as he pulled her up.

As they went their separate ways, she found herself cuddling into a warm blanket and thinking about how much things have changed. She closed her eyes as the heaviness began to overcome her body.

#

"Where are you, little girl?" whispered a voice that echoed through the room. She lay on her stomach while feeling the coldness from the hard floor pressing into her skin. Footsteps moved closer, and she could see the shiny black shoes that the man wore. The voice sounded no older than a teenager, and for some reason, it scared her. She didn't understand the twisted gut feeling and how she could hate someone she barely knew, but at that exact moment, she wished not to be found. As the footsteps grew closer, she covered her mouth, afraid to let out a scream. Then she heard a bird whistling as there was a racket from outside. He walked off, and she let go of her mouth while gasping for air.

#

She awoke from her dream to the rustle of leaves near the tent. As she slowly pulled the tent open, she caught a glimpse of the perpetrator behind the noise. She pulled aside the tent door slowly and saw a deer in the leaves. Rare in its beauty, it reminded her of a soft blanket of snow.

It was shuffling frantically as if it were in search of something. She grabbed some nuts from her bag of food and climbed out of the tent, then tossed them toward it while keeping her distance. She climbed back into the tent just to be sure not to frighten it. The deer nibbled at the nuts and walked around the tent. She wanted to pet it but knew that was a bad idea and waited for it to move away from the tent instead.

Once she found herself out of the tent Sylvian stood freshly clothed in a lightweight white long sleeved cotton shirt and black pants. She sighed while wishing for a fresh shower and toiletries. Instead, she brushed out her knotted hair, took care of her teeth and placed one of Sin's red and silky long-sleeved shirts on along with grey sweatpants to cover her legs.

Sylvian laughed, "That's quite the appearance."

She rolled her eyes, "At least it's comfortable."

"Awe, and Sin's, I see."

Her cheeks flared red. "We were in a hurry."

"No need to explain to me, Dandelion, let's get moving."

Dandelion? She remembered jumping into a field of dandelions as Sin had glared at her from the window then she snorted.

They packed up all their stuff and ate a quick breakfast. The deer wasn't too far from the trees, and she caught a glimpse of it staring her way. A shiver ran up her spine at the thought of someone watching. She noticed certain creatures had appeared as she navigated the land. First the blue jay and now a deer with fur the color of a daisy's petals. What could this mean? Should I be worried?

CHAPTER FOURTEEN

As Sylvian led Erin down a particular path, she couldn't help but notice the darkening of the plants in their surroundings. There along the trees stood a barbed wire fence with large vibrant carnivorous plants. Erin shivered as she watched a bug become its next meal. Poison oak and ivy ran along the sharp edges of the bushes on each side of the trees. Wild bright red and black berries grew on the vines, but Erin cautioned herself not to touch them.

They finally arrived in front of a gate that had two grotesque statues on each side. The black beaming eyes seemed to follow their every move. Sylvian reached into his pocket to reveal a red ruby and raised it toward the statues. If the gates hadn't pushed forward to open, she would have declared him insane. He nodded for her to follow behind.

She paused. "Is this safe?"

"As long as you don't do anything stupid."

Rolling her eyes, she continued forward as the leaves crunched beneath her feet. Sylvian halted as Erin mindlessly bumped into his back. She followed his gaze and observed a large steel dragon with details of scales carved into it. Its teeth and claws appeared razor-sharp, and she looked up at the massive figure.

She watched as Sylvian inserted another ruby into its gaping mouth. "How many of those are you just carrying around?"

"Enough for food or weapons if they were needed." He shrugged. The ground beneath them shook as the dragon collapsed and revealed a set of underground stairs.

They took caution with each step as Erin clung to the back of his shirt for leverage. "So, how did you know about this place?" she whispered.

"When you're the son of a craftsman, you learn the secrets of the town and the people that live in it."

"You would tell me if you were leading me to my death, right?" Erin joked as he pulled her further down.

"You have nothing to worry about."

As they approached, there were two golden doors that displayed a variety of jewels such as amethyst, emeralds, and sapphires. Admiring the artistry, she was ecstatic as she slid her fingers across the jewels. A gust of air blew through, and the lights shut off.

Erin latched on to Sylvian's arm. The doors opened, revealing a floor that glowed a bright blue from pebbles underneath an aquatic surface.

Then she felt as though a weight was lifted from her shoulders, and clarity embraced her mind. They walked slowly down the path and arrived at a pool of water that had steam rolling from the surface. In that water, a slim woman dressed in a long turquoise dress appeared to be floating on the surface. Erin could barely make out her face because of the darkness.

"Come in," the women said to them in a siren-like voice.

Erin felt compelled to listen to the woman as she walked into the water without worrying about her clothing. The water was warm enough to embrace her limbs comfortably. The air smelled of mint and sea salt while reminding her of a spa.

Floating on the water, she closed her eyes. She didn't understand why she felt so at ease, but at that moment, all her worries faded. Her mind felt clear as she fluttered her eyes shut.

#

Erin was transported back into her previous dream where she had hidden underneath a bed. She crawled out from underneath the bed and observed the room. The walls were painted with red and orange vibrant lilies. When walking past a mirror she saw herself with long brown hair, a ponytail with a white bow with two tails, and a shiny red dress with white ruffles that feathered down to her knees. A noise captured her attention as she tiptoed towards it.

As it flung open, a boy with shaggy blond hair and Caribbean blue eyes climbed in from the window.

"Zach!"

His chest puffed in and out as he took a moment to catch his breath. "Are you okay? I didn't mean to get you into any trouble," he whispered.

She nodded but stayed silent.

"Listen, I don't know what's going to happen, but I overheard my dad and yours, and they want me to look after you. I promise I won't let anything happen to you. I will protect you," he said, holding her hands.

Footsteps approached the door as they both stood still. Zach grabbed her arm and led her to the window, and she glanced down at Sin standing at the bottom, holding onto a ladder.

"Go!" Zach demanded.

#

She awoke to the smell of burning incense filling the room. The woman that she had seen in the water was sitting in front of her. She had long black hair that fell to her lower back, and her dress was even more beautiful out of the water. She noticed a quartz crystalized necklace that the woman wore. The woman also wore a mask filled with red ruby jewels to cover her face.

"Who are you?" Erin asked.

"My name is whatever you would like it to be, for I am not tied to one. I am a safe space for any woman in need. What is it that you desire?"

Erin noticed that Sylvian had disappeared. "Where is my friend?"

"He is outside of my domain where all men shall be. You shouldn't be naïve when you cannot foresee all the intentions a man may possess."

She wondered why the woman had such a negative view toward men.

"What happened to you?"

The woman just stared at her, unwilling to share anything about herself.

"Why don't you stay down here with me?" Her voice echoed through the cave as her words were steady.

Erin didn't like that idea as the hairs on the back of her neck stood up.

I will not allow her to trap me down here.

"I need answers about my parents. My name is Galena. That's why I'm here."

The woman-maintained eye contact with her. "You're the princess of Rosanafalls," she said, intrigued.

"Are you going to help me or not? What do I have to do?" Erin became more irritated and claustrophobic as each moment passed.

The woman walked off, then grabbed a golden box with a blue jewel on the front. As she opened it, she found a diamond-shaped silver key inside. "This is a skeleton key to your mansion. Don't worry about my debt; it's been paid. Also take this." She tied a bracelet around Erin's wrist that was made of a tan twine. An opal-colored rock the size of a quarter pressed against her skin. "It's an illusion rock."

"You remind me a lot of your mother."

A sudden rush of hope flooded through her mind along with sadness.

"I wish I remembered her" Erin admitted.

The woman brushed her cheek with a feather-like touch and stared into her eyes. "Time and growth coexist. Don't let the past alter your present choices."

Erin shook her head at the riddle as her vision of the woman blurred. She blinked to focus her eyes. A feather-like touch brushed against her skin. The sky was a bright blue without any clouds in sight. When she rose from her position, she spotted a frantic Sylvian who ran toward while helping her to stand. "I was so afraid something happened to you." He pulled her into him and hugged her tightly.

"That was a great idea, the woman knew my mom and she provided me tools to help along the way." She pulled out the key that the woman had handed her to show him along with her bracelet.

His face brightened as he relaxed his shoulders. "I knew it was a smart idea."

"Have you thought of what your plan will be when we arrive? I am afraid that the guards may not welcome our company."

Erin agreed with that—she hadn't exactly trained to be a ninja assassin.

"Sylvian, I will protect you," she promised.

He bent over while laughing at her comment. "Okay, warrior princess."

Unamused, she lightly punched his side.

Suddenly his hand is on the back of her head while the other her inner arm as he offsets her stance sweeping her off her feet and falling on top of her. He hovers his head over her with a wide obnoxious grin on his face. "Work on observation, you need to be vigilant or else you will get kidnapped again."

Erin nodded. "Understood, now get off," she wiggled.

He dropped his head closer to hers and whispered, "Make me."

CHAPTER FIFTEEN

"What the hell, Sylvian?" Zach glared at the two lying on the ground. Erin felt a rush of heat flood up her chest and neck as the weight of Sylvian pressed on her. His legs wrapped around her waist as his arms were on each side of her head while holding his torso up. Sylvian released the hold on her legs and pushed himself up from the ground while offering his hand out.

She took his hand and used her feet to push herself up. Then a hand on each side of her waist pulled her back into a hard surface. She gasped at the sudden jerk of movement while inhaling familiar scents of sandalwood and musk. "Do you not remember what I said about running from me, little Jack rabbit," Sin whispered. Their kiss reappeared in her mind as she stomped on his foot for him to release his hold.

"You guys are the worst, leaving me all alone back there!" Flora yelled out, stomping on the leaves.

She wore an olive-green sundress with white daisies attached to the sheer fabric. The outfit was paired with white sandals that wrapped around her legs with a tied bow in the back. Her golden curls were loose as two pieces framed her face.

Erin's eyes widened. My friend is a nymph goddess. An arm brushed up against her, "Who is that?" Sylvian asked as his eyes sparkled, and his face appeared lost in a trance. She turned towards him, "You didn't meet her last night? Oh right, you decided not to join us," Erin nudged his shoulder.

Erin wasted no time greeting her friend as her smile brightened when she neared.

"Flora!"

"You need to give me the details. I see you have stirred up quite the pot." She laughed while glancing over at the brothers and then finding her way to Sylvian's gaze.

"Flora, you haven't formally met Sylvain.

Sylvian stretched his hand out for her to take, "Pleased to meet you."

"I am not sure how feel about you taking my friend into a forest filled with danger," she cut her eyes at him.

He slacked his shoulders while forcing his gaze downward and dropping his arm to his side.

She flashed her eyes back up at him and smiled, "But you also had the courage to betray Sin and Zach and therefore as long as she is safe, I can let it slide."

He stepped into her space, "Don't worry she is always safe with me."

Flora stepped even closer, "Likewise."

"I can't tell if you two are about to kiss her kill each other," Erin joked.

#

"I don't know what kind of power you have but hearing that Sin's lackey disobeyed him was magical. It took me a minute to realize it, but now I understand why they're all at your beck and call," she said more seriously. "You are the princess and soon-to-be Queen of Rosanafalls!"

Erin twisted her lips into uncertainty. "I don't believe I am fit for that title; it was taken from me when I was a child."

Flora locked eyes with Erin. "The girl I remember was quick on her feet, smart, and wouldn't let anything change her mind. I know that same person is still in there." She poked at Erin's chest with a bright smile. "We also need to work on regaining your memories. Nobody should go through life without remembering their childhood."

"Since I have been here, I've been having random dreams—I believe they're memories from my past."

"That is a good sign. Maybe you're regaining them since you are home."

Erin thought about what that meant, home. Did she mean the place where she was born or the place where she was raised?

"This place will feel more like home when I get my family back and can understand where I came from."

"Don't worry, everything will fall into place."

"You will understand why things happened the way they did, but for now just enjoy the company." She smiled.

The guys walked toward them with dinner and fixings for s'mores. Zach stood next to her while nudging her shoulders. "We come bearing gifts, and something to make it feel a little more like home," he said.

As they lit the fire and cooked dinner, everyone sat around the warmth together. Flora brought a speaker and played music as she began to sway back and forth while drinking her wine. "Come dance with me," she pleaded.

"I'd rather not." Erin laughed. She only danced when nobody was watching.

Everyone laughed at each other's jokes while roasting their marshmallows in the heat of the fire. She felt a bit more intoxicated with each sip of red wine Flora had offered her. It was fun, letting go for the first time in a long time. Flora pulled on her arm until she eventually gave in to the pressure. They danced and sang along with the music while the darkness surrounded them, and the moon shined through the trees.

Erin glanced at Flora, "I will be back."

She wobbled down a path through the woods for privacy. She enjoyed taking a break even if it were for just a couple of minutes. Her mind wandered to more than one sleepless night, and how many of them involved finding the big and little dipper from the night sky. They reminded her of a steady and safe place that remained constant, no matter how quickly things shifted in her life. As she was lost in thought, she heard footsteps from behind.

Is Sin here to discuss that kiss?

"I don't want to talk about it right now," she blurted out.

"Talk about what?" Zach asked. He appeared from the shadows like a demon in the night with bright blond hair and sharp blue eyes. Her chest tightened as she thought about what she should say, but she couldn't control how her eyes observed the flow of veins in his muscular arms.

"I wanted to check on you," he mumbled while walking slowly toward her.

She remained silent and paralyzed.

He was only a foot from her now, and her body felt weaker than normal.

"I'm sorry for hiding your past from you," he said softly. "I guess I was just afraid of what would happen, or change." He remained eye contact while placing his hand on the tree above her head.

"Protecting you became my life, and I crossed a line. I hope you can forgive me."

Erin sighed. "You're important to me, but no more lying."

His eyes grew intense with hunger as he stared into her eyes and then dropped them down to her lips.

Her stomach tightened. She had wanted him to look at her like this for years. Her mind brought her back to the moments of yearning for his touch. She placed her arms around his neck. He pulled her into him as she wrapped her legs around his hips, and she thudded against the bark of the tree.

Then it was too late, and he forced his lips onto hers while she tasted the salty carbonated beer on his lips and tongue. His kiss was hard—like he had wanted this for a long time. It felt good, but also not right, as the kiss with Sin crashed through her thoughts.

Erin pulled herself away from him while allowing her jelly-like legs to stabilize themselves on the ground. She couldn't escape the hurt from his eyes, especially since this was something she had wanted forever. "I just need some time to think about everything. A lot is happening so quickly."

"Yeah, alright, but don't keep me waiting too long," he said while running his hands through his hair. He held her hand while pulling her back to the campsite.

Everyone had already parted ways for their sleeping arrangements. Erin was thankful for that, as she didn't want to run into Sin. "Goodnight, princess." Zach bent down and kissed her cheek.

Erin stepped into the tent that had already been prepared for her and Flora.

Noticing a green light shining from an object beside her bag, Erin gently picked it up. It was a rock that illuminated a vibrant neon green, and she wished she could pull the name from her memory. It was beautiful, and it made her feel safe somehow.

Although she had not wanted to travel too far from her friends, she remembered Flora mentioning a hot spring nearby. She reached for her dagger and the mysterious glowing rock to take for precautions. She knew that walking in the woods alone was a bad idea but having a clean body outweighed the risk. I have a dagger. I will be careful.

CHAPTER SIXTEEN

When she arrived at the spring, she felt taken back by the view as a cloud of steam rolled from the calm and steady surface. She didn't waste any time to remove her clothing and step into the water. The earth felt still, and tension decreased from the warmth that hugged her muscles. She floated onto the water and closed her eyes while taking in the air.

"Gorgeous," a deep and low voice said, breaking the silence.

"Of course, you would be here." She groaned. Sin was already in the water; he must have followed her.

"The little jackrabbit can only run so far from my reach. However, I'm unhappy with your recent actions." Her cheeks flushed. He must have seen Zach and I kissing.

"I will admit he's brash for kissing my girl before I had a say—luckily you pulled away before I had a chance."

She crossed her arms. "I guess I should add stalker to my list of why I shouldn't be with you."

His expression changed from playful to serious as his eyes darkened. He moved toward her like a serpent in the water.

"Don't come any closer," she said, her voice threatening.

"Or what?" He smiled crookedly.

She realized she was the vulnerable one without any clothes on in a hot spring.

Pay attention to your surroundings.

"By the way, did you like my present?"

She recollected her memory of the glowing rock that sat on top of her clothes.

"It's an interesting item. Where did you get it?" Her breath hitched further as he approached.

"It was my mother's. There's history behind how she got it from my father. I wanted you to have it. Something to illuminate your path in life when it becomes dark."

Erin relaxed her face with a gentle smile and sunk her body down into the water.

"What do you remember about me from our past?"

Sin captured her gaze with his dark honey eyes.

"Your imagination was quite something. We'd battle each other, and I'd let you win in the end."

"Is that so?" She laughed. Hearing about a memory she'd lost was exciting, like a mysterious photo that had been revealed from the realms of time.

"I wouldn't mind reenacting. Although, I wouldn't be easy on you. I need to teach my girl how to fight." Sin glanced at Erin and then down at the waters.

"You know, my dad was hard on me. He taught me that love weakened the mind. I understood where he came from, and that's why I forbid myself from having animals. Until I stumbled across an injured fox. I felt so bad for it . . . weak, alone, and vulnerable to predators. Until I took on the role of protecting and nursing its injury. My father wanted me to become a beast like him— powerful and mean. To me, there's strength in caring for something, giving it the freedom to make its own choices.

Erin was interested in his kinder side. "That's sweet."

He was now much closer to her, so close that she could feel his breath on her skin. "You're not like that fox, though—in fact, you have the power to hurt me. Therefore, you're more like a rose with thorns," he whispered in her ear. "Strong, brave, cunning, and deadly." He wrapped his hands around her wrists.

Her heart pounded, and the electricity in her body pulled toward him like a magnet. Maybe he would try to kiss her again. She craved his lips, but that felt dangerous. He gently let go of her and instead stepped out of the water.

He glanced back at her with a towel wrapped across his waist. "I think that you are my weakness." His eyes flashed with desire, and his lips curved into a grin. He allowed her privacy, but not enough to leave her alone.

When she finished, she walked over to where Sin had been sitting.

"Tell me another memory that we shared together."

His eyes softened, then closed as he recalled a memory. "I remember a time you were playing by yourself in a field full of daisies and dandelions. The sun was out, yet the scenery wasn't what caught my attention."

Erin closed her eyes as she tried to imagine the setting.

"I was just on my way to meet my father for training, but when I saw you, everything just went blank. I decided to walk up and ask what you were doing. Instead of answering me, you said 'Close your eyes, blow, and make a wish' while placing a dandelion in my hand. I didn't ask why as I closed my eyes and blew the flower petals into the air. You smiled at me, not realizing you'd already taken my breath away."

Erin pictured them as children playing in a field full of weeds that were more than just an eye sore on someone's front lawn. "Just like that I knew you were mine," Sin said softly. He ran his hand along Erin's cheek and down to her lips. She almost felt like kissing him just then but remembered Zach's kiss from earlier.

"Let's return to the campsite and rest," she said, hoping nobody learned of their disappearance.

She couldn't understand what Zach or Sin saw in her, and she didn't feel like she deserved their attention. As he walked beside her, he brushed his hand against hers but didn't demand it just yet. His dark hair was slicked back from the water; his sandalwood and amber notes engulfed her senses. She felt robbed of her time with him, the moments they shared as kids.

What would I feel for him if I could remember?

"Sin." He slanted his head toward her while preparing for the question to break from her lips. "Why didn't you come looking for me?" To claim to be in love with someone and not attempt to search for them wasn't quite convincing.

"If I had, I'm not sure I could've resisted the urge to take you away from everything you had ever known. I wouldn't have been able to let you go. I had already allowed you to consume my thoughts. It broke me to watch you disappear from the world we created. I wanted to be selfish, though. When I found you swimming underneath the fall, I lost it. My heart that had slowly mended itself had shattered once again."

He stopped walking and turned to face her. Then he placed his hands on each side of her waist. Losing herself in his amber eyes, she noticed a hint of green behind them. "I apologize for hurting you, but I will never allow you to fade from my life again. If you had stayed away, maybe it would have been different."

The brush of his fingers just above her collarbone sent shivers of desire down her spine. She could feel a pull toward him, as though just being near him was simple and exactly where she should be.

Wolves howled through the forest, but instead of being alarmed, she stood there while lost in his hold. He leaned in, and even though she knew she needed to stop him from moving closer she stood in place. When their lips touched, a spark of energy awakened her body. Like jumping into a refreshing pool after being in the summer sun all day.

The soft breeze shifted as he pulled her into his body. She succumbed to his lips as he lifted her legs and let her wrap them tightly around him. Grasping his neck, she clawed the back of his shoulder.

He sucked in and pulled away. "Careful, little jackrabbit. Tease me too hard and I will never let you go."

CHAPTER SEVENTEEN

The splash of loud waves sent vibrations through Erin's ears; it was a familiar sound that she could never forget. As she opened her eyes, she realized she was in a dreamlike state. She could feel the gritty sand between her toes and the warmth from the sun. It was a dream filled with orange and red colors, comforting ones. She felt safe as she watched a woman standing in the water staring back at her. The women appeared to have short blonde hair and hazel eyes.

When she glanced down at her feet, she noticed a sand dollar and carefully picked it up. It was a full piece with a star on the top, surrounded by white. She could tell that it had already decomposed due to the dull appearance and dried out texture. Although the sand dollar was dead, Erin found beauty from the skeleton. It left its mark on the world while viewed as an object of desire.

#

An orange glow pierced through the tent as Erin blinked her eyes open. She tiptoed out of her tent and walked to the designated restroom spot. Then she walked back toward the campsite until she noticed a man standing against a tree. He looked to be around her age, with ruffled bright-red hair and freckles, and he wore an army-green button-down shirt and beige pants. He stared at her way with an interested look beneath his green eyes.

Before she could move toward him, he was out of sight. Walking slowly, she felt an unsettled twinge from her insides. She steadied her pace until she felt a pull on her ankles. She looked down and realized two snakes were staring at her with slithering split tongues. One was a vibrant red with yellow diamond patterns and the other had black diamond patterns. Don't panic, they're not going to hurt you. At least I hope not. But just to be safe I will make no sudden movements.

Then the red-haired man appeared. "I see you have met my beauties, Scarlet and Rye. I promise they won't hurt you, if you do what I say."

She tried to remain calm as her pulse quickened. Shouldn't have wandered off.

He didn't appear as dangerous as the snakes, but she wasn't testing that theory. They tightened their grip as he waited for her to comply. All her belongings were in the tent along with her weapon. She noted to have that on her next time.

"What do you want? I don't have any money." Is he working with that man that previously kidnapped me?

"There is something that I want to show you, Galena."

Her face scrunched in confusion. "Who are you?"

He walked into her space as the vibrant red snake with black diamonds wrapped itself around her throat and the other her shoulders, "I will explain, but I'd rather do it in the privacy of my own home."

"What if I don't want to go with you?" Her muscles stiffened from the fear of the snakes sinking their fangs into her. She tried not to show that she was terrified as her hands began to shake uncontrollably.

He smirked, "I wasn't asking what you wanted, little toxin."

Her fists tightened by her sides as he pulled out a black cloth from his pocket. He walked behind her, used the black cloth to cover her eyes, and whispered into her ears, "I will lead you—just don't try anything stupid."

I am sure my friends will find me, I hope. She had no idea what his intentions were and the feeling of possibly being trapped frightened her. For now, she had to stay calm and do what he said, at least until she could figure out a plan. He grabbed her hand and guided her in an unknown direction.

When they seized walking the man untied Erin's blindfold. When her vision cleared, she was able to examine her surroundings. The home reminded her of a house that a horror fan would enjoy. It looked like a two-story home judging by the height and windows while painted black with a built around porch. I seriously hope he isn't going to chop me up into pieces.

He led her up the stairs and opened the black doors to the house. A woodsy and sweet smell filled the air as they stepped inside. Neon green paintings of snakes surround the dark walls. He seems a little obsessed with snakes. She followed him into a large room with a leather sectional in front of a bricked fireplace.

He nodded his head in the direction of the couch. "Take a seat."

Her skin pressed into the cold leather of the couch as she allowed it to support her weight.

"I will be right back, don't move?" He walked to her while putting his arms out for the snakes to travel onto.

She noticed the uniform and spotless room. The atmosphere was cold and sad. I wonder if he lives here alone. Either way I need to find a way out of here. She glanced at the corner where the front door was and wondered if she should attempt her escape. But before she could decide, Shane walked back into the room while holding two white mugs.

As he handed her one of the mugs the scent of vanilla and honey tea awakened her senses.

"It's not poisoned," he reassures as he sits next to her.

She sipped just a little to appease him, tasting bold and earthy tones along with the sweetness from the honey and vanilla.

"My name is Shane." He sips on his tea. "I happen to know your father."

A rush of hope crossed her mind. "Do you know his whereabouts?"

He placed his mug down on the wooden table in front of them.

"No, he doesn't like for is location to be known."

She sat up straight while placing her mug next to Shane's. "Why?"

"He would have to tell you himself."

She leaned back onto the couch while closing her eyes. Shocker.

"So how did you meet him?"

"My mother and father died when I was young. As a child I developed an interest in venomous creatures, which made me an odd kid to take in. Luckily, your father found me, and helped me out, while allowing me to stick to the shadows I call home. He could have easily called me out, and my life would have been over."

"Instead, he paid me to learn about the chemical agents of venom and how to create an antivenin. He told me he would return to collect and deliver a payout. He provided this home. My orders were to bring him the antivenin and his daughter to him. But I'm unsure of his location currently."

"Alright, but if you had led with that, I would've come with you."

"So, you would have agreed to follow some random stranger—you are a weird one. "He grinned.

"I am the weird one?" she said with a sarcastic tone.

"The future Queen of Rosanafalls should be more careful," he said while taking her hand into his.

"That will never sound normal to me."

"Shane, you know you took me away from my friends who are literally on the same mission?"

A loud thud interrupted their conversation. "I see you made friends with this bastard," shouted a familiar voice from the other side of the room.

Shane nearly jumped out of his pants when he saw Zach across the room. "How the hell did you get past my snakes?" he roared, glaring.

"You mean these," Zach said. He lifted his forearms to show the vibrant red creatures slithering and squirming. You forget, I created a bond with these damn ugly things." Zach placed them onto the floor as they slithered away. "While you were researching, I was learning about how your friends work."

Zach sat next to Erin. She felt a rush of relief spread over her body as she smiled at him. "Are you alright?" She wrapped her arms around his neck as he placed his securely around her waist. His scent reminded her of the salty water from the chaotic ocean. It made her feel as though she was home again. "I am now that you are here."

"Don't tell me you have fallen for the princess," Shane said, giving Zach a friendly push.

Erin could feel her cheeks filling with blood from the remark.

"Honey, I'm home!" Sin shouted as he barged in.

"I need to work on my security," Shane roared.

"Oh, come on. It's just like the old days when we would chill as kids." Flora slapped Shane on the arm.

Shane's eyes softened. "Yeah, I do remember those days. I guess I will work on food arrangements and then we can talk about what we need to do next."

"I'll help." Sylvian followed Shane to the kitchen. Zach and Sin sat on each side of Erin. Feeling a little closed in, she stood up from her spot while looking for the way to the bathroom. Sin and Zach glared at each other as if there were competition.

"I'm going to get drinks." Flora smiled and walked off.

"First door on the left down the hall," Zach said.

"You know me so well." She nodded. But instead of stopping there, she decided to investigate Shane's home. She still did not trust him, and right now he was distracted.

She pushed a door open to reveal walls that were covered in a dramatic forest green while creating a moody atmosphere. His mattress was a king with a black comforter. She walked toward a desktop which had three connected computer monitors attached to it. The setup reminded her of the place she woke up in when kidnapped. Could he be connected to the man that recently kidnapped me?

Knowing she wouldn't have time to turn on the computer, she looked through the small desk drawers. She found small syringe needles with a yellow tint of liquid inside.

What is he doing with those? Not daring to touch them, she quietly closed the drawer back.

As she made her way out of the room, she noticed something lying on the counter next to his bed. It was a small sand dollar necklace. Holding it in her hand, she examined the pale white exterior while wondering why this was lying on his table. It instantly brought memories of her recent dream. I am sure it's a coincidence. She placed it back down and stepped out of the room.

She finally found the restroom and was invited by the warmth of a bright light inside. It reminded her of a rainforest, with green and blue marble on the floor, and turquoise painted walls. There was a large tub, and right beside it stood a miniature waterfall.

A soft tap thudded against the door. She walked over and opened it, finding Zach holding her toiletries. "In case you want to get cleaned up."

"Thanks." She smiled. This time he hugged her more tightly, and it made her feel warm inside. When his hands dropped down to the middle of her back it sent a flutter of tickles inside of her stomach.

"Erin, will you be mine?" he whispered. His hot breath made every inch of hair stand up. She wanted to give him an answer, to say yes because this is what she had wanted for such a long time. *I need to explore my feelings for Sin.* "Please allow me time."

His face fell, and he nodded, then left her alone.

CHAPTER EIGHTEEN

Shane brought a book out that had a metal exterior with white pages inside. He opened it up and revealed drawings of waterfalls, caves, hideouts, and designed weapons on each page, including Erin's dagger. As she reviewed each page, she realized her father had written descriptions next to the weapons.

"Your father is a smart man, and he made sure to stay two steps ahead of the game. He didn't want anything to happen to you, and he planned to kill the man who stole your mother," Shane explained.

Then she found a letter addressed to her:

Dear Galena,

I can only hope you do not pursue this any further, but just like me, you might wish to fulfill your desires. In that case, this book will lead you toward the correct path. There is quite a journey mapped out for you. Of course, you know this place we live in is based around the famous waterfall, named after your ancestors. This waterfall is the powerhouse of our land, and there are multiple waterfalls with hidden treasures.

Unfortunately, I'm going after a man that found this out, and he needs to be stopped. Once he finds the magic rocks, not only will he hold all the power to our home, but he will also destroy it. Just be careful. He has people who are always watching. Don't trust anyone. Last thing—Shane has created an antivenin. You may use it for yourself, but if you consume too much venom, it could kill you.

I love you, Galena. I will find you soon.

Your father,

Bastian

This was good news; she had a lead to follow, and in return, she would find her father. It was a lot to take in. Her heart raced from the excitement and nerves. Deciding to take a break, she stepped outside for air. She wished she were more prepared, yet she knew that with her friends, she'd be alright. "But still why leave me in the first place?"

"He may have been protecting you, but he could have gone about this another way," Sin said. He sat down, placing a friendly arm around her waist as she laid her head onto his shoulder. "I felt like I never belonged in the home I grew up in. I watched other kids join sports and participate in camps or clubs. Meanwhile, I sat in an empty home, alone. I would wish for the perfect family, but I quickly realized that wasn't the path chosen for me. And here I am, picking up the pieces left for me to figure out."

"I will help, you don't have to feel alone anymore." He wiped her tears.

"Why would you want someone like me?" she asked softly. Feeling his body twitch, she wondered if she made a mistake, as she still didn't know how she felt.

"That's it. I am taking you out of this place to make you mine—forever." He lifted her from the ground.

"Sin, as much as I would like to be whisked away and taken to an exotic land, we need a plan." She laughed.

"Deal. Where do you want to go when this is all over?"

"Somewhere by the water, with lots of sun and cold drinks with those cute umbrellas."

"Anything for my jackrabbit's happiness. If you promise to never run from me again." He smiled, and she raised her eyebrows, then escaped back into the house.

Before she opened the door, he grabbed her waist and pulled her body into his. "To answer your question from earlier, it's your imagination. There's a world of beauty that only exists behind your eyes, and it's inspiring. And I just want to smile when around you. You charge my internal batteries," he continued, gently kissing her neck. She felt vibrations run from her body as she wiggled free from his arms and walked inside.

Zach's eyes veered toward them, a hint of anger flickering behind them. Knowing she was in a world of trouble, Erin decided to focus on the task ahead of them instead. "Okay, so we need to split up to cover the grounds," she said, dropping the book onto the table. Everyone's eyes were on her, and she felt thankful for all their help. It was nice to have a large group of friends compared to her former days.

"We will split up into pairs, find the magic rocks, and report back to each other." Erin tore pages from the book that had the locations of each waterfall and handed them to Shane, Zach, and Flora. Shane received amethyst, Zach received ruby, and Flora received emerald.

"Choose your partners." Sin rolled his eyes. "We all know who Zach is choosing."

"Erin, you're coming with me," Shane said. "Besides I can discuss more with you," he said to her.

"I call dibs on Sylvian," Flora said.

Zach looked at Sin in disappointment. "I guess you're stuck with me." She was a little relieved—a break from the men and to focus on her goals would be beneficial.

"We will all meet back at the center point of these waterfalls; they are only a couple of miles away from each other," Erin said. "We can start our journey in the morning and pack tonight."

"Everyone, follow me," Shane said. As they entered the room, there were multiple weapons displayed on the wall. Handmade guns, knives, swords, and bowing arrows. Sin began by taking a sword and handgun while Zach grabbed the rifle and dagger. Flora grabbed the bow, and Sylvian grabbed a handgun and knife. Shane grabbed a handgun and a combat knife.

Erin was the last one to pick. She had a sick feeling in her stomach, as she had no desire to hurt anyone. "Look, I'm not going on a manhunt, Shane. Don't you think this is a bit much?" Sin let out a loud sigh to break the silence as he grabbed a small handgun and placed it in her hands. "It's only for your protection. You don't know who you're dealing with, and you would rather be safe than sorry."

She felt the weight of the cold metal in her hands and thought about how pulling one finger could end someone's life. She shoved it back into Sin's hands. "No, I have my father's weapon and prefer not to resort to that. I am confident without it."

Before Sin could say anything, Zach wedged himself in between them and grabbed the gun from Sin. "She doesn't want it. Now leave her alone," he said while placing it back.

Both guys glared at each other for a moment before Shane broke the tension. "Alright, prepare for your mission. We will meet in the middle of the waterfalls in three days in the morning. If all of us aren't back, then we will come looking."

Everyone went on to do as Shane ordered them, but Erin hung back for a second. The thought of ending someone's life made her quiver. I will use this only as a last resort. Then she grabbed the gun Sin had given her earlier. As she walked back upstairs, Sin embraced her. "I'm not sure I trust you alone with this guy," he whispered.

"I will be fine," she said while flashing him a portion of the gun.

He grabbed her arm gently. "Please be safe." Then he held her face and pulled her into him while brushing his lips against hers. "You don't want to see the bad side of me. But if I had my way, nobody would come between us."

His dark eyes were handsome, and her body betrayed her heart as she soaked in his warmth. "I will be okay. Don't worry about me," she said and pressed herself gently from his hold. She could tell Sin didn't want her to go but he had no choice. As she walked away, she felt his eyes on her.

CHAPTER NINETEEN

Everyone prepared for the morning's adventures as the sun's rays warmed the earth. Erin allowed herself time to admire the glowing bright yellow along with the softer shades of red that sifted through the blue sky.

"Ready?" Shane said to her from behind. She stood up and stretched, then nodded in Shane's direction.

She pulled out her map and began down the trail that would lead them to the waterfall. It was fun to walk through the forest and mountains while studying the trees along the way. It was crazy to her how long trees lived, and the forms of life they witnessed through time. "5,000 years," she said aloud, and Shane blinked at her curiously. "That's the age of the oldest tree."

"Interesting. Too bad we don't live that long," Shane spoke.

"Would you live that long if you had the choice?"

He shrugged his shoulders, "I don't know. I mean, I would have so much time to accomplish a better life, whatever that would mean. You?"

"I believe we could learn a lot, but it's possible to lose sight of the value of life. On an uplifting note, I am sure these trees hold all sorts of secrets." She giggled.

His smile turned into a straight-lined serious expression as she noticed a flick of secrecy in his own eyes. "I guess we will never know," he said.

The crackling sound of thunder roared from a distance as the temperature outside began to drop. "When you're indoors, thunderstorms are the best mood stabilizer." Erin looked back at Shane, a little worried. "We need to get to this waterfall before the storm."

Her legs may have been on fire, but she was relieved to have made it to the waterfall. This one seemed to split into two falls and resembled a drawn curtain. Erin noticed there were stone stairs at the foot of the waterfall. There was only one way of getting through—swimming across.

She slid off her dress and put it in her bag, then slowly dipped her body into the icy water. When she was on the other side, she had Shane toss the bags over to her. She looked back and noticed Shane staring her way, causing her to feel uneasy. He pulled off just his shirt and jumped into the water, then swam quickly over to her side. Both shivered, safely underneath the shelter of the cave from the cloudburst.

It comforted Erin, reminding her of the days she would wrap up in a warm blanket and read her favorite book.

"What was your life like before you ended up here?" Shane asked.

Erin thought about school and her teachers, how the concept of the future was their focus. What career do you want? What college will you be going to? Where will you live? When will you create a family?

"There was always a need for implementing goals, worrying about the future." "I was taught to follow a mapped-out path of goals to achieve through life, but it was exhausting, and stressful." Erin dropped her shoulders and sighed. "It was a lot of pressure."

Shane's green eyes showed a glimmer of sympathy. He placed a hand onto her shoulder. "When you feel anxiety from worrying about the future remember to watch either a sunrise or sunset." "It can clear our headspace and remind us of the present."

"Thanks, I will have to try that."

He smiled but his grin shifted into a frown. "Time to get moving," he said.

What was that about? She followed him into the cave while proceeding with caution.

It was quiet in the cave, and dark. Erin remembered her green light and pulled it out to illuminate their path. Thanks, Sin. Suddenly, she lost her footing and slid down a slope of rocks, causing her to slide into a bottomless black pit.

She caught her breath and calmed her anxiety when she realized what had happened. A burning sensation on the back of her arms and legs caused her to wince in pain. She looked up to see if she could catch a glimpse of Shane.

"Erin are you alright?" he shouted.

"Yes. I am going to try to find a way up." Slowly, she pushed herself from the ground and looked ahead. My clumsiness is treacherous, but at least I only have a couples of scratches and possible bruises. As she continued down a path, she heard a trickling sound.

The noise grew louder as she arrived at what sounded like rushing water. Vibrant lavender and violet hues illuminated a large waterfall as her jaw dropped in awe. Then she remembered words from her father's book and immediately pulled it out from her bag.

"Beneath the cave waterfall lies a powerful and magical elemental rock that belongs to the guardian and wielder of the Claw sword." She placed the book down and walked toward the pool of water. Luckily, it was shallow enough to study the bottom. She dipped her feet carefully into the water and picked up a rock that appeared to be calcified.

As she pulled it out, she noticed that there was a lavender color shining from the inside. She climbed out of the water and hit it against the ground, hoping it would break. It took a couple hits until it broke apart and dropped out an object. The amethyst stone was carved into a wolf, and she could feel energy from the vibrations of the cold stone. It was like a jolt of tingling electricity—not enough to physically hurt her, but to inform her of its power.

Then a memory from her past emerged. She remembered her father handing over a sword to Zach and Sin when they were younger. He proceeded to teach them sword-fighting techniques—yet another memory that mysteriously appeared as she rolled the palm-sized object in her hand.

She grabbed her book and flipped through the pages. A few minutes later, she came across a page that had drawings of multiple weapons that resembled Zach's. One of the drawings of the swords had a long slick black charcoal finish, with a silver blade and a black leather rope hanging from its handle. Looking closer, she noticed an insert that was shaped like a dog or a wolf with the word amethyst written above it. This amethyst wolf pairs with the sword drawing from the notebook.

As soon as those thoughts crossed her mind, she noticed that there was a small note written across the sword—something one would have to look for. As you grow older, this will protect you. You can find the sword where you were born.

I wonder if this message was meant for Zach. As she stood up, she heard a large rumble, and quickly stashed the wolf into her bag.

A loud crash resounded a couple of feet from where she had fallen. She walked toward the noise and rolled her eyes while looking down at Shane. Now we're both stuck down here.

"I had no choice. We have unexpected visitors," he whispered. As she heard mumbling from above them, her heart sank.

"Okay, let's try to find a way out," she whispered, grabbing his hand to help him off the ground. His expression shifted into an evil grin as he tightened his grip around her hand and immediately yanked her down along with him. He held her body tightly against his and yelled "Down here!"

"What the hell?" she screamed, struggling to free herself from his grasp.

"Sorry, Erin, but I had a job to do, and you made it too easy."

As she bit into his hand, he loosened his grip. Then she twisted herself out of his grasp and kicked him in the crouch before he could get up.

"Shit," he grunted irritably.

She pulled her gun from her bag and pointed it at him, trembling with anger.

"I don't have time for answers right now, but you better stay down. Don't follow me," she said, shining her light through the tunnel. I should have known better than to trust a snake.

She browsed the dark cave for any sign of light. Feeling fatigued, she slowed down her pace. I didn't come this far just to quit. Then she ran her fingers along the walls as she felt for any kind of air movement. She came to an opening that inverted itself into a gaping hole and raised her light toward it. Tight spaces frightened her, so this would be a challenge, but at this point, she had no other option.

Crawling onto the rough surface, she was careful not to harm any more of her skin. As she had learned to breathe through her anxiety, she sent her mind into a calm state while retrieving a memory to distract herself. Wasn't she fond of hide-and-seek as a child? Then a memory flashed through her mind.

#

She was running down a red-carpet hallway while trailing upstairs as someone counted. She ran her hands across the wooden railing, she tried to walk on only her toes, while being quiet as a mouse. Before the seeker arrived, she had found a hiding space.

"Ready!" he warned.

She sat there in her red velvet dress, red bows on each side of her short brown hair, lying on the cold floor. Peeking out just a little, she saw Benny pass her while looking all around.

"Found you," whispered a voice behind her. She turned and saw Zach with a smug grin.

Before she could say anything, she heard an older man's voice outside the hallway, and she looked to see who it was coming from. It was a tall man with a dark beard and dark eyes to match, and he looked angry at Benny. Erin realized he was wearing the same boots from her last memory. Feeling worried, she looked back at Zach and put her hand on the wall to push it open.

Zach said, "No, you will only make it worse—just let him be." She felt bad but did as he said, although she wanted to help him.

#

She fazed out of her memory as the crawl space became more cramped. At this point, she was sweating and struggling to breathe. Thankfully, there was an out, but it led her to another part of the cave as she dropped down. She stretched for a second, thankful to be on her feet again instead of crawling on a rough surface. Then she noticed words written on the walls.

She ran her fingers across the letters carved into the rock and followed them down until she found stairs leading further into the cave. She didn't want to go any further but needed to explore. Once she arrived at the bottom, she noticed a door that was handmade with real cherry oak wood material. On the outside, the word Rosana was written in cursive. She pulled a red notebook from a shelf that was built into the wall and flipped it open.

Each royal daughter will continue the family name, Rosana. She will be born with a gift to protect the land and maintain peace among the people. This wasn't the case long ago. There used to be arranged marriages, but that all changed when a witch and princess collaborated for the freedom of choice in love.

Now, her husband will take on her last name and become her protector. He shall not obtain power and will be taught to fight in battle. This is meant to lower the chances of placing power into a reckless man's hands. If one has chosen the correct partner to rule, then all will prosper from the land. There will be no pain, suffering, or malnourishment.

The largest waterfall has become a special landmark for Rosanafalls. It holds special healing properties with the use of royal blood. Within each waterfall displayed across the land is a cave guarded by its people's ancestral history. Rosana is the last name a woman is born with and must pass onto her partner in marriage.

This place is for anyone with the Rosana last name. It is a sanctuary for protection from outside threats.

Most of all, welcome home, Royal One.

CHAPTER TWENTY

ZACH'S POV

I stare at the wolf den that rests above the waterfall ahead, continuing toward it as I glance back at Sin. It's surprising that he's made it this long without running back to Erin, but I remind myself that she still hasn't chosen—though I fear she might be falling for his charm.

Sin catches up to me and bumps my shoulder. "Let's get this over with. I can't stand to see her alone with another man."

As I walk into the dark cave, I decide to follow the wolf imprints on the ground.

"You know, she has already made up her mind," he says.

I continue to walk because I know this is an attempt to crawl his way underneath my skin. The cave growls as though there's a large wolf hidden behind the walls.

"She is already mine," Sin says.

The muscles in my jaw tense from his words.

"Regardless of what you believe, we won't know until she makes a choice."

"Those lips tasted divine, though. I can't explain how intoxicated I feel when I'm kissing her."

"Sin!"

"Don't touch her. She's mine." He repeats himself as though he has already claimed her.

Being in love with the same person feels like a never-ending game of tug and war. Although, I do not play a fair game, and I am sure that at the end of this one, she will become my wife.

There's a door at the end of the hall with two crossed swords on the front. Both have placeholders for wolf inserts, and they are silver with a metal handle. I look over my shoulder and see that Sin has already disappeared. "Of course,"

I yell. "Like a dog running back to his owner—damn fool."

Grabbing the sword closest to me, I pull it from the door. I remember that it was one I had trained with long ago. I glance at the door and wonder how I am supposed to open it.

"Need some help," A voice sounds. To my right is a man with icy white-blond hair and crystal-clear blue eyes.

"I haven't seen you in years, cousin." He pushes from the wall and walks toward me.

"I've been busy," I say.

"Tell me, does busy have a name?" Ezra says.

I've decided it is best not to tell him about my love interest. "Do you think you could help me open this door?"

He looks at me as though he's deciding if he wants to push harder for information. Then his shoulders drop, and he grabs the other sword. He stands directly in front of me and pulls the sword in front of his face, and I mirror his movements. "A fighter must solute before battle. It's a sign of respect against their opponent," he says.

He bows, and I follow along with the charade. Lastly, he cuts his sword in the air. "You must cross my sword." The swords clash against each other, and then a feeling of vibrations shifts underneath my feet. There is a click, and the door opens for us.

"How did you know all of that?"

"Zach, clearly you have never wondered about our ancestors." He shakes his head.

"Nope, been busy with the one person who's taken over my thoughts for years. Without her, nothing matters."

"So, there is someone," Ezra says, reminding me of his presence. I almost want to kick myself for saying that aloud.

But then there is silence, and just like everyone else, Ezra vanishes from my sight. I picked up the sword he had held and walked through the door. Lights flash on from all around as though I am in a hospital. I catch a strong smell of bergamot and leather as I glance around the room. There is a fireplace on the right and a brown leather couch in front of it. There appears to be a kitchen with a bar set up.

As I walk through the halls, I find a restroom and even a master room. "Who keeps up with all of this?" I wonder aloud. "Maybe Ezra can direct me to the source." The room is full of bookshelves, and I immediately think of Erin. "She loves her books." The last room that I find is larger than the others.

Hanging on the walls are multiple swords in a glass case. Each sword has a name carved on the front. Written on the wall above are the words. The swords of the fallen, Protectors of the royals who guard the land.

Then I come across a familiar sword as I scan them. Engraved in the blade is Alzaar Zayn Claw. A shiver runs through my spine as I think of the cruel man behind that sword.

He has low tolerance for weakness and zero mercy. Behind it is a slab with information written on it. I readjust my eyes to read it.

Shall be passed down to only son, Sin Felix Claw.

Must be a mistake. The sword, just like the others, has a wolf imprinted on them with a silver blade and metal handle. They appear to be crafted by the same person.

Then I saw the name Kayleon Calvar Sharp.

Wait, what the hell? Written underneath Sons it says Zachary Silas Sharp.

Obviously, Erin and I aren't related because her real name is Galena, and the Rosana blood runs through her veins. I grasp both Sin's sword and mine while confusion settles in my chest. Has my whole life been a lie? A

Sitting in another display case is a bright-red ruby shaped into a rose. It reads underneath the display case: To be passed down through the Rosana generations, safeguarded here until the next in line is available to become queen.

This will surely brighten her day. Then I remember a certain irritating brother—

Half-brother—who has already run back to her.

Be there soon, princess.

CHAPTER TWENTY-ONE

SYLVIAN'S POV

I follow Flora as she strides through the forest at a fast pace. Her copper curls are twisted tight, and she wears a turquoise eye shadow and dress to match. The dress is beaded with silver jewels and flares just above the knees. It wraps around her neck and leaves her arms bare, and it compliments her brown skin. My eyes lower while scoping out her petite figure. I realize just how much I am staring as she turns around.

I catch up with her and maintain her pace.

"It's about time," she says, breaking the silence.

"I was just admiring what's in front of me." I smile.

She bites her lip as if holding back a grin.

"What's your deal, Sylvian? Why do you stay with Sin?"

As we walk through the trees, I notice that her eyes match the color of the vines that wrap themselves securely around their bark.

"I was supposed to be returning a favor. To be honest I just kind of lost my purpose."

She smiles, and I feel like my heart has stopped. "Good thing about life is that you can find a new path to follow. It just takes the courage to start."

"Wise words."

"I know a thing or two." She winks.

Our arms brush against each other. "I should stick around you more often."

She pulls her body away while leaving me frustrated with the distance between us.

"After you help Erin, what will you do?"

She is quiet for a moment, and I allow the silence. The wind moves through the trees as the sound of crunched leaves echoes beneath our feet. I hear the rustle of a creature in a bush beside us.

"I want to learn more about my abilities and my background," she says. "My mother hasn't been around to teach me about my magic, and so I have been stuck researching on my own. Before my grandmother passed, she spoke of attending 'Owlery falls.' It's a place full of women and men who practice magic. They use the symbol of a white owl to represent transformation. She would say 'Growth and education are infinite; our desire to continue that can alter our transformation.' I plan to grow stronger and wiser, to become an advocate for us.

"We have been manipulated, used, and slandered by people through time. I understand why many have found homes in isolation and are afraid to learn about their ancestors. I have learned that royals and witches have bargained for peace among the lands and in return help each other. Although, there are some in power that are more focused on taking advantage.

"Which brings me back to why I need to be there for Erin. Royals and witches are alike regarding having power. But when handed down a heavy responsibility it becomes a burden. Your life is controlled and guarded by the dangers of power-hungry people. And she is in a position where she knows nothing about her past, the life of a princess, or the power that has been passed down to her. She needs me."

"I love the idea of learning about yourself. And standing up for your people is brave. The error I find in your words is allowing yourself to be consumed by obligation. Maybe it is wise to stand back and lend out a hand when necessary?"

When I find her eyes again, they widen with a shimmering sparkle in them. She places a gentle hand on my arm as a sense of tingling spreads through me. Her touch is energized, and my heart may spark if she leans in any closer.

"Careful, Sylvian. Your words offer an interest in my well-being and that could lead towards dangerous waters."

I almost tell her that I am more than willing to travel through hell if she were waiting for me when I found my way out. But then the sounds of rushing water distract her from the conversation, and the moment is gone too soon.

"We're finally here." She tosses her hands up in the air with a twirl. In front of us is a massive waterfall; its peak is hidden in the clouds. She grasps my hand and pulls me forward. "Sylvian let's stick together," she says, and then the floor moves from beneath our feet. Darkness surrounds us, and I hold onto her hand firmly.

"Don't worry. We will be alright," she says. When the movement stops, all I see is neon green. Then people in green and gold robes with embroidered white owls on the right side of the fabric. A tall man with arm tattoos, spiky black hair, and an angry expression appears.

"Gene, it's great to see you!" Flora shouts.

He nods in my direction. "Who's the pretty boy?"

"Oh, this is Sylvian." She places an arm around my shoulder. "He won't say a word, I promise."

"He needs to see the leader. Send him her way, and then you can have your usual room."

"Alright, Gene." She smiles and grabs my arm.

Before I can speak, she pushes me into a room and covers my mouth. "I would advise you to keep quiet about our intentions, pretty boy."

She winks, and I lean down next to her ear.

"What are yours?" She leans closer, and I smell the sweet fragrance of lavender and jasmine. "I already told you, but I know you have a small number of people you trust."

My mouth is already curved into a smile because I realize that I would trust this woman with my life. I make haste with a decision to catch her off guard and plant a kiss on her lips. They're filled with fire, and I feel an urge to consume her, but I pull gently away instead. Her eyes lock me in with a fierce jade green. Then a sudden knock at the door shifts our focus.

Flora led me to sit on a beige leather sofa as she opened the door. A woman with a striking beauty and an assertive demeanor walked through the door. Her eyes are dark brown, and she has bronze skin with black braids that fall down her back. She wore a green-seaweed colored vintage dress and tethered sleeves that hang at her elbows. Her leather brown boots are up to her knees, and a necklace with the same white owl attached to it rests on her chest.

"Sylvian, it's nice to be in your presence. My name is Sakura." She reaches out her hand, and I accept it.

"Nice to meet you." Before I continue, a shocking sensation runs through my body. I feel paralyzed, like my life is flashing before my eyes. Pictures of my youth flood through my mind, and I watch my memories play back like a television show.

The last thing I see is when my first love leaves, and then I feel the excruciating pain cut through my chest. Then the pain is pulled away, and I am staring back at Sakura and Flora. I can see the worried expression on Flora's face as her eyes narrowed.

"Sylvian, I've discovered that magic abilities lay dormant inside of you. I'd like to invite you to our headquarters," Sakura says.

I placed a hand on my forehead from the splitting migraine she caused me. "What just happened?"

"No harm has been done to you. I just needed to know that your intentions weren't malicious. We have enemies and outsiders that would take the opportunity to steal our people for their gain."

"I understand."

"As for your powers . . ."

I hesitate to respond because my parents were normal, as far as I knew.

"I'm not sure what you're talking about."

Sakura smiles wide. "When the time comes, you'll learn of your ability. It'll be when you most need it. For now, I invite you to stay and learn more about the art of magic and transformation." She hands me a card with a castle on it. "When you're ready, this is where the rest of us are located."

She proceeds to hand Flora an emerald-shaped wolf. They both nod at each other as though they have a secret language. Sakura leaves, and I am left with confusion and my migraine from the events that transpired.

"Well, that was easy." Flora smiled.

I pierced my gaze towards her, "Maybe for you."

She places a hand on my shoulder, "So, you've been holding out on me?"

I widen my eyes. "I never knew."

"To tell you the truth, I never knew either; I found out in the worst way." My eyes soften, and then there's a knock at the door.

Flora runs to it. "Gene! What a lovely surprise."

He grimaces. "You have outsiders roaming around—take care of them, or I will."

CHAPTER TWENTY-TWO

Erin cracked the door open to reveal the inside of the room. When there appeared to be no visible threats, she walked in. There were lights placed on the walls, and a red carpet rolled out between two comfortable-looking brown leather-style chairs. Antique tall clocks leaned alongside the cave walls, and bookshelves were placed throughout the place.

Porcelain dolls were placed on top of wooden tables; their black and dark-brown hairstyles tied with bows. She found the room with a queen-sized bed and a sheer red curtain hanging around it, golden silk sheets, and white decorative pillows on the top with the letter R embroidered into them. At the foot of the bed was a brass-colored book with silver pages. She opened it up and began to read:

Dear Royal,

This is now your sanctuary, and here you shall stay safe from anyone outside of our bloodline. A spell has been placed upon these walls to only allow the sacred inside. You may have already learned this place holds powers, passed down through generations to the eldest daughters to become powerful rulers and guardians. My name is Jenevia Mae Rosana, the Queen of Rosanafalls.

The name Rosana has presented itself through time as a protector of the land. We have learned how to guard our homes and fend for ourselves away from the cruel world outside. We also possess the necessary power and allies to help with this form of protection upon the land. If you are a woman in the bloodline and are next in line to become queen, you will keep the Rosana name, and the man shall acquire it. Just because a man takes the name does not mean that he is in the bloodline until he proves himself to be genuine and loyal to his new home and family.

If this is my granddaughter, Galena, then I am pleased that you have made it safely home. I wish I could welcome you with my arms. You will learn the secrets hidden for good reason in the family. I know that you will help to provide peace in Rosanafalls as you lay your mark on our home.

Love,
Jenevia Mae Rosana

Erin gently closed the book. She felt a little nervous about the information. Is this really the life I want? Not too long ago I had been setting goals for college. I know nothing about being a princess or becoming a Queen.

As she rose to her feet, she looked at the books on the case and noticed that one stuck out to her. It was made of red-colored leather and cream-colored pages. On each page written were poems, and on the cover read, "Each petal tells a story." Then she placed the book in her bag.

I will read this when I have the time.

This place would be here for her to return to, and she wanted to track down the others before Shane got to them. She had to find a way out as she scanned the room all around for a clue. At the back in a corner, she saw what appeared to be a door, but it blended in with the walls of the cave with gray and sharp edges all around. She pushed on it as it opened to the other side, allowing the warmth from the sun to embrace her skin. Hearing the waterfall from a distance, she realized it was above her.

Then she ran as fast as she could into the woods to hide herself. It looked as though it would be a couple of miles on foot to the next waterfall, but what choice did she have at this point? As she insisted on running further into the forest, her ankle became caught in something that immediately yanked her body upside down.

Anxiety crawled through her stomach. The sounds of leaves crunching caused her to still. Damn, my luck is not looking up right now.

"I'm sure glad your knight and shining armor has come to the rescue," Sin said as he cut the rope and allowed her to fall into his arms.

She closed her eyes as the blood rushed back to its designated areas. Then as her feet touched the ground, she hugged him back, thankful for the rescue.

"Are you okay?" he asked.

"I am managing." Then they broke free from each other, and she tamed her hair and dress. She realized that he had been alone. "Where is Zach?"

"I may have left him once we found what we were looking for. I didn't trust Shane with my girl."

"You were right about Shane. My instinct is usually on point; I could smell the snake from the moment I walked in his place. I just don't understand what he wanted." She groaned.

He placed his hands on her shoulders. "He wanted you to lead him to what your father and family have hidden and protected. From now on, you're not leaving my sight. You're a princess, and you need to start acting like one." He held her gaze. The caramel ring around his eyes glowed from the sunlight peaking its way through the forest.

"Fine—at least until I can defend myself," she said with defeat. He began to move in for a kiss until a noise interrupted them.

"To be continued," he said while grabbing her hand and leading her deeper into the forest. "We have to get to Zach and warn him and the others."

"I do not want anyone hurt on my account," Erin said.

"I can take you to Zach. We found a hideout in the cave."

The sunset shone underneath the trees as they walked to the next waterfall. Erin pulled out her water bottle and rested against a tree, exhausted from climbing around in the dark cave. She was glad to have found what she was searching for, along with more information about her family history. "Rosana," she said, and the word rolled from her tongue.

Sin tore off his shirt to wipe the sweat beads from his forehead. Her eyes widened at the thickness in his arms and how defined his chest muscles appeared. Her gaze followed the curves that narrowed towards his beltline. Her heart began to race as heat flooded into the lower parts of her stomach. She breathed heavier and imagined teasing the fabric that clung against his skin and what he may do. Why am I drooling over him so hard? It's like I haven't had a taste of sugar in months, and he is the candy teasing me.

When she snapped out of the trance it was too late as honey warm eyes stole her breath.

"Those glazed over eyes share secrets, Erin." he said and moved closer. "Want to share?" His eyes, captivating and dark, caused her breathing to quicken.

"Not at all," she said and stood up. "I won't forget you holding me against my will—you're lucky I saved your ass."

A hand wrapped around her arm and pulled her back. "Maybe you liked it a little," Sin said, sending shivers down her neck and spine as she unlinked herself from him.

"Or maybe you're delusional. No more touching, or I will use this on you," she said, revealing her dagger.

"You wouldn't dare," he choked.

"Try me." She smiled.

Zach appeared, gripping Sin's shirt tightly like he was about to lay a punch.

"Stop it," Erin yelled, forcing herself in between them. Zach looked up at her with an awkward smile as Sin pushed him away. Then Zach got up and immediately gave Erin a tight hug before she could say anything. She could feel the air in her lungs decrease as she allowed him to hug her.

"Let her breathe, dumbass."

"I'm glad you're alright, Erin," Zach said. "I guess Sin was right about Shane?"

She nodded at him. "Unfortunately."

"I have something that I believe belongs to you," he said. He ruffled in his pocket and pulled out a beautifully shaped rose crafted from a ruby. It was a flawless deep red and carved without any noticeable imperfections.

CHAPTER TWENTY-THREE

Erin pulled her dagger out of her bag while studying the handle. She noticed an inverted place that could fit such a piece and tried to place it as if it were a puzzle. It slipped in perfectly and was a nice finishing touch to her dagger. "I'm not sure of the correlation, but I know your mother was fond of flowers," Zach said.

She smiled at the thought of growing closer to her parents. "Thanks, Zach. I appreciate it."

"Anything for you, princess." He smiled and took her hand. She could feel the tension building from the way Sin glared at Zach. "Quit your staring. I got you a gift as well." Zach tossed an object toward Sin. He pulled out two swords—one displayed a white wolf, and the other had a black wolf painted on the handles.

"I remember this sword. I had forgotten all about it," Sin said.

Erin remembered the amethyst piece she found as she knelt to find the piece from her bag. She walked over toward the swords to match the piece and found that it fit perfectly in Zach's.

"I found this secret room; it had our ancestral history and mentioned the stones were created to protect the royals. There are secrets from our past that were hidden. If you had stayed, you would have known that." Zach glared at Sin.

"Protecting Erin is my priority—whatever else comes after, I will research on my own," Sin said.

Zach stepped into Sin's space. His fists tightly bawled. "She isn't yours to protect."

The muscles in Sin's jaw twitched as he straightened his posture.

Erin places a gentle hand on each of their arms. "I need you to ease your anger. We should focus on finding Flora and Sylvian before Shane does first."

The tightness in their arms settle. Their gazes fall onto Erin. Zach speaks first. "You're right. We should settle for the night and begin our journey in the morning."

"Then I guess one of us will need to be on guard duty for a couple of hours. It's not safe for a fire either—could lead them our way," Sin said.

As they set up the tents and prepared for the night, Erin hoped that Flora and Sylvian did not run into any trouble. She leaned against a tree and pulled out the book she had found in the cave.

As she opened it, the first page said:

Memories are a gift; they remind us how quickly time can freeze into eternity.

To my daughter, Galena,

Emotions do not mean weakness but instead reveal the genuine parts we cannot hide. With you I wanted to share these poems as they have helped me to cope.

Remember, never be afraid to express yourself, we are unique in our own way and have a voice to share with the world.

Thinking of you brings me to the sea

I remember your smile when I pause on life to rewind
The past feels distant yet when I reach through my memory it isn't hard to find
Like a ghost you haunt me from a single song or smell
Where it comes from, I could never tell
The essence from the salty sea engulfs my memory
From the times we would walk on the beach
I would flash a smile, as my soul felt at peace
While spending time with my favorite person
Who could never be replaced with another version
I will forever feel this pain from loss
And I hope that one day our paths will someday cross
Until then I will keep you close to me
With each memory that reveals itself like us admiring the sea

Erin closed the book as cold wet tears dampened her cheeks. I wonder who she wrote that poem about. My heart yearns for my mother, I wish I could remember her.

Zach sat next to her with a concerned expression on his face, "Are you okay?"

She wiped the tears from her eyes and wavered a smile, "Yes, my emotions get the best of me at times."

"That's alright. I would rather you express them instead of keeping them pent down inside." He placed a hand on her chest.

Her sweet Zach—what would she do without him and his comforting words?

"You know I care about your safety; I just didn't want to leave without answers." He placed his hand on top of hers.

"You did the right thing. You found the stone, and information about your past."

He gently placed a hand on her cheek. "Yeah, but it took a lot not to go back for you. If anything happened, I wouldn't have been able to forgive myself."

She nudged him with her shoulder. "You can't protect me forever."

"Want to bet?" He tensed his hand, looking serious.

She rolled her eyes while shifting herself, then stood up. "I better rest for the night. Wake me if you need anything."

"Night, beautiful. You have a place beside me if you would like."

His smile was soft, and she felt bad that he had to stay up, but she could feel the fatigue setting in. She also knew that if she fell asleep on Zach then Sin would flip out in the morning. "I'd rather not piss off your brother tonight," she joked.

He stood up, "Don't worry about him. You should focus on what you want. I am a selfish man, and I am not giving up easily on you." The pull from his ocean blue eyes were consuming as they became inescapable. He closed into her space as they grew with an intense desire.

She couldn't find herself pulling away as he leaned down to claim her lips. A flutter of tickles spread through her stomach. He placed a hand underneath her chin and went in for another kiss but instead of forcing the act he kissed next to them and then on the side of her cheek.

"See you in the morning, princess."

#

She remembered running through a field full of corn stalks as Sin and Zach chased her through it. Outside grew darker as it began to rain, and Erin winced from the leaves that felt like razor blades against her skin. When she realized she'd lost the boys, fear crept through the back of her neck, causing her to shiver.

"Guys," she yelled. Her heart thudded against her chest as she grew afraid to walk farther into the cornfield.

Then a noise shuffled from behind her, she turned around slowly, then stopped at the sight of glacier-blue eyes staring back at her. The wolf's fur was the color of snow, and it just stood there looking serene, like something from a picture.

She had learned to be cautious with wild animals, so she stood still, not wanting to anger him. Somehow, she felt unafraid, as though it were someone she had known her whole life.

#

The sun peeked behind the trees as a cold crisp cut into the air. She enjoyed waking up to this view. Although she loved this camping scene, she missed the luxury of utilities so that she could feel cleaner. She grabbed a bottle of water and decided to brush her teeth and change into a clean black long-sleeved dress. Then she ventured a bit for her privacy.

Admiring her dagger, she wrapped it back around her leg and started to walk back to the campsite. She started a fire, then placed a cast iron skillet above it while preparing eggs. Then she took a sip of coffee, inhaling the earthy dark aroma, waiting for the power of food to wake the two men.

After grabbing plates and cups, she set everything down on a blanket as if it were a picnic. She paired the eggs with fresh fruit and smiled at her creation when she finished.

"Good morning," she said.

"I miss my damn bed," Sin said, while stretching. His eyes widened as he focused on the food Erin prepared. "Looks amazing. He slid his hands around her waist and pulled her in for a hug.

She elbowed him to back off with a playful smile, and Zach lunged at him. Once everyone finished, they cleaned up, and the guys walked off to change and prepare for the day.

Erin thought about her recent dream, remembering how realistic it felt. I am lucky that the white wolf never attacked me. It could have been bad if it wanted to take me for dinner. She shivered from the thought of running through the cornfield from the beast. Though it was one of the most beautiful creatures she had seen, she knew to be wary of its intentions. "Even the prettiest things have claws, like roses and their thorns."

Sin came running back shirtless, distracting her from her thoughts.

"Thanks for breakfast."

She needed to break their closeness. He wasn't helping her think clearly, especially without a shirt on. Damn muscles.

He embraced her, but she pushed him gently away.

"I figured it would help to reenergize us."

Smiling, she grabbed a shirt from his bag and handed it to him. Time to shift my focus on finding Flora and Sylvian. Then I can find my way home.

"I will be right back, I am going to grab our stuff," Sin said after throwing on his navy-blue cotton shirt.

Erin nodded as she proceeded to lose herself in the thought process of her plan. I hope that Shane or his men haven't hurt them. I didn't want them to get caught up in my mess.

"Everything will work out," Zach said as he walked Erin's way. "I've known you long enough to see when you're mustering in your thoughts," he said. As the wind blew her hair into her eyes, he placed it back behind her ear gently and locked eyes with her. She stared back into his eyes, the deep blues. They reminded her of the wolves' eyes. Did he see the wolf? Does he remember?

"Do you remember a time we played in a cornfield?" she asked.

He was quiet for a moment while trying to retrieve an old memory.

"Yeah, how could I forget? I went crazy looking for you in the rain that night."

"Did you happen to see anything unusual?"

"Nope, not much to see, since it had gotten so dark. Why?"

"Just wondering," she said and shook it off. "You can talk to me about anything."

"I know it's frustrating to have fragments of the past invade your mind," he said.

"I hope that we can be together, Erin." He placed a hand on her shoulder. "Take your time, but don't let me wait too long. You don't know how badly I want to keep you for myself at times. If I could go back in time, I would have never allowed you to end up here again." His expression fell, as if he realized he had just said the wrong words.

Erin took a step back, feeling a rush of emotions. "What do you mean?"

He ran his hand through his hair, "I didn't mean it like that."

Anger began to rise as it climbed from the pit of her stomach and into her chest. He would never have told me the truth about my past. I would be living my life based around lies. And he would have just allowed it. For how long?

"Zach, you should have told me the truth. I felt like a prisoner in my home for so long, like I didn't even know who I was." Tears streamed down her cheeks.

Zach's face was filled with guilt, but also something else that she could not read.

She was afraid of expressing her anger with words she could not take back, so she did what she could do best—turned around and began to run. The wind brushed against her skin, and her emotions felt like a mess. She felt a burning in her stomach and a sting against her cheeks.

Suddenly, arms wrapped around her body. She began to fight until she looked up and realized it was Sin.

"Let go!" She twisted and turned from his hold.

"Not until you calm down. I don't want you hurting yourself, especially in this state of mind."

She worked on catching her breath to calm down.

He held her gaze and pulled her arms above her head. "Breathe."

She obeyed and deeply inhaled in and out while watching the rise and fall of her chest.

Once her pulse was at a resting state Sin let go and allowed her arms to fall to her sides.

He stared into her eyes, "Are you alright?"

She sighed. "I will be."

CHAPTER TWENTY-FOUR

Erin peered down the edge of the mountain that they stood upon. Her heart sank as she imagined herself tumbling down it. She shivered at the thought until Sin stepped on her side to hide the view. "I won't let you fall—only into my arms."

The tension in her shoulders eased as his warm eyes filled her with a feeling of comfort.

A soft touch caressed Erin's arm. She looked over to see Zach with a hint of sadness in his eyes. He stood close to her as their arms brushed against each other and instead of speaking his body language said it all. That he was still her protector.

#

It seemed as if this waterfall was a little harder to reach. Erin wondered how Flora and Sylvian were managing. They finally could hear the rush of the water nearby. Zach took careful steps and held out his hand for Erin. Her stomach churned at the height of the drop as she shook her head.

Zach jumped while falling gracefully onto his feet. "I can catch you," he said.

"I'll find another way," she yelled. The drop was dangerous, and she couldn't believe Zach's flawless landing. Erin looked at Sin and the bag he had on his back. "Do you have a rope in that bag?"

"So, I can tie you up?" he laughed. She rolled her eyes as he began to unzip his bag to hand her a rope. "Perfect," she said while grabbing it from him and searching for the nearest grounded rock. She found one from her peripheral vision on the far left, then walked over to it and checked to see how sturdy it was by pulling it.

She looked at Sin. "You think this will hold our weight?"

"Yeah, looks good to me," he said.

She continued to tie a knot around it. "Do you have any gloves?" He shook his head. "Okay, no problem."

"Zach, I'm going to climb down with this rope—just watch me in case I fall," she said.

Sin placed his hand on Erin just before she began. "Be safe—we don't need our future queen breaking any bones, or worse."

Erin's heart felt like it was ready to cave. She was not a big fan of heights, and now she had to climb down without killing herself. Rappelling herself down the side of the cliff carefully, she focused on her footing.

"One slow step at a time," she said. As she climbed down, she noticed the pain in her hands was increasing from the friction of the rope. She could feel the sweat dripping down the back of her neck, and her hands were close to losing grip. Her weight became too much to endure, and as her hands slipped from the rope, she began to fall. As she shut her eyes her thoughts silenced. Once she opened them again, she realized she was lying on top of Zach's body.

"I got you," he said, breathing heavily." They stared at each other and sighed. Erin dropped her head onto his chest.

Erin pushed herself up from Zach's body. She extended her arm out to help him. "I didn't hurt you too bad, did I?"

He shook his head and took her hand.

"I would gladly allow you to fall on me like that again."

#

When they arrived at the waterfall, it appeared to be the tallest they had ever seen, as it reached far into the clouds. Black clouds hovered in the sky. The water rushed down the rocks violently forming a massive waterfall.

The sharp edges on the rocks point up towards the sky. On the ground, an image appeared in the colors of the rainbow—a picture of an owl. Erin walked over to the colors and stood in the middle of them while looking around for the symbol that was causing the shape. Before she could catch her breath, the rocks from underneath her shifted.

The ground floor moved as though it were an elevator, forcing her underground. She fell to her knees and froze. When the movement finally stopped, she slowly stood back up. She found balance in her equilibrium before she moved on. Then she stepped off the platform as it shot back up to where it belonged. What just happened?

The cave had green lanterns with fire lit up along each of the walls. She noticed that the floor had a black marble surface. Bats flew around the area as if it were their home in the dark and damp space.

At the end of the hall was a door with the same image of the owl in the colors of the rainbow. She pushed the door open and found her friends Sylvian and Flora in front of her, smiling.

"You're alright!" Erin smothered them with a hug.

"Wow, you look great! Now we need to bring Zach and Sin down here."

Flora was wearing a green robe soft as velvet, with a white dress underneath. Sylvian wore black slick pants and a long white dress shirt with a matching green robe.

Flora tapped Erin's arm, "First, let us explain the rules," she said.

The area was massive. It was just as big as a university. Erin became intrigued at the five-pointed star enclosed with a circle in the middle of the floor. Surrounding it were five doors with unrecognizable words as each knob was made from either amethyst, ruby, emerald, pearl, and sapphire jewels. A flood of green smoke filled through the halls as they walked down them.

When they approached a wooden door Flora opened it and pushed Erin through first.

Sylvian walked Erin to a leather couch and had her take a seat.

"I'm glad that you're okay," he stated.

"Likewise," Erin said.

Her head spun out of control from the confusion as she leaned her head back against the couch. At least they're safe. She let out a relived sigh. Then she forced her head back up and set her gaze onto her friends.

Flora sat next to Erin. "This information I reveal cannot be shared with anyone."

Erin nodded while listening to her words. Flora's eyes were darker in the cave, a sharp piercing green. She reminded her of a dark fairy, one that would lure you into your death if she wanted.

Erin maintained eye contact and placed a hand onto Flora's.

"Your secret is safe with me."

Flora smiled. "We call this cave, Owlery Falls. We are among the beings that can master magic. Royalty and magic are connected in this world, and so that intertwines with your fate, Erin."

Sylvian walked over to stand in front of them. Erin shifted her gaze up at him as his face was expressionless. Flora pulled a knife from her pocket and cut a small slit on Sylvian's forearm as blood dripped from his wound.

Erin gasped, but before she could scream, Flora grabbed her mouth and held it shut.

"It's alright. Let me see your hand."

Erin held out her trembling hand, afraid of Flora's next move. She held tightly onto Erin's index finger and pierced the tip of the blade down. Erin flinched from the pinch of pain. Then she hovered her finger over Sylvain's wound and allowed just a drop of blood to fall inside. They all watched as Sylvian's broken skin slowly began to close and heal, with no evidence of a laceration.

Then she remembered healing Sin when he became poisoned.

"What does this mean?"

"We are still working on understanding all of that, but this has to remain a secret," Flora said.

"If anyone found out about your healing abilities, then they would want to keep you for their own," Sylvian said. "There are a lot of people that would kill for your protection, and a war would start if that were to happen."

The door was forced open as a tall man with large arms and dark spikey hair shoved Zach and Sin into the room.

"Get rid of them. You know they shouldn't be here," He rumbled through is chest in a growl.

"Got it, thanks." Flora answered. She placed a cloth onto Erin's finger and applied pressure.

"Your knights must have needed to get to their princess."

She stood in front of the two men.

"I can't take your blindfolds off. I must lead you back out of this cave."

Sin peeked before Flora could stop him as he ran to Erin.

"Thank the stars you're alright." He grinned.

Flora snapped his blindfold back down. "No more peaking, or I will chop one of those precious fingers off."

"Okay, but I also would like some answers."

Flora grabbed Sin's sword and placed an emerald-shaped wolf inside of it. "These swords are bonded with special magic from the wolf spirits. You shall see what powers they hold as you wield them. They must be used appropriately, or they can truly harm innocent people. If you do so, you will answer to the counsel, and they will form an appropriate punishment."

"Noted," Sin said.

Erin turned to Flora and placed a hand on top of her shoulder.

"Flora, thank you for watching out for me. I may not remember all our memories, but you have proven to be a great friend."

Flora smiled and handed her an envelope. "These are letters written between the two of us when we were young. I found them in a room that was set up for me. It hurt when you were taken away. I honestly thought I would never see you again. I am staying here to learn as much as I can, so that one day I can become a powerful witch to stand by your side."

They both hugged and shared tears but knew it wasn't a permanent goodbye.

"Sylvian and I are going to lead you out of this cave.

Sylvian stepped into Erin's space.

"I trust these two will take care of you." He hugged her and held her hand.

Flora grabbed Zach and Sin's arms and led them out of the cave.

They all stood on the platform as it lifted them up to the top.

The breeze carried drops of water that splashed against Erin's skin while reminding her that she was out of the cave.

"Erin, there is a whole world out there with answers, and I know you will unravel them. Just be careful," Flora said. "You may have the ability to heal, but not yourself, and I believe each time you do; it affects you."

Erin acknowledged her words with a nod. "I am not invincible, got it," She joked.

"Truly, I am glad that you're by my side. I hope you learn everything you need and become one of the most powerful witches."

"And I will be rooting for you to become a magnificent Queen." Flora reached for a hug and then stepped next to Sylvian onto the platform. Then they were gone as Erin felt a tug of loss. She knew it wouldn't be the last time seeing her friends, just for a little while. See you soon.

"It's not forever and just think—when we're done with this journey, we can all meet up at my place and have some drinks." Sin laughed while pulling a bottle of brown liquid from his bag.

"You know what, let me have some of that."

He twisted the cap and handed it to her. As she poured the liquid down her throat, notes of honey and a sensation of warmth filled her body.

"We have a long journey ahead of us." She handed him back the bottle and slouched her shoulders while walking backward, staring at them.

"Are you sure you to are ready for this?"

Zach and Sin's faces displayed a heat of anger and before she could speak, strong arms grabbed her by the waist.

"Told you I would find her," Shane spoke.

Erin began to wriggle from the hold she was in, "Run!" She screamed at Zach and Sin while hoping for once that they would listen.

She didn't want them to get hurt because of her. She would find a way out of this but if he hurt them then she wasn't so sure that she could hold herself back from causing harm to Shane.

"Shane, if you hurt them—"

He clasped a hand across her lips before she could finish out her sentence.

"You may want to consider your next move," He threatened.

There were only a couple of men surrounding them, but it was enough to overpower them, especially when each of them held a shotgun in their hands.

Shane tightened his grip on Erin.

"Nobody moves. I take the girl, and you two stand still."

CHAPTER TWENTY-FIVE

The moon illuminated the sky with a cream-colored halo while appearing close enough to touch. The atmosphere felt eerie, as the only surrounding sounds came from nature itself. Then Erin's arms were freed, and she felt a soreness from how taunt Shane held onto her skin. When she was able to look toward Sin and Zach, she realized they were not standing there anymore. What replaced them instead were two massive wolves the size of bears.

The white one's eyes reminded her of something familiar again. They had that same intense sharp light blue, and the fur resembled the color of a blanket of untouched snow. The black one beside it had emerald-green eyes with a golden-brown halo iris, and fur as black as charcoal. Their teeth were razor sharp with claws larger than her head. She could feel the heat from their breath as they both growled fiercely.

Shane's crew backed up, then as soon as the wolves stepped closer, they ran.

"You didn't say anything about wolves!"

The men ran off like cowards, not even attempting to shoot their weapons.

The wolves did not back down as they ran after their prey.

Erin twisted out of Shane's grip. "Looks like it's just us."

She pulled her dagger out and grabbed Shane's throat before he could move.

"This game ends." She forced the edge of her dagger against his neck.

"Careful, little toxin I wouldn't want you to get your hands dirty," Shane spoke.

Erin tightened her hold against him, "Too late."

Flora appeared with a rope to tie up Shane's hands.

"How—?"

"Gene told us what was happening up here. Eyes are always on you." Just as the words spilt from Flora's mouth a flutter of wings and the noise of a hoot sounded through the area.

Erin caught a glimpse of white wings and a pair of yellow eyes hidden in the trees behind the waterfall.

"Why?" Flora asked Shane with an edge of anger in her tone.

"Don't worry about it."

Flora flashed her deep green eyes toward him with a glare. "Fine—then don't count on mercy. You know we would have helped you. Turning on us was a mistake."

"You should have never come back," he said before Flora slapped tape across his mouth.

"No need to be an ass," Flora said as he cut his eyes back at her. "And to think, I thought you were a decent guy, but I guess it's true what they say. What you hang out with is what you become like—a snake."

Shane jumped at her, as though he would intimidate her, but she just stood there and laughed.

"As for tonight, Erin, let's go back to the cave. The guys will be normal again in the morning. I know I have a lot of explaining to do." Flora groaned while pushing Shane towards the platform.

#

"Flora, why did you keep this all from me to begin with?" Erin asked.

"Would you have believed me? That the two men who have fallen head over heels for you are secretly wolves, and that your best friend comes from a descendant of witches, or that unicorns are real."

"Wait, what?" Erin's eyes widened.

Flora laughed while holding on to her abdomen. "Got you on the unicorn thing. But yes, everything else is a big—"

"What the hell!"

"Well, yes, if you told me all of this in my world, of course I'd think it was made up. It's all so unreal, almost like a story."

As Sylvian walked in with food, the smells of onion and pepper seasoning filled the room.

"I haven't had a good meal like this in a while." Erin smiled while taking a bowl from him.

"Luckily, they allowed me in the kitchen." Sylvian laughed. Erin smiled as she took a sip of soup. Flora handed her an earth-green silk dress with a low V-neck and a soft ruffled skirt-like hem.

"I'll escort you to the restroom," Flora said. Erin nodded.

The bathroom was a decent size and filled with white marbled walls, a porcelain tub, a shower, and glittering lights that sparkled through the dark room. She used some of Flora's lavender essential oils to fill the inside of the water. I did not expect this change of events.

Then she remembered the book with the poem she had read and dried her hands off to flip to another page.

Howling is comforting to the soul.
 A freedom only a few know.
When the wolf howls, I listen
The harmony reminds me that the place I live in is a prison
One with walls, and rules that must be abided
Even if they are designed by the one-sided
Sometimes I wish I could take place of the wolf at night
To be feared, fearless when caught in sight
My cries are silent and hidden
Living in this cruel world I realize my kind heart could never fit in
So, as I open my ears to consume the howls from the mysterious creature
I wonder if I howled at the top of my lungs would the ropes become weaker
One day I could join your release
Then I would have the courage to stand up and speak

Although the poem portrayed a deeper meaning than the wolves, it reminded her of Zach and Sin. I wonder how lonely they must feel. She wondered if they were alright, and she could feel an ache in her chest as she worried about them, though she knew Flora would not agree to search for them.

Regardless of how strong they appeared, everyone has a breaking point, and she would not just go to sleep until she set eyes on them. A faint knock silenced her thoughts as the door creaked open. Sylvian tiptoed in while covering his eyes.

Erin wrapped a towel around her body. "Sylvian what the hell?"

"I know you, and I want to help. We should look for Zach and Sin while Flora and Shane are asleep."

"How?"

"I may have put a little sleeping potion in their food tonight." He glanced up at the wall and shrugged.

"Sylvian!" she whispered, though she was impressed.

Sylvian turned around. "Come on, we are wasting time."

Erin dried herself off and pulled on her dress while combing through her hair.

"Ready." Her green dress brought out the green in her eyes, and her light-brown waves cascaded down her lower back.

Sylvian's jaw dropped as he stood there silently for a moment. "Stunning," he said with a smile. He placed the bag on his back and grabbed her hand as they tiptoed out of the bathroom.

Erin witnessed Shane's head lying on Flora's shoulder as they were asleep. Erin giggled a little, knowing how pissed Flora would be after this, and then she felt a little guilty. She noticed Sylvian was staring off into the distance, lost in thought, and wondered what was on his mind.

"Alright, let's find our wolves," he said, taking the first step.

CHAPTER TWENTY-SIX

"I assume this isn't strange to you?" Erin asked Sylvian as they walked toward the sounds of howling.

Sylvian gave her a quiet stare as he helped her down from a rock. "I've lived with Sin for long enough to know most of his secrets. To be honest, Sin hasn't changed into a wolf until tonight. When you live in a steady environment, you lose interest to respond to outside threats until someone you love is involved. I believe that tonight was the first both Zach and Sin have shifted."

"I will warn you that dragging them along any further will only damage your heart. One day you're going to be the queen, and in return you will choose a king. It's not to be taken lightly because partnership involves committing to each other's differences. You won't always agree, but working together for common ground will allow for a greater outcome."

She smiled. "I agree—which is why I need to take time."

A noise resounded through the woods as Sylvian pulled her behind him. Crunching leaves and a dragging noise alerted them. "It's Sin," Sylvian said. Erin pushed past him and gasped at the sight of Sin covered in blood, then watched him drop to the ground. She rushed to his side while watching his chest move faintly.

Erin thought about the first waterfall, the one that had healing properties along with the roses. She glanced back up at Sylvian while trying to calm down her heavy breathing. Her hands began to shake as her body threatened to spin into a panic attack. I must focus on saving him.

"I know where we can take him."

Sylvian pulled out a large blanket for them to slide him on. "This is going to suck," he said aloud while tugging on one end of the blanket. As they finally arrived at the large waterfall, the smell of fresh roses rolled through the air as they both stared at the pool.

"Now to get him into the water," Erin huffed.

Sylvian went ahead and jumped in. "Okay, now slide his lower half down, and hold his upper body upright."

As she helped slide Sin carefully into the water, Sylvian held his bottom half steady. Erin fell to the ground, wrapping her arms tightly around his torso as she slid into the water. The roses gathered around his body as their floral scent wafted through the waters. A few minutes passed as Erin and Sylvian waited. "Oh, come on, water. What is taking so long?" she asked.

Remembering when Flora used her blood to help Sylvian, she swam toward her bag while grabbing her dagger to release her blood into the water. Then the water grew livelier, as though it were vibrating from underneath her. The moonlight glistened onto the waters as they turned a turquoise blue, and the roses became a vibrant red.

Sin floated onto the waters as though they were carrying and mending his body back together. Then he finally opened his eyes while recollecting his consciousness.

"Welcome back, friend." Sylvian smiled at him.

Sin half-cocked a smile while swimming in Erin's direction.

His hair was a shadow, and his eyes were dark and full of hunger. Her pulse quickened as her nostrils flared heavily. She was terrified. He has already stolen my heart. When he closed in on her space a sudden rush of heat flooded between her legs.

She gasped as she backed herself into the wall.

He placed a steady hand on her cheek. At first, he gently kissed her lips. When she found her way back to his eyes, she noticed that his had glossed over.

"Mine," he whispered. Her heart fluttered at his words.

Then he grasped the back of her neck and dived further in as he pried her lips open for him. She closed her eyes and allowed him to control the movement of their tongues. A spark of passion filled her veins as they deepened their kiss. She moved her hand onto his cheek and wrapped her legs securely around his waist. He wrapped his arms around her torso and spun them around until they pulled apart.

"I owe you a second time, my little jackrabbit." He flashed a smile. She felt weak but electric in that moment, like nothing but the two existed and it felt right. Sylvian had already jumped out of the water and walked away as Sin helped her onto the rocks. As he pushed himself up, she admired his muscles.

She envisioned a banished angel as she admired his features. His dark wet hair was slicked back, and each muscle—partially hidden by the shadows— glistened in the moonlight, contouring his perfect body. She caught herself staring, unable to look away from his caramel eyes.

"You scared me—don't do that again." She trembled as he stepped closer. He grabbed her wrists before she could flee and stared into her eyes as if he could hear her every thought.

He tilted her chin up as she became lost in his gaze.

"I love you, Erin."

CHAPTER TWENTY-SEVEN

Sin just professed his love for me. And I said nothing. To be fair I am still working on my feelings for him. Erin pulled her red bag over her shoulder and darted toward the trees for privacy. She rolled her lavender dress over her head. Its straps were made into violet ribbon bows that sat on the top of her shoulders. The breasts and midline revealed a row of green vines and pink flowers, and the bottom flared out down to her knees.

"Stop being selfish," said a deep rough voice from across the way.

A man wearing a dark black hood, dark eyes, and light-brown shaggy hair appeared. He was handsome, yet something about him seemed threatening as her instincts bubbled through her lower abdomen. She noticed he had two swords strapped to his back, and two visible daggers shined from each side of his pants.

"Selfish?" she stuttered as a chill crept up her back. His face twisted into a vicious smile as if he were trying to be charming and frightening at the same time. It made her feel more frightened, just the thought of what he could do, or how fast he was with those weapons.

"You might change your mind when you hear my offer." He shuffled his hand in his pocket and pulled out a silver ring with a white wolf emblem on it, then tossed it to her.

She remembered that Zach always wore that ring—she never questioned him about it but knew it was important to him. "Where did you find this?"

He stepped closer, and she could feel the space between them close in. She stood in place while grounded in her spot. "If you come with me without resisting, then you will get your precious friend back safely."

"There's not much time to decide. You only have a couple of seconds before your friends realize their girl is standing in the woods with a stranger."

Erin knew in her soul that this was a bad idea, but she wanted to save Zach. She lifted her hand and placed it into his, as he had extended it out for her answer. The night air caused her to shiver as she thought of all the endings this could lead to. What if he is leading me into another trap?

She spotted flames of light as they approached a cabin with torches surrounding it. Before they walked any further, he stopped and pointed at the wire that was barely visible to the naked eye while reminded her of a spider's web. Before she could lift her feet, he scooped her up. "Hey, put me down. There is no need for this," she yelled while hitting him.

"Hush. I can't have you setting off any alarms," he said.

She was uncomfortable being carried around like a doll, but had to put up with this man to get to Zach, so she decided to remain cooperative.

Once they were inside, he steadied her back down onto her feet and watched as she took in her surroundings. It was a relaxing little cabin with a fireplace that glowed a soft orange as the room was surrounded by red-colored furniture. It smelled like pine and cedar, and it reminded her of the time she and Zach went camping.

It was around summertime, and up in the mountains, the earth was still. She was surprised he didn't try to make a move then. Times were simpler, and she would have agreed in a heartbeat. Erin studied the fire as the memory brought her back in time.

It was just for the weekend during spring break. Upstate in the mountains, she was able to clear her mind while watching scary movies, roasting marshmallows, and laughing at Zach's attempts to play the guitar. She would look up at the stars, realizing how comfortable she felt. That was the time she first walked to a waterfall. She dragged Zach along and observed the smoke that trailed behind the mountains and the water streams. Then when they arrived, she snapped pictures and pulled him into the water as they splashed at each other.

It was one of her favorite days, one that she was hoping would lead to more but never had. After that, she decided one day she would work up the nerve to confess her feelings. As life continued, she realized that her desires were changing their ways like the direction of the wind. She drifted off on the couch as the light from the fire flickered in the back of her eyes.

#

The stillness of the silence felt abnormal as Erin awoke to an empty cabin. She noticed a pillow underneath her head and a blanket covering her body. The light shined through the windows as the smell of bacon awakened her senses. When she rounded the corner to the kitchen, she saw Zach standing over the stovetop. She rubbed her eyes vigorously and walked toward him. "Zach?"

"You need to stop being so naïve and gullible," he said softly with a smile.

"I was worried about you," Erin said while grabbing his hand. "You're my best friend, and I will be here for you whenever you need me." He smiled back without saying anything for a while.

"So where is that guy?" she asked.

"Oh, you mean the guy you decided to trust. I took care of him; he's tied up in another room. Now run along and wash up."

"But we need to find Sin and Sylvian." She stopped at the door that Zach had the man tied up in and slowly pushed it open. He was lying on the bed; ropes tied to his feet and arms. It was then that she realized it had been the man that led her to the cabin. He began to mumble, but before she could understand, the door slammed in her face.

"What are you doing?"

Erin looked up and noticed his eyes were not the same breathtaking clear blue water, but instead hazel. He grabbed her chin and pulled it up, gazing at her for a moment.

"You will be the perfect bride for me," he whispered as he planted a kiss onto her lips. At that moment, she knew this was not Zach, and she pushed him away from her.

"What's wrong with you?" he said with an angry twist in his voice.

CHAPTER TWENTY-EIGHT

She immediately tried to run toward the door, but he pulled her back into him. "Who are you?" she screamed while trying to wriggle free from his tight hold.

"Be a good girl and take a seat." He thrust her onto the couch.

If she didn't think of a plan, she could be in a swarm of danger.

"You don't want to hurt me," she said.

"Oh, and why is that?" he asked while grabbing her face and squeezing her cheeks.

"I'm valuable. I'm the Princess of Rosanafalls."

"Hmm, no wonder he had his guards on search for you," the man whispered to himself. "So, what you're telling me is I can deliver you for a price? Sounds like a great idea—let's go." He pulled her up by her wrist.

"Wait," she yelled. "I won't go with you until I find my friend Zach."

"Oh, that must have been who you thought I was when you threw yourself at me. I am an illusionist, so the person desired shall appear."

He let go of her wrist and stared into her eyes.

"Yet someone recognizing my power is intriguing."

That's useful. "Let's make a deal," Erin said.

"Okay, you're cute," he said while running his fingers down toward her breasts.

Erin smacked his hand away. "Not that kind of deal!"

"I could just take you right now if I wanted." He grinned.

"Yeah, and you will have two angry wolves, a warlock, and a witch after you, so you might want to rethink that. But if you help me, I will grant you full permission to live in the palace."

"I would do anything for your hand in marriage." He grabbed her hand.

She pulled her hand away. "That is not up for negotiating."

"Okay, fine, but if you go back on your word, then you won't like what will happen."

"Alright, so we might want to get out of this cabin," Erin warned.

He put out his hand for a negotiation shake. "Name's Ron."

"Galena, but I go by Erin," she said while shaking his hand.

"We will need to find my friends to help us."

Ron folded his arms into his chest while leaning against the wall.

"Yeah, that sounds like a good idea. The guy who is running the palace isn't such a nice man."

"What can you tell me about him?"

"For starters, the man that abducted you was lying. He wasn't going to help you with whatever he promised. Right before I popped in, he was about to take advantage of you while you were sleeping. You really shouldn't just fall asleep so easily; you would have woken up to a violent surprise. But of course, I rescued you."

"You would be a great bodyguard," she said while examining his arms and torso. She noticed his green eyes had a brownish tint around the irises, his hair was ash brown with locks of curls, and he wore a short-sleeved brown shirt with khaki pants and tan boots.

"Never again." He rolled his eyes. "You may want to tread carefully in the royal world, as there are secrets and lies that can separate the truth from reality."

She nodded, feeling a new level of anxiety. As she shifted against a tree, Ron placed his arm above her head. "I'm not sure of your plans, but walking into that palace is a trap."

She never thought of that possibility. That the man who tried to kidnap her could have planned this all along. "That's why I have to be careful, and I have your help." She winked. "I have this strong urge to protect this place, its beauty and mystery.

I can't leave it to the destruction of an evil man.

"Another thing—he has collected strong poisons to use at his disposal and has used them on many people. He may threaten or use them against your friend."

Erin immediately thought of Shane. "That traitor." She sighed.

"I will kill you," roared a familiar voice from across the way. Sin already had Ron in a chokehold as they thudded against the ground.

"Sin!" Erin yelled, trying to pull him off. A force pulled them apart as they flew across the woods.

Flora and Sylvian walked up beside Erin. "See, I told you Erin could take care of herself." Flora was wearing a gorgeous light-blue strapless dress and had Sylvian by her side.

"Erin is that man a threat to you?" she asked while pointing at Ron.

"No, he has helped me, and he is going to help us get into the palace." She walked over to Ron and lent him a hand off the ground.

Sin quickly grabbed Erin away from Ron and squeezed her body into his. "She's mine."

"I am nobody's." Erin retracted from Sin as she grabbed Ron's hand and pulled him toward Flora and Sylvian. "Ron, this is Flora, Sylvian—and the pain in the ass you already encountered is Sin."

Ron nodded and grabbed Flora's hand, then kissed it. "You are one beautiful woman. Thank you for your help." Flora looked impressed and smiled at him at Sylvian, who seemed a little uncomfortable.

"We have to save Zach," Erin said. "Ron has agreed to help us as we construct a plan to save Zach and overthrow this imposter of a king."

"We must be careful, though, because he is a dangerous man—"

"Okay," Flora said. "First off, we all need to go back to Sin's place so that we can organize this plan and figure out how far we will be walking on foot. At dinner, we will discuss what needs to be done. I know you're exhausted, and you need to relax," Flora said while putting a hand on Erin's tense shoulder.

Erin didn't want to just go chill; she needed to save Zach. An overwhelming feeling of exhaustion came over her as she drifted back into Sin's arms.

"Was that necessary?" Sylvian asked. Sin grabbed her arms, pulled her body to his, and began leading the way back to his home. "You are a weird group of friends," Ron said while following them and watching his step.

"You underestimate this girl's force. She will do anything in her power to save the ones she cares about. I first realized that as kids."

"What happened?" Ron asked.

"In my younger years my anger showed the true nature of what kind of destruction my powers could cause. I watched in horror while feeling helpless as my home was engulfed in flames. But I didn't realize it, until it was too late. Erin ran toward me and tried to shake me out of it, but my emotions consumed me."

"Erin knew I would blame myself if my family died in that fire, so she darted into the house to save my parents. The stupidest thing she could have done, but we were kids, and she didn't think things through. I fell to my knees when I realized what I had done and began to cry. Then I immediately got back up and ran to Sin and Zach's father's house for help. We always knew who to run to for help.

"Before I got to the house, I heard a name calling out to me. 'Flora,' screamed Erin from a distance. I turned around, and there Erin held my mom up as she struggled. 'Help,' she screamed out. I ran back toward her only to see Zach and Sin with their father helping my mother. They were not thrilled with me as they both glared at me for allowing Erin to run blindly in a house of flames.

"Zach and Sin helped Erin treat her burns, and I wished my powers hadn't existed. My father had shockingly disappeared from the scene that day. The worst thing to have happened to me after that incident was losing Gal—I mean Erin."

"What happened to her?" Ron asked.

"I learned from Zach and Sin's father that it was best that she went into hiding. I wanted to know more but they wouldn't offer much information. It was meant to be kept secret. That night I had not only lost my best friend but also my father. He had disappeared, whether he died from the fire, I will never know because his body was never found."

I stayed with my mother to train and learned to control my emotions. While I blamed myself for a lot of things, I chose to become stronger for the ones I love, and to protect her like she did me."

"She is lucky to have a friend like you by her side," Ron said.

Knowing that you went through such trying times in your lives should strengthen your friendship and understanding of one another. My only word of advice is to stop protecting her—she doesn't need it. You should tell her the truth."

Flora's eyes widened as she grew quiet.

How could he know?

CHAPTER TWENTY-NINE

Erin opened her eyes as the moonlight revealed itself through the room. As she pulled herself up and tossed the covers from her body, she pulled open the window for air. There was a cool breeze that made her feel lucky to be in a warm room, unharmed.

The day Zach crawled through her window appeared in her mind. He was soaked from top to bottom, and yet he made it his mission to still see that she was all right, knowing she was all alone in a house during a storm.

She walked over to the table and rummaged through her bag for her book and dagger. Then she rolled her fingers over the ruby and wondered about its purpose. She had so many questions and not enough answers. If only her memory would fully restore itself, then she would understand. Perched on the edge of the bed, she opened the book she'd found back in the cave and turned the page.

Daughter, you should not have to sacrifice your own free will

Bringing a child into this world could be cruel and unfair
Yet you had me under your control with just your stare
Growing up, my world felt constricted like a prison
As I had learned to contort myself into someone else's perfect vision
It was not until I became older that I learned to grow
Out of the bud and into a blooming flower to glow
Until he came around to pluck me from the ground
Where I would lay safe and sound
It wasn't until then that I knew what I had to do
To keep the peace and hide you away
For you do not deserve to pay for the mistakes your mother has made
I had let my guard down without sight
My barriers fell, and I became soft

But when I did, I learned quickly what it would cost
Free will for you, for our little family
And like a blue jay, I know now that I must set you free
So, as you read this book of poems, please try to understand
That your gift and beauty should never be placed in another one's reckless hand

Your mother,
Amaryllis

Erin brushed a tear from her eye as she realized she was robbed of her childhood without her mother. She only wanted time back but knew that was impossible. She wanted to find the man behind the destruction and cause him pain and suffering. A knock at the door disturbed her thoughts, and she answered for her visitor to come in.

Sin pushed the door open—barefoot, wet hair, pale skin, and muscles visible through his blue cotton long-sleeve shirt. The smell of eucalyptus interrupted her senses, and she began to forget her worries. The sharp edge of his jawline, the darkness in his eyes that seemed to glow when he laid eyes on her.

Sin grasped her face gently, but she pulled away for fear of losing control, especially when her body screamed to invite him in. But her mind fought harder to maintain distance.

"Dinner is ready, and Flora has a plan if you want to join the discussion."

He seemed cautious, as if afraid to scare her. His concern was adorable, and she smiled while looking the other way.

"You don't understand how much I love you, Erin. I know you have had my brother in your life for years, but I looked for you before then. When we were younger, I vowed to protect you no matter what. I love your timid attitude toward strangers, but bubbly demeanor around friends and family. The way you laugh at the smallest jokes even if they aren't that funny, and the softness in your eyes as you see an animal from afar. To me, everything about you illustrates beauty. As long as you've been on this earth, you've been the one for me." He held her hands and brought them up to his lips.

Her body felt warm and tingly all over, and she felt as though nothing mattered, and the world was still. It was as if she had her feet buried in warm sand and was listening to the crash of waves. "When I was away why didn't you come to see me, or why weren't you chosen to protect me?"

"I wasn't sure where you were, and it was already decided and too late for me to do anything about it," he said.

She could not help but wonder what life would have been like if it were him and not Zach there, what kind of memories they would have made together.

She placed a hand on top of his chest.

"I guess what matters is the present."

He pushed her back onto the mattress while trapping her between his legs.

A flood of warmth rushed through her. Although she was at his mercy, she wasn't afraid. She felt safe and wanted to stay there in his presence. Then he leaned down to kiss her, and she allowed it.

He slid his hand underneath her dress and ran his fingers across every inch of her body. Then he leaned in towards her ear and whispered, "Does this mean that you are mine?"

She did not think she could feel weaker, but that caused her to ache in lower places. Before he continued to kiss her, he stopped and waited for her answer. She began to cave as she opened her mouth until the door made a noise and Flora yelled on the other side, "You two coming?" Guilt rushed through her at the thought of their plan to save Zach. Yet she wanted to dive back into Sin's mouth while feeling his tongue caress her own.

"To be continued," she said with a devious smile.

He tightened his legs and placed her arms above her head. "I am not letting you go until I have an answer. "I want you to be mine, and I won't stop until you tell me to," he said with full intensity.

She sighed. "You win," she said between each kiss. "I am all yours, Sin."

Kissing her lips and her neck, he said, "You won't regret those words." Then he pulled her up from the bed.

"Go out there while I get dressed." She gave him a light push and smiled. He turned around, smiling wide, and winked at her as he twirled back around to exit the room. Her lips were sore from all the kissing, and she hugged her body from the excitement. After walking to the mirror, she fixed her hair and opened the closet for a dress to throw on. She picked out a ruby red dress with lace that ran down both sleeves.

She tossed herself back in bed just to remember Sin's touch and how alive it made her feel. If she had the choice, she'd do it all over again, and she wasn't going to let herself feel bad about it. She'd made her decision and now would have to face Zach, although she may have Sin keep quiet at first.

Her stomach ached as she worried about Zach. Okay, time to save my best friend, she thought as she jumped out of bed and ran to the door.

CHAPTER THIRTY

Erin opened the door, and the house filled with laughter and music from the kitchen. Her friends were like family, and that filled her with joy. She hadn't had much of that, so it didn't feel normal, but she hoped one day it would. As she walked down the hallway toward the noise, a hand covered her mouth, and arms pulled around her waist. This has got to stop happening, she thought, pissed as she caught a glimpse of blond hair, sapphire crystal eyes, and the smell of honey and cinnamon as she fell into Zach's arms.

#

Water flooded through her ears as she sat on a rock by a waterfall. The sky was orange and yellow, and the scent of lilacs filled the warm, inviting air. She noticed a person was with her. It was a woman with shoulder-length light-blonde hair, skin the color of white silk, wrinkles that curved around the eyes and mouth. This was the person she remembered feeling the safest around, "Grandmother," she whispered. As a mist of water brushed against her cheeks, she couldn't find words to express her feelings.

#

The image became fuzzy, and light pierced through sharply as she awakened from her dream. She felt pained that the dream had not finished and questioned the reason behind it. For years, she had missed her grandmother and never knew how she passed. But the memories were like the taste of dark chocolate on her lips—brief and bittersweet.

Her head pounded as she realized she was not in her usual bed. The bed was soft with white sheets underneath and a large satin sage-green comforter on top of her. As she looked around, she realized the walls were plain white without any pictures or vibrant colors.

The door creaked open before she could gather any more of her surroundings. Footsteps swiftly walked toward her, and as she went to move her hand, she realized a cold chain was wrapped around her wrists and ankles. "What's going on?" she yelled as she felt the weight of the bed shift.

"I'm sorry," he said. She looked up at a face she had known for years, and he looked back down at her with tears in his eyes. "I guess now I owe you the truth."

"Zach, we can talk later—unchain me." As she squirmed back and forth and yanked the chains, sweat beaded on her forehead.

Erin felt vulnerable and hurt, but she would not give up on the Zach she knew deep down. It was like jumping off a spinning ride at the fair. The dizziness remained as the earth stood still. "Whatever you did, Zach, I forgive you—now let me go," she yelled.

"No," he screamed with an edge that Erin had never heard before.

"Zach," Erin said, but her voice cracked, and her throat dried.

The soreness and tightness in her chest rose, and the wetness from tears rolled down her cheeks. She loved Zach with every ounce in her body, and even this made her want to forgive him. "I will do anything, please." She coughed as her tears came flooding. He wiped her tears away, pain in his eyes.

"Erin, the only way out of this is if you marry Kayleon's son. He promised that nothing would happen to you. He told me that if you did that, then he would allow you freedom"

Erin was quiet for a moment and took time to understand what exactly Zach was saying. "Zach, why would you want me to just give up everything?"

He leaned down next to her. "If you can just go with this charade for a bit, I promise I will protect you from him. But first, I need you to agree to everything I say, and then I can release you."

She nodded while feeling a sense of relief wash over her. Zach leaned up against her body and unlocked her chains. She felt his body press against hers gently, and with each brush it made her uncomfortable as she began to think about Sin. What would he do if he knew that she had chosen to be with his brother? Would he betray her then?

She did not want to think about that as she rubbed her chafed skin.

"Zach, what are we going to do?"

He grabbed her hands and hugged her. "I'll figure this out." He almost went in for a kiss, but Erin quickly turned her head away.

The door flung open as a man wearing a black suit with a sage-green tie appeared. His eyes were brown with a yellow halo around the iris. He half-cocked a smile, and she studied his thick brown hair, wondering why he looked familiar.

Then it hit her. "Benny?"

"It's Benjamin."

She felt her stomach twist and turn. *No way would I marry my old bully.*

"How are you even here?" She coughed.

"None of that matters because you're my possession as soon as I take your last name and become a part of the Rosana lineage," he said in a dark voice.

Erin wanted to scream. *In your dreams.* She was done allowing men to decide her future. She would play along just until she found her way out of this mess. She stood up from the bed slowly and walked over to Benjamin while taking his arm.

"Why don't you show me around the palace?"

He leaned in to kiss her on the cheek as he stared directly at Zach. "I would be thrilled to."

CHAPTER THIRTY-ONE

Zach's Pov

If I had my way, Benny would be dead by now. I'd sink my claws into his carotid artery and watch him bleed out. But I also must watch myself because my actions can cause consequences for Erin. And Kayleon made it clear that he had information on our friends, probably from Shane's help. I wouldn't be surprised if they were on their way to the palace, especially when they find out she is missing.

I knew that if Erin walked into the palace blindly then she and everyone would be at the mercy of Kayleon's trap. He had been pulling the strings this whole time, but what didn't make sense was the reason behind it. He knew that the Rosana princess must choose their partner solely for the purpose of love and protection. What did he have to gain from all of this? And why bring her back here? Unless he was working for another?

Either way I obtained death angel mushrooms to end him and his precious son. Then Erin can have her palace and thrown that is rightfully hers. She can rule as Queen with me by her side. She will never have to worry about anyone hurting her again because I will be there for her protection. Luckily, I offer my own power as a Shapeshifter.

I watched Benjamin prance around like he owned the palace. Like he was finally gaining the upper hand. He wanted Erin this whole time. He may say he is going to allow her freedom, but I call bullshit. Since we were kids, I could see the way he looked at her.

But Benny had been a bully to Erin through her childhood years. She didn't deserve that treatment from him then, and she surely doesn't deserve it now.

Don't worry. I got you, Erin.

Her turquoise eyes caught my attention. "Is there a restroom I can use?"

I grinned and pointed to the room down the hall. "It's right there."

"Are you sure she won't try to escape?" Benjamin asked.

I snapped my eyes at him while trying to hide the anger.

"She is a woman of her word. You don't have to worry."

He folded his arms into his chest with a smirk over his face. "This must be hard for you, losing to me. Especially the woman that you had been chasing for years. And you never confessed, how pathetic."

My shoulders tense as I clenched my fists. I can knock him out right now. It was such a tempting thought until I noticed a guard staring our way. I remain silent and decide to play it safe, for now. He will pay for what he said, just a matter of time.

On the pillar behind the wall in the shadows stood a woman. She had long wavy brown hair, wore khaki tan pants and a green army colored shirt. Who is that?

"I'm going to go use the restroom as well," I say.

Lucky for me she was close enough to the men's restroom that I could walk that way.

I nodded to the guard as he stared at me with a stoic face. Not friendly, got it.

Then I slip behind the wall and tap on the woman's shoulder. When she turns around to face me my jaw almost drops.

"Erin?"

It looks like her, but the eyes aren't quite the same as they appear brown and green instead of her turquoise color.

"Who are you, and why do you look just like my friend?"

The woman standing before him laughed. Her long wavy brown hair shifted into a darker blonde and shortened with a messy appearance. Her chest flattened and shoulders broadened. This was not a woman, and it was not Erin. "What the hell just happened?"

"Nice to meet you, Zach." He handed me a note.

"I have to go before they notice me," he says while disappearing into the restroom.

My shoulders shiver when imagining him shapeshift from a woman to a man. But with all the magic in this world it doesn't surprise me that there would be an illusionist. I've never met one before as they are rare.

Kayleon isn't here, so you will meet him later tonight at dinner. For now, I will send you back to your room—or allow you freedom, just as Zach is there to keep you in order."

Erin rolled her eyes, and I laughed at how adorable she was when she obviously hated someone.

Benny focused his attention on Erin, "I have business to take care of, so I will expect to see you all cleaned up tonight, and you shall sleep in my corridors since you will be my wife."

When I reached for her hand, I had forgotten how much smaller it was in comparison to mine. I held onto it securely while never wanting to let go. As I led her to the kitchen I pulled out a snack for her to eat. It was just a chocolate croissant but the way her face lit up made my heart fall.

"I would love to meet the people in town. Remember when you promised me that?" she asked as her shoulders fell back.

"Yeah, it would be a good idea for you to meet your people," I tell her.

She stopped chewing her croissant, and a look of sadness spread across her face.

I directed my gaze onto her eyes.

"It will be alright—one thing at a time."

Then I remembered the note in my pocket and pulled it out. Zach was written on the front.

"He must know."

"Who?"

"Sin."

Her eyes lit up as she straightened her posture. She walked towards me and leaned in to see the note.

"Read it."

Zach,

I'm glad that you're okay. Thanks for protecting me back there. I'm going to make this concise. Tonight, we're going to sneak into the palace. You have already met Ron, I'd assume, since you're reading this note—hopefully he did not get caught. Ron is our insider. Believe it or not, he used to be a guard at this palace, and you have witnessed his power.

We're saving you and Erin, so just be prepared. Don't do anything stupid and please protect her.

-Sin

Erin jumped up with relief, hugging Zach. "Sin and the others should be here soon enough and then we can finally take back our home."

I would never get used to her saying his name. It should be mine on her lips. Not his.

I'll be damned if I lose her to him.

CHAPTER THIRTY-TWO

Erin's stomach twisted into knots when Zach hugged her because she'd have to confess to him soon. She didn't want to hurt him, her best friend. For so long, she'd thought they were soulmates until she realized that he was the comfort through the storm.

His eyes anchored her in the deep blue sea as she lost herself in them. She still had feelings for Zach, and those would never leave her soul. But she'd have to be okay with that when she broke his heart. Now was the best time—at least then, if he wanted to leave, he'd be given the choice before the fight began. As she opened her mouth, Zach placed a hand on top of her thigh. His touch caused her to straighten and tense from the warmth it pooled in between her legs.

His sharp blue eyes captured her gaze, "We will be in separate rooms. I am not planning for you to be alone with him, but if you should, please protect yourself."

She nodded. "He is just my childhood bully, and this time I am not that scared and vulnerable girl from my past."

A smile brightened his face. "You are more of a force to be reckoned with, and I see that now." He lifted his hand and stood up from the chair. The warmth from her leg vanished as she relaxed her body again. Telling him my feelings will be harder than I thought.

#

A knock at the door alerted Erin as she opened it to see a woman with silver hair styled in a bun and warm brown eyes. She wore a black dress with buttons down the front of it and an apron tied around the waist.

"Hello dear, my name is Mary.

Erin straightened her posture and smiled. "Nice to meet you, my name is Erin."

The woman's eyes set on the top of Erin's hair and trailed down to her feet as she circled her.

Suddenly, Erin felt uncomfortable. She would have to get used to this when she became Queen, but she still felt like that reality was surreal. *I am going to make a terrible Queen.* She dropped her shoulders and gazed down at the floor.

"Chin up, remember only you have the power to show the world your emotions. Facial expressions, posture and clothing can play important roles in proving your identity."

Mary's face softened as she relaxed. "You will be a great Queen dear, don't put too much pressure on yourself."

My emotions most be obvious.

Then Mary stepped into the doorway while snapping her fingers as women dressed in the same black and white uniform flooded into the room. They curled Erin's hair and powdered her face with the prettiest makeup along with applying floral perfumes that made her sneeze.

Catching a glimpse in the mirror, she couldn't even recognize herself as she touched the velvet red bow holding half her hair up. Her dress was made from soft red silk material, lightweight and breathable as it made a V-neck down to her breasts. The top revealed her curves as it was fitted, and the bottom flared down to her ankles. Her arms were bare, and she wore red velvet heels.

All this just to meet this stupid man felt frivolous. She pulled back the royal gold curtains and looked up at the crescent moon hanging in the sky. Then she walked toward the door while trying to conform to heels as she wobbled. She took a deep breath and let it out as she reached for the doorknob.

Zach stood on the other side, wearing a black tuxedo, looking much more uniform than he ever had. Her eyes widened at how handsome he was, and his eyes lit up while examining her from top to bottom. "You're breathtaking." It struck a match in her heart and caused her stomach to catch butterflies as she took his arm for him to escort her.

"Why are we so dressed up?"

They walked down a staircase with wooden rails, and there was a red and gold rug that led to a ballroom floor. Music and people filled the room as Erin nervously walked down with Zach. "I may need a drink."

"Might be hard with all eyes on you." He nudged her in the side.

Everyone stopped to look at them as they entered the ballroom floor for the first time. She could see Benny talking to a tall dark-haired man in a gray suit. Then she met Sin's eyes.

Sin stood at the bottom of the staircase, wearing a dark-blue suit with a white button-down shirt underneath and a navy tie. Her eyes widened until he caught a glimpse of Zach's arm moving toward the arch of her back.

"Look at you, stealing the light from every star tonight." Sin smiled.

Her cheeks burned as she tried not to smile too wide. "Where is everyone else?" she whispered, now walking with Zach on one arm, Sin on the other.

"Patience, little jack rabbit," Sin said.

Flora, Erin wanted to scream but held in her excitement as they found her standing next to a table with a glass in her hand. She wore a turquoise mermaid-style dress, with golden curls, green eye shadow and a bright-green lily pinned to her hair.

"Sylvian and Ron aren't here because they're planting the poison Zach gave them into Kayleon and Benny's room. Erin, you're going to have to get it into Benny's system, and I will take care of Kayleon," Zach said.

"The guys are going to make sure that the guards are knocked out with the sleeping potion I made," Flora proudly whispered.

"If this works properly, then you can take back what is rightfully yours," Flora said.

Erin nodded, a little worried about what was coming next. Sin squeezed her hand as if to assure her that everything would be all right.

Then she noticed Kayleon and Benny walking their way as everyone dispersed through the crowd, leaving Erin to herself. As they finally reached her, she took in Kayleon's scent. It was a strong sharp cologne and a hint of dark liquor that nauseated her senses. When she looked up at him, her heart immediately felt a strike of pain along with confusion. It was her father, the one she grew up with. "What's going on?" Erin demanded as she felt a tinge of anger.

"I know I betrayed you, and I hope that you can forgive me one day," he said in a low, unapologetic voice.

"You neglected me! You were never there; I can't count the times you left me alone in that house and treated me like I was nothing. Then you decide that I need to come back here."

She was shaking from anger and although she wanted to punch him, she stood in place and glared at him. "You took everything from me. What was it all for?"

He stepped closer into her space.

"You may not understand my intentions, but someday you will. It was all for your own protection."

Erin took a step back and scowled at him. "I was never yours to protect, where is my real father at?"

His brows pinched into anger. "I am done entertaining your questions."

Benny backed up, and a confused look appeared on his face while the room grew quiet.

"You are done screwing with my head, my family, and my friends. I will never let you win." Erin promised.

As she turned around, Kayleon grabbed her arm and shoved her into Benny. "Benjamin, why don't you take care of your future wife?

Benny clung to her with a fierce hold.

Sin stood up, ready to pounce, but Zach held him back.

"Don't draw attention to us. We've got this," Zach said while inhaling deeply.

Erin decided not to fight as Benny led her to his room. He slammed the door shut behind him and pushed her onto the king-sized bed. As Erin's back hit the mattress, she felt nothing but a fiery rage running through her body.

"I will never marry you," she glared as he locked his hands around her wrists and pinned them down.

"You know, Erin, you and the rest of them may think that you're all better than me, but one day I will prove my worth to you all."

"Nobody has ever said that you were worthless. But this behavior is low even for a bully like you."

"Bullshit. From the day I came into your lives, I've been an outsider—the idiot that you didn't want to be seen with—and instead of me protecting you, it had to be one of the golden wolf brothers. Your life was already mapped out before I could even try to introduce myself to your father. He made his choice. Until Kayleon offered an opportunity that I couldn't refuse. He told me that if I held back and did what he said, you would be mine.

He laughed while grabbing her hair and pulling her head back. He wrapped his legs around her and held tightly as if trying to assert his dominance like an animal. Erin would not allow it; she worked too hard to find the missing pieces of her past.

An epiphany interrupted her thoughts. She was meant to protect this place. She had a choice to either fall victim or rise above to reclaim her throne, her home. I will make this right. I will find my parents and make this world safe again.

She managed to pull her weight while flipping him over and grabbing his arms.

"Benny, you have a choice whether you're with or against us. Choose wisely." She backed off from him while still holding on to hope.

"What's in it for me if I help you? I won't get what I want in the end."

Erin adjusted her hair and dress while looking back at him. "That's life, Benny. If you choose to continue down this path with Kayleon, you will lose. Power will never fill the void in your heart. That is something you must work on."

His face scrunched in distaste, "What would you even know about that?"

She sighed, "The fact that I didn't have my real parents or memories isn't enough?"

He pointed a finger in her direction, "You had Zach."

"Benny, if you weren't too busy bullying people, then you would have had me too."

He looked as though he had let his guard down for a second, and then Erin could see some vulnerability in his eyes.

He stood up from the bed and stalked toward her.

She tensed while wondering what his next move would entail.

Then he backed her up against the door and placed his arm over her head while looking down at her.

"Do you think you could find it in your heart to forgive me?"

She released the breath that she sucked while placing her hand on his chest, she looked deeply into his eyes. "Don't mess it up."

As she pushed him away, he smiled wide, and she noticed a sparkle in his eye—one she had never seen before.

"You know, for what it's worth, I'm sure you would make someone happy one day," Erin said as the door swung open, and she fell back and into Sin's arms.

He was out of breath with blood and bruises near his right eye. She gazed at the bruises and touched the side just barley, "Sin, what happened, are you okay?"

He grabbed her hand and gently kissed the top of it then his face twisted with anger as he placed her behind him.

He twisted his hands into Benny's shirt and pinned him against the wall.

"Next time will be your last, watch yourself."

Erin jumped in and pulled Sin from Benny. "He is on our side."

"I don't buy it," Sin said as he forced Benny's body against the wall with a thud.

Benny placed his hands up in surrender, "She is right, I am done with this game."

Sin glared at him, "Fine, but if you ever pull this shit again, your dead."

Sin turned back around to Erin as his shoulders dropped, and his eyes focused on her. From the look of his sincere eyes, it seemed that he had bad news.

"We have a problem. Kayleon has fled with Flora."

Erin gasped. "What? Why would he do that? It doesn't make any sense. He is trying to hurt me through my friends. He will pay for this. Her face twisted in frustration.

Where is Zach?"

"Present," he said along with Sylvian and Ron. He ran toward Erin and hugged her tightly. "Are you alright, princess?"

She shook her head and hugged him back.

"Sin had to rescue you first," Zach said.

"Hey, you had her for years. I can only imagine what you had done, the poor thing was probably tortured." Sin locked his arms securely around her waist and pulled her into his chest. "Besides, Erin finally made a choice and it's not you Zach."

"She is mine—paws off," Sin claimed.

Erin's body tensed up as she could feel the heat from Zach's eyes burning into her skin.

CHAPTER THIRTY-THREE

Zach's eyes lowered onto Erin's. His expression slack as his shoulders dropped from disappointment.

"Tell me he is joking, Erin," Zach said.

"Can we focus on the fact that Flora is gone?" Sylvain interjected.

While trying to focus her attention elsewhere, Erin gravitated her attention towards Benny.

"Do you know where he could have taken her?"

"I may have an idea."

"Will he hurt her?" Erin asked.

"I don't believe so. During my time around him, he never abused the staff."

It would be a bad idea to navigate through the woods at night, but I hate to leave her in the hands of that monster. She stood upright and made eye contact with each of her friends as they stood there while waiting for her direction.

"First thing in the morning we will find Flora."

As everyone dispersed and went their separate ways she mustered in her thoughts. Zach's expression killed me. Sin should have known better than to bring up my decision so casually. I should have told him to keep us a secret. She sighed heavily while sinking her body into the porcelain tub.

Relaxing her muscles in the hot bath, she closed her eyes, hoping she could calm her nerves.

Will this nightmare ever be over? I haven't come close to figuring everything out.

Just one thing at a time.

She pulled on a white nightdress and brushed her hair. After slowly pushing the door open, she noticed that the palace felt still and silent. Tiptoeing around the halls, she observed the antique glasses stocked on a shelf—glass figurines of bluebirds.

"White suits you, little jackrabbit." Sin said. He was close behind her as his breath sent chills down her spine. He planted a long kiss on the side of her neck as a moan escaped from her mouth. Instantly warmth fluttered between her legs as she twisted around to catch sight of his ember eyes.

His hair was wet and slicked back, and he wore gray slack pants and a white shirt. He ran his fingers along her jawline, and she felt tingles rush through her skin.

"I have been yearning for this since you left." His hands dropped to her lower back, and he lifted her as she wrapped her legs around him. Then he parted her lips and slowly slid his tongue into her mouth.

In that moment, she forgot where she was, who she was, and all her problems. He had the power to distract her, which she didn't mind. But then she thought of Zach and suddenly pulled back from Sin's lips. Her chest ached at the confusion in his eyes.

As she dropped to her feet, Zach walked in and found them.

"So, it's true," Zach said with a spike in his voice. "I can't do this." Then he turned around and walked away.

Erin went to run after him, but Sin grabbed her arm before she could. She twisted herself from his grasp and ran after Zach with tears in her eyes.

It hurt her heart to see him that way. She could feel a sharp pain in her side. "Zach, it wasn't supposed to happen like this. You're my best friend." Tears streamed down her face.

"I've loved you for so many years."

"I've felt the same, Zach," she said while grabbing onto his arms to steady herself as the icy cold cement pried into the bottoms of her feet.

"Just tell me, why him? Of all people, my brother. Are you sure he's the one who will make you happy? You've only known him for a couple of months. Don't just give up on us.

I know you chose him amid this chaos, but you could have me instead," he said gently.

The warmth from his hands embraced her cheeks. Although she still had feelings for him, they were not the same.

His love was easy and simple like the comfort of a blanket. He pulled her into him and kissed her softly, as if trying not to press too hard. She liked the way Zach tasted and became lost in his embrace, but then she felt awful.

Slowly, she pushed him away. "I chose Sin, but I still love you too, Zach."

"Erin, if you can't be with me, then I won't stay. It's breaking my heart."

"No, don't go," she pleaded. Tears fell from her eyes, "We need to save Flora."

"You'll be fine. You're a princess, remember? You don't need to count on a man." His blue eyes glossed over as he looked away.

Her heart shattered as all the memories from their past flooded through her mind. She felt as though she were losing him, and she did not know what to do. If she chose him, Sin would leave. She wanted to go back to the beginning when they first met.

"You lied. If you love me, you wouldn't leave." Her eyes filled with tears again.

"If you want me to stay so bad, then choose me."

Erin stood still, unsure of what to do because either way would complicate things. "That's what I thought. Once we save Flora, you will never see my face again." He turned around and walked out, and the door shut behind him.

As she slid down, her legs scraped across the cold hard ground. She felt numb, unable to imagine living in a world without him. What was she going to do? She wanted to hold him so tightly and give him everything he wanted. If Sin hadn't existed, she knew Zach would be the one.

She needed her mother's advice. But her mom wasn't here—she hadn't been for years—and that just made her want to wallow even more. Mom, I need you.

Then she felt a hand interlock with hers. Sin sat there with a sad look in his eyes.

"Are you alright?"

Erin slowly lifted her body and noticed he was holding two mugs, one of which he handed to her. The warmth embraced her hands and helped with the frost from the night air.

The aroma of dark chocolate, sweet marshmallows, and vanilla filled her nostrils as she smiled. As she sipped on it, she tasted the smooth, honey-spiced flavor of alcohol.

"I added some rum for a little kick—figured you would enjoy it." He smiled at her while sipping from his red mug.

She liked the rum; it soothed her soul and relaxed her.

"Erin, I know you care about Zach."

"Sin, I chose you, and that won't change." She lowered her eyes at the mug.

"But you could have waited to tell him about us."

He placed his hand on her knee. "I just don't want him to keep trying. It needs to be clear that you're not his."

Erin provided a weak grin and gazed up at the night sky.

He placed a kiss against her cheek and wrapped an around her shoulders.

"Let's go inside. We have a big day ahead of us tomorrow."

She knew that she had to save her best friend. There was no time to dwell on Zach's emotions. The stars glistened in the sky, and she remembered the nights she would fall asleep under them with Zach beside her.

"Sin, what do you see when you look up at the sky?"

He slid the back of his fingers down the side of her cheek, underneath her chin while tilting it up.

"That I don't want to waste another second without you're light in my world."

"I will never let you go," He placed a kiss on her lips.

"I still can't believe you tied me up, though," she teased.

"I can do it again, but this time it will be fun," he said.

"I think I would like to retire from being held down. First the kidnapper, then you and now Zach."

She covered her mouth. Her eyes widened.

His face hardened as she realized she had said too much.

CHAPTER THIRTY-FOUR

Erin shifted her legs as she tried to find the words to explain.

"Zach kidnapped and chained me to a bed in the palace. It was part of his plan. Nothing happened, and he released me once I agreed."

"I should have known." He shook his head while covering his face. "I will kill him," he said and stood up. Grabbing his arms, she pulled herself toward him and kissed his lips. She wrapped her hands into his hair, forcing herself into his space while interlocking her tongue with his. She couldn't understand her pull to him; it was rather different from Zach.

Her soul felt as if it would leave her body, and she lost herself in the seductive smells of honey and chocolate on his breath. I shouldn't do this, but I want to surrender myself to him. Erin pulled back for a second and lost herself in his dark eyes. "Want to take this to my room?"

His smile widened as he picked her up and spun her around. "Is my little jackrabbit going to be still like a good girl?"

She grinned and pressed her fingers on his bottom lip. "Only if you promise to use that mouth of yours."

His eyebrows lifted as he drew out his tongue and licked the tip of her finger.

She grew weak in the knees and began to tremble. Why must he tease me?

As they closed the door behind them, the palace was quiet. She giggled as they tiptoed through the halls while trying not to be caught. They found a room to hide in while being careful not to make too much noise.

The door shut behind them as Sin pressed himself against her and kissed her neck and down her collarbone. He rolled his tongue steadily along her neck, to her jawline, and then back to her lips while running his fingers down toward her breasts.

"I've wanted this since you disappeared after our playtime," he whispered in her ear. His words jolted her senses as she let out a small moan and ached for his lips to touch hers.

"It was a tease, but now I have you, and you're all mine." He grabbed her face and pulled it into his. Her head was empty, as if she had taken morphine and it cured all the pain. She managed to release herself from their bond and pulled him toward the bed.

He stopped as she backed her legs against it. "Are you ready for me?" he whispered in a low growl. The darkness suited him, and she realized she'd offer her soul to him if he asked for it.

She slid from her dress, unsnapped her bra, and then locked eyes with him as she tossed her underwear to the side. The light from the moon crept in, providing enough light for him to catch every curve of her body. His eyes grew dark with a pang of fierce hunger.

His eyes darkened, "Breathtaking." He pulled his shirt over his head to reveal his muscles and then stalked towards her.

Her nerves sent chills through her body as her eyes dropped lower the moment his pants fell to the floor.

As she fell onto the bed Sin pulled himself on top of her while kissing each inch of her skin.

"You have me in command for the rest of your life," he said as though he were signing a contract with his affection.

She closed her eyes while picturing him on a throne beside her. If they were to split ways now, it would tear her apart.

Her thoughts dissipated as his tongue went deeper into her mouth. He slid his hand onto her clit while rubbing her bud steadily. She could feel herself climbing an imaginary hill as the spot he worked on grew sensitive with the pressure and speed of his fingers. Then there was a rushing sense of peace as she let go of all the tightness while moaning into his mouth.

"I am ready for you," she panted.

"Is that so?" He rolled his tongue down her neck and slid a warm and wet trail down her body. Then he moved down to her ankles and kissed the insides of her thighs. An aching desire pulsed in between her thighs as she bit the bottom of her lip.

"Sin," she pleaded.

"Be patient, jack rabbit. I have waited a long time for this moment, and I am going to take my time enjoying every inch of you." As he kissed her clit and gently bit it, she rolled her eyes back. He thudded his tongue against her as she arched her back from the shock of pleasure. Then he brought tears to her eyes as she moaned from the orgasm, he gifted her.

Then he thrust his cock to fill her with a delicious satisfaction. A moan escaped her mouth. "Fuck, Sin." She felt a pain from the stretching and then instant relief as he pulled out and forced himself back down.

"I love you," she forced out in between breaths.

"I love you too." He slammed himself inside her with another thrust. Pulling her arms above her head, he sucked on her nipples as she moaned louder. She clenched her legs as tight as she could as he worked his way deeper. They both climbed together as he rolled his finger back down to her clit.

Tendrils of black swirled through her mind as she rolled her eyes back. Tears fell from her eyes.

"Erin," he moaned into her neck. "Your body is mine. I will never give you up, little jackrabbit."

She smiled. "I wouldn't dream of it."

Feeling relieved and giddy, she planted a kiss on his chest and turned to climb off the bed. She didn't go far as Sin grabbed her around the waist and pulled her back to him. "Just where do you think you're going?"

She felt comfortable in his arms and didn't want to move as she soaked in his warm embrace. "For one, I need to run to the restroom," she said while pulling herself away from his hold and throwing her clothes back on. "Also, I don't think anyone would be too happy to find me in here in the morning."

"Screw what they have to say."

"I will see you in the morning, my future king," she whispered in his ear. She could almost feel his body tense.

"Damn, you just keep getting sexier." He smiled while placing one last kiss on her lips.

She softly shut the door, hoping not to make a sound as she walked through the halls. But before she was able to reach her destination, someone pulled her into another room.

Her screams were muffled when a hand covered her mouth with light pressure.

"I don't know what I have to do to prove that I'm the one for you," Zach said.

She tried to escape him by pulling his hand away and reaching for the door, but he grabbed her body and threw her onto the bed. Her body began to shake from the sudden movement. Her lower lip began to tremble as she bit it to fight showing her fear. She didn't want him to have power over her, even if he was scaring her.

"What are you doing?"

He pressed himself into her body while holding her in place.

"I won't let him have you."

She didn't know what to do; this was not the Zach she knew. It was as though something had taken over his body.

She tried to push him away.

"You don't get to decide."

Zach thrust her back down and kissed her intensely. A feeling of dread came over her as she pushed him away. Then he grabbed her face and pulled her back into him. She could feel the tears ready to flood until she heard a loud thud and watched as Sin pulled Zach from her.

Sin held onto Zach's neck with all his strength as Erin allowed herself to breathe, tears crashing down her face. She came to her senses as she watched Sin raise a fist towards Zach.

"Sin, enough," Erin screamed.

He stopped and took her hand, then led her to the shower room that she was supposed to go to before all this mess. He turned the faucet on as the steam flowed around them like a warm compression.

Erin collapsed into Sin's body as they both rinsed off in the shower together.

"I never thought he would go that far," she said, feeling depleted of energy.

"Me neither," Sin said.

"He didn't do anything crazy, did he?"

"Just the kissing, but if he had, I think I'd have killed him myself."

"You're staying with me tonight."

Erin didn't argue; she wanted to forget this whole night and was thankful to be in Sin's arms as she cuddled into him. She relaxed herself and fell into a deep sleep as the night wrapped around them.

CHAPTER THIRTY-FIVE

Rays of sunshine peeked through the window as Erin woke. She realized that Sin was gone. Probably for the better.

As she recollected the events from last night, she pushed them to the side to focus on saving her friend. Time to save Flora. There was a knock at the door that made her body tense until they spoke.

"I was sent to have you dressed," the woman said as she opened the door. Kathleen was stitched on the right side of her uniform.

He couldn't bother to remember her name?

Kathleen didn't speak as she handed Erin a satin-pink dress. It was soft and smooth with lace in the front and ends. The sleeves ran down to her wrists, and the fabric hugged her curves. The lady brushed her hair and placed it in a bun that matched her honey-toned makeup.

Then she used a white flower-styled clip that pulled the look together.

"This was your mother's." Kathleen smiled.

Erin's eyes brightened, "You knew my mom?"

"Yes, dear. When she resided within these walls, before." A hint of sadness reflected in her eyes as she grew silent. "I know that you want to find your friend, but if you leave, we will be abandoned—something your mother would have never wanted."

That didn't cross her mind since Kayleon, and his guards disappeared from the palace altogether. "I will figure something out. I promise."

Erin walked into the dining room of the palace as the aroma of bacon and sweet pastries filled her senses. She sat down in the closest chair, placed her hand beneath her chin and let out a sigh. Guilt is eating me alive when I should be on my way to save Flora.

Sin took his place beside her, dressed in a black suit but a satin-pink tie to match Erin's dress. "We look cute," he said while placing a hand on her thigh. Her back straightened as he began to slide it closer towards her panties. She placed her hand on his to prohibit the movement while cutting her eyes at him.

The tension in the room rose as Zach seated himself on the other side of her. Sin squeezed her leg to distract her from raising anxiety levels. When everyone was gathered around the table she figured this would be the perfect opportunity to bring up what Kathleen had told her earlier. I can't leave this palace unprotected.

"We have a problem," Erin announced.

All eyes were on her which felt intimidating. She released a breath and puffed out her chest to portray confidence.

"We can't leave the palace unattended. Someone must stay and protect it and the people," she said.

"Well, you are the princess," Zach said, smirking.

She cut her eyes at him and smirked at his arrogance. "I am the one that Kayleon wants, therefore I'll have to go."

"Zach and Ron should stay," Sin blurted out. "Ron knows the ends and outs of this place, while Zach can help to protect it."

Zach looked dissatisfied. "No, I will go with you, Erin."

Sin slammed his glass on the table. "The hell you are after the events that transpired last night."

"What happened?" Sylvain raised a curious eyebrow.

I just want to forget about it. She mustered in her thoughts.

"Nothing." She refused to feed into the drama.

"Benny can take me to the spot Flora is being held captive," she decided.

"I can be of use when it comes to Kayleon," Zach said.

"How convenient, I wonder why?" Sin snarled.

He just wasn't going to give in, and Erin's head spun from all of the stress.

"Fine." She cut her eyes toward Zach.

Sin clawed his nails into her leg as the words fell from her mouth. She winced from the pain and pushed his hand off.

"Benny and Zach go with me as Sin, Sylvian and Ron protect the palace," she ordered.

Everyone finished their meals in silence and ran off to their rooms.

Erin walked into her room as Sin slammed the door behind her.

"I do not trust him alone with you after that stunt he pulled last night."

"It'll be fine. I'll protect myself," she said while placing her hand on his chest to calm him down.

"Remember, I am the ruler, and I chose you to be the King of Rosanafalls."

The tightness in his muscles softened as he pulled her into his chest.

"King Sin—I could get used to that name."

She pulled back to look into his eyes.

"I must learn how to protect myself and strengthen my abilities."

"I will have a word with Benny, and you better promise to be back quick and unharmed." She nodded as she noticed her red bag lying on the bed.

"You brought my stuff."

"Of course I did. I knew you would need it," he said.

He placed his hands onto her cheeks and bent down to kiss her mouth. Then he slid his hand down her dress and pushed her lightly onto the bed. "I want you."

A sudden flush of arousal heated between her legs. She felt the desire to be filled.

If only I had the time.

A knock on the door interrupted them as they quickly pulled from each other.

"You ready?" Zach said.

Erin and Sin both rolled their eyes, and she said, "Give me a second."

"To be continued," Erin said while picking up her bag, ready to get this over with.

Sin grabbed her hand and slipped something onto her ring finger. She raised her hand to examine a diamond imprinted onto a black wolf along with diamonds circling the band. Its eyes were emerald just like Sin's eyes when he turned into a wolf. "For my future wife."

Grinning, he grabbed her face and gave her one last goodbye kiss. "I love you," he said as she whispered the same to him and turned around for her new journey. If she stayed any longer, she wouldn't be able to leave Sin's side.

She was thankful that he was allowing her to manage her decisions. This time he realized that she could take care of this on her own. She never had given herself credit, but it was time to gain confidence. If she were going to become a leader and protector, then she would have to learn the ins and outs. It was the only way she could fulfill her role as a queen one day and make her parents proud.

#

As the leaves crunched beneath Erin's feet, she watched her footing. Then she stole a glance at Zach, who looked uneasy. "So, what are Kayleon's weaknesses?" Erin broke the silence.

Zach's gaze twisted into a devious grin. "Information comes with a price."

Erin was appalled. How could he ask for anything after what he did? Why was he suddenly the bad guy now? Erin decided to play his little game to cure her boredom. "What's your price?"

"To be named later."

She dropped her shoulders and stopped in front of him while putting her hand out for him to take. "Fine, shake on it?" He took it, squeezed and didn't let go as she tried to pull away.

"Kayleon isn't human," he said.

Erin knew Zach was a jokester and didn't know if she could believe him, but then there were a lot of things that would make sense if that were true. She vaguely remembered her fake parents had started to leave at night more often.

She sucked in a breath. "Wait, is he a vampire?"

"Sort of. He made a deal with a witch for eternal life, and in return, he must bring a human body to her to keep his soul from leaving earth. She obtains the body's soul in exchange for his life."

She placed her hands onto her hips.

"That's not a vampire, and that sounds awful and exhausting."

Zach grins, "So technically, he doesn't die when he's harmed." "But like any contract, I am sure there is a loophole."

Erin shifted her weight to her right side.

"Nice, so he is like the bad guy that just keeps coming back." She frowned.

"Unless we can work in a deal with the witch," Zach questioned.

"We don't have time for that. And what if he uses Flora's—"

"He won't. It must be a man's soul, and he wouldn't dare harm another witch."

She narrowed her eyes, folded her arms in and leaned back.

"Did you know this whole time? You could have told me that I was living underneath the roof of a killer."

"I didn't want to stress you out." He placed his hand on her shoulder, but she pushed it off.

"How do I find this witch?" She felt the need to exhaust her options.

The shuffling of boots reminded them of Benny's presence.

Erin turned her head towards him.

"Benny, why don't you go ahead and find Kayleon? I may have a plan, and I believe splitting up could be beneficial."

"I was ordered by Sin not to leave your side," Benny explained.

"Benny, since when do you take orders? Aren't you tired of that?"

He straightened his back, "If you feel safe then I will go find Flora, but she may not accept my help."

Erin nodded, "You have a point. You could help us to sneak inside," she said. Hold on, she thought, pulling out a piece of paper and a pen to write a quick note. "Give this to Flora. She will trust you after reading this, and then you two can sneak out of there. Then we can defeat Kayleon. At least then, she'll be out of danger, and if we fail, then we can come up with another plan."

Benny pulled out a map with coordinates and the location of Kayleon's castle.

"Erin, be careful. Sin will not be pleased if anything happens to you nor would I."

She smiled and wrapped her arms around him.

"Thank you for helping me. I am glad that we are not enemies anymore."

The smell of cedar and spice filled through her senses from his shirt. It was a comforting feeling; one she hadn't known.

"Okay, see you soon." He placed the paper into her hands.

It was the only way to divide and conquer. As she walked back to Zach, he smiled, not hiding how happy he was that they were alone, as if he planned for it. "How do you know the witch's location?" she asked.

"You forget that I have wolf blood, and Kayleon goes to her every year, so it's not hard to pick up the scent."

"From miles away?"

"Honestly, she's not that far away from his castle, and she keeps an eye on anyone she collaborates with."

She rolled her eyes. "You know a lot, don't you?"

"It's safer and wiser to accumulate information from enemies." He shrugged.

"Yeah, well I have so much to gather, my brain hurts thinking about it."

"It'll be alright. I'll help you," he said while wrapping his arm around her neck and pulling her into him, but she pushed him away.

"Okay, I won't touch you again." Zach put his hands up in surrender.

"It's not a game. You scared me." She stood in front of him to block his path.

"You promised you would never hurt me, and you did."

"You hurt me too," he said while walking past her. Silence edged them apart. Soon the woods grew darker, and the night sky appeared above them.

Zach dropped his bags. "Come on, let's set up camp here."

"No, I can keep going," Erin said as she kept on walking.

"I can tell that you're past your limit." He grabbed her arm.

"You don't know that." She sped away from him.

Arms wrapped around her waist and pulled her feet off the ground.

"Zach, put me down," she kicked her legs. He tightened his grip and walked backwards. Suddenly they were falling and crashing into the dirt and leaves. When Erin caught her breath, she realized she was facing down Zach's chest as she inhaled the scents of warm vanilla and sweet honey. "What just happened," she huffed.

"I may have lost my balance," Zach admitted as a dimple revealed itself next to his lips and his face flushed red.

Erin realized her legs were wrapped around him as she slowly pushed herself up from his chest. He grabbed her waist, pulled her back down and rolled them over as he toppled her.

"Zach," she warned with a heated glare. "You're too easy to play with princess."

She tensed.

"Can you stop joking for once in your life? Zach, I chose your brother, and that's final. I'm not sorry that I hurt you, just as much as you're not sorry for lying to me. So, if we could make this trip less painful and aggravating, then that would be nice."

A pain flickered in his eyes as he released his hold on her and helped her to her feet.

I hope that I set him straight with my words. As she set up her sleeping area to her comfort, she noticed Zach had already begun a fire with no tent in sight. Erin stomped up to him. "Where is your tent?"

I didn't bring one, but I will sleep by the fire.

"Okay, fine." She didn't argue as she sat down to feel the heat brush against her skin.

His blue eyes darkened.

"Can I just ask one question? Why my brother?"

She steadied herself next to the fire and frowned. "I didn't mean for it to happen; it just did. It's like he became colors I had never seen before, as if I were opening my eyes to something brand new for the first time in my life." She observed the patterns of a clay-colored leaf. "I've had feelings for you too, though. If you'd shared your feelings with me before, I may have been yours." She lowered her gaze from his. I want to be honest with him as well as myself.

"I want to cash in my prize."

Erin looked at him and wondered what he would throw at her.

"Let me kiss you one last time. If you feel nothing, then I will accept your relationship with my brother. I know you said you already chose, but maybe you could use a little more time and convincing."

She dropped her shoulders. "Fine."

Zach quickly rose from his position and walked over to her. Her heart sank a little, as she was worried and feeling shameful all at once. Zach sat down next to her and cupped her face in his hands. They filled most of her face and were callous, yet gentle. As he pulled her into him, he smelled of sweet berries from the fruit he'd eaten that morning.

He put his tongue gently into her mouth and pushed her lightly down onto the earth. She kissed him back, eyes closed as she let herself go, consumed by the warmth of his lips. As he continued, she felt weak all over. He ran his fingers up her thigh, and she could feel the tingling sensations from all over her body. She didn't want to stop but knew this was wrong, but also amazing.

Once his hands moved further up, he continued kissing her while sucking on her lip. Her body desired him, and she couldn't pull away. She knew she had to stop before it got to that point, so she lightly pushed his chest. He indulged himself with her for one last kiss before gently pulling away.

He turned around quickly as she laughed.

"What are you doing?"

"Unless you're going to make it better, it's no concern of yours." He looked like he was concentrating on something.

"Not a chance. You are on your own." She ran into the tent, then zipped it. "Goodnight."

Why am I so stupid? She could hear Zach laughing on the other side, and now she had more problems. Sin is not going to be happy, and what are these feelings toward Zach?

She pulled out her book of poems, hoping her mother could offer guidance.

Love comes from a safe place

Learn to fall in love, but do not become naïve
Don't wear your emotions for all to see
Hide the darkest parts until you find someone who understands
Who can be a true protector of your heart and a friend
Time will reveal people's true colors
Don't be fooled by lust, and carefully trust others
When the time is right you will be set free
By the one who's meant to be
In the sense that they will love you without control
They will love you enough to let your soul go

As she gently closed the book, she realized the meaning behind the poem. I can't rush love; I need to take my time. She wrapped herself inside of the blanket and snuggled against the journal. "Soon we will meet, Mother."

CHAPTER-THIRTY-SIX

Erin could feel a weight on her body as the heat from the sun warmed the tent. She tossed and turned until she realized she couldn't move as someone's arms pulled her closer. Zach lay there sound asleep, his arm holding her body against his. She shook from his hold as he awoke with a smile.

"Well good morning beautiful," he said with a yawn.

I am not even going to waste my energy. She hurried to brush her teeth and threw on a black dress, this one flowy and made of cotton. As she gathered her things, Zach collected his belongings while dressing right in front of her.

Luckily, she turned around in time. "Let me know when you're finished."

Warm breath entered her ear. "Finished. Ready to meet the witch?"

"I guess." But she was not prepared, especially since they willingly helped Kayleon. On top of it, the witch was a soul collector, and that was a terrifying thought. As Zach led Erin along a dark path, she knew there was no turning back.

He grabbed her hand and pulled her to his side. "You should stay close, just in case."

She decided not to fight him as she noticed bones of all sorts hanging from the limbs of trees along the path they traveled. The leaves turned red beneath their feet as the wind picked up, and a cave several feet from them appeared. Erin took a long breath as they walked inside.

"I sense powerful beings nearby," echoed a voice in the cave. It was not long before Erin was in total darkness and alone. Lost in thought, she didn't even feel him pull away from her hand.

"It's an honor to be in the presence of a royal daughter," the voice said.

"I am here for a favor," Erin said, trying to hide the quiver in her voice. The cave was colder than normal, and she could feel goosebumps rise on her arms as she waited for an answer.

"I don't provide favors, my dear, but I can fill a request for the right price," the witch said.

"What is your price, and why don't you show your face?"

"I am the face of multiple witch ancestors that come from all over. We can all hear you." "The witch you speak with is Viola. What is it that you desire?"

"I want you to release Kayleon from this earth. He has caused nothing but destruction."

A rising fear caused Erin to hug her body tightly. This could be a bad idea.

"That isn't something I can offer. You see, he provides me with souls. These souls provide me with the power to fill desires, and so Kayleon is helpful in satisfying those needs."

Erin dropped her head down from defeat. "I guess I will be on my way then."

"You know, I wouldn't mind possessing a gift like yours," the witch said, and Erin felt a rush of wind lift strands of her hair.

Erin thought of her powers. Control over venomous creatures, and healing victims from poisons and wounds. She didn't want to give them up, but if it were the price to save her friend she wouldn't hesitate. I worry about the consequences later.

"Deal," Erin spoke to the darkness in the cave.

A rush of cold air brushed past her shoulders. The cold chill crept up her neck and caused her to shiver. Then a thudding noise clunked to the ground at her feet. She jumped back while wondering if the witch intended to harm her. As she knelt to pick it up, she noticed it was wrapped in a metal golden snake and that the blade was silver.

"I need a drop of your blood. This dagger won't affect you, but you may use it on Kayleon, as his soul will become confined to it. What you do with it after is your choice."

Erin pierced the tip of the blade down until a drop of blood surfaced.

Multiple voices began to speak through the cave.

"Do you accept the terms and conditions to this contract with Viola?"

"I do." She accepted her fate.

A force knocked her down to her knees, and her body felt drained.

"What's happening to me?" she wheezed through faint breaths.

#

Waves crashed, and the salt in the air invaded her senses.

"What have you gotten yourself into, child?"

Grandmother. A bright light and haziness clouded her perception.

Erin tried to rub her eyes.

"Where am I?"

The woman's eyes softened. "You're in the Astral Dimension. Your soul is here with me until your body wakes. I'm here because I can't peacefully pass on until our world is safe."

"It's not like I have a book to teach me the rules. Besides I must help my friend and if it involves giving up my gift then I am alright with that," Erin admitted.

"That gift is uniquely yours, along with many that have been passed down through generations," she said with an assertive tone.

"I'm sorry things have not been easy for you, but the Rosana bloodline depends on you as well as our people."

"What happened to my mother?"

Cold hands touched her shoulders. "Soon, you will open doors that will reveal the past, but for now, focus on saving Rosanafalls, becoming the queen, and bearing children," she said while lifting a hand to Erin's cheek.

Erin smiled, simply happy to have a moment with her grandmother, one she never could have imagined. "Okay," was all Erin could manage to say, but she had so many questions.

She could feel time ripping away from her as her body pulled itself back to reality. Time felt endless in this place with unknown doors, visions, and people from the past.

CHAPTER THIRTY-SEVEN

Erin awakened to hands pushing down on her shoulders, and she slowly opened her eyes and saw Zach hovering over her. He resembled an angel as the halo from the sun appeared above his head, and his bright blond hair fell just below his light-blue eyes. "You're glowing," she said.

With a smirk on his face, he laughed. He pulled her up onto her feet and embraced her with a strong and warm hug. "Erin, you scared the hell out of me. One moment you're by my side and the next you're gone." He sounded panicked.

She felt as though she had been hit by a train, as her body felt bruised, sore, and dehydrated. Perking up, she remembered the dagger. Ignoring Zach's words, she looked around.

"Looking for this," he said and pulled the dagger out from his back pocket.

"This will help us defeat Kayleon," Erin said, taking it from him.

Zach looked worried. "What did it cost you?"

"Just my gift," Erin said, and his eyes widened.

"Why would you do that?"

"To save Flora," she answered.

Zach placed his hand on his forehead, trying to shake the frustration. "I hope nothing bad comes of this, Erin. I might have to make a deal with the devil just to save your life."

Erin rolled her eyes. "You will not. It'll be alright—I promise." She placed her hand in his. "We will get through this."

"You may, but Erin, I am tangled in your web with no way out." He pulled his hands away. "Come on, let's go save Flora so we can finish this." Then he turned around and began to walk.

Erin's shoulders dropped as her chest felt tight with guilt. She felt a painful twinge in her forearm and looked at it, noticing a dark pattern tracing her veins. Strange.

"Are you alright?"

"Yes," she said while lying her arms against her side. Once they arrived, Erin couldn't believe how massive the castle was compared to the mansion they had come from. It reminded her of a historical building from her history books. A metal gate wrapped around the castle as a barrier against unwanted company.

It had a peculiar grotesque build with black-and-white stone. The spooky glaze from the hazy clouds and lightning in the sky illuminated the eerie tension behind it. "We shouldn't just walk in the door; we would easily be caught."

"Let's wait till nightfall," Zach said.

Erin agreed as they fell back into the woods to find a place to rest. She wanted a fire, but she decided to wrap herself with a blanket instead while making sure to hide her arms from Zach.

"Zach, we must get him alone. I'm sure he has multiple guards."

Zach implied, "I was thinking, maybe I will go in the front door. That will provide time to sneak in and find Flora and Benny."

"I don't want you to get hurt, and you can't fight them off on your own." She groaned.

"No, but I can lead them into a dark forest."

Erin didn't like this idea, but she knew they had to do something. "Okay, but first you must help me sneak in. I'm not ninja-certified." She laughed.

"One day." Zach smiled.

As the air grew colder and the night sky darkened, they tiptoed around the property while looking for an opening. Zach pointed out ledges they could climb over while Erin watched. He placed a hand in between the sharp edges where flat metal spread while kicking the other leg around and tumbling to the ground.

"You, okay?" she whispered.

"Yeah, come on," he whispered back while dusting himself off from the dirt on the ground.

Erin steadied herself while climbing the gate, worried she might fall. Once she got up to the top, she followed Zach's lead and pushed herself off, then fell ungracefully. Zach caught her before she slammed onto the ground, and she felt instant relief while looking at him.

They began to sneak around the castle while looking for a way in.

"There must be some kind of secret passageway.

Erin spotted an unusual brick wall hidden behind spiked dark green bushes filled with bright red roses and vines growing on the outside. It pushed open like a regular door, and they moved inside quickly. The hallways lit up with old-style candle torches, and she watched as the dancing flames caused shadows to appear on the walls. Zach took hold of her hand as they slowly walked through the hallway.

Focusing on the warm pull of Zach's hand, she tried to accumulate the plan. She needed to be on guard with whatever obstacles would be thrown her way. Save Flora, find Kayleon and end him. What could go wrong? Only about a million things because somehow life had a funny way of tipping my world upside down.

As they moved through one hall and around the corner, it felt like they were just walking in circles. Erin leaned against a wall as she grew tired of walking through the endless maze.

"We're looking past something," she said, trying to determine what kind of puzzle they had to solve to reach the other side. As Erin heard a faint noise, she leaned in closer and recognized the cries. "Flora!" Erin yelled. The voice became silent as she pushed onto the wall.

She leaned back, took a breath, and examined every inch of the bricks. Then her eyes spotted a flickering light. "Zach, lift me so I can grab one of those torches."

He bent down for her to wrap her legs around his shoulders, then held onto them tightly. "Don't drop me."

"Not planning on it."

As he allowed her back down onto her feet, she grasped the black handle of the torch. Then she took the torch and swayed it over the wall, searching for any sign of an entrance.

The light from the flame outlined the shape of a door. She pressed in the brick that was shaped like a handle, then watched it disintegrate its layer in front of them.

Erin was pleased with herself as she and Zach stepped onto the other side and watched it close back up from behind them. The walls were covered in gray stone that resembled a prison dungeon.

As they rounded the corner, they found Flora shackled in chains, looking drained and helpless. Erin's back straightened as she balled her fists up. "Kayleon will suffer." It was a sight she never thought she'd have witnessed, and it angered her.

"Flora," she said while wrapping her hands around the cold black bars.

"Did he hurt you?"

Flora shook her head but didn't speak.

Erin wanted to break the bars that separated the two.

"Where is the key, she began to pace around the room."

Zach lifted a comforting hand onto her shoulder. "Calm down. We will fix this."

Her body was trembling from anger as tears began to roll down the sides of her face. "Zach this is all your fault! You kept me from this world. You didn't tell me anything. Now I am stuck trying to fix a mess that could have been avoided." She began to cry harder.

"You don't know that, Erin. This is why you needed to leave, to be protected from people like Kayleon."

"My choice was stolen from me. My memories erased and my ability to save anyone is gone because I have no idea who I am or what I am. I don't have my mother or father, and I have felt lost for years. You don't get to stand there and tell me that it will be alright."

"Not only did you hold this from me, but you have been closer to Kayleon than you led me to believe. For all I know he has a darker plan up his sleeve. And here I am a woman who is supposed to save a world that I know nothing about nor how to even start by picking up the pieces that my parents left scarcely for me."

There was a flicker of pain in Zach's eyes. She couldn't feel bad for him. He tried to walk towards her, but she put her hands up to stop him.

"No, I need space. Help me find a key, I want Flora out of those chains." She held the dagger the witch had given her tightly around her fist. "I am going to find Kayleon and make him pay. Don't follow me, just help Flora," she demanded.

"Flora, I need to investigate the castle and look for the keys. I will be back for you," she said with certainty in her eyes.

Flora shook her head as she seemed to have hurt behind her eyes. She must feel bad for what I said.

Erin found her way inside of the halls of the castle. She rounded an unexplored corner and found a door in front of her. Pushing the door slightly open, she watched for any foot traffic. The halls were quiet and empty.

What a waste. Hearing footsteps approach, she found a wall to hide behind as she covered her mouth with her hand. As the footsteps grew closer, she held her mouth tighter.

CHAPTER THIRTY-EIGHT

Erin held the dagger in her hand while raising it up just in case the footsteps proved to be a threat. Once they stopped, she wondered if they were turning around. She peaked around the corner. Suddenly she was pushed back onto the wall as a hand wrapped around her wrist and the other grabbed her waist. Her pulse quickened.

Sandalwood and mint took over her senses as she glanced up into fiery brown eyes. His hair was a shadowy mess as he wore a red button-down long sleeve shirt and dark pants.

"Sin," she sighed from relief. "Wait, you're supposed to be back at home protecting it!"

His eyes darkened.

"I couldn't just stay there. I would kill anyone who lays a finger on you. You may be inclined to your own choices, but I protect what's mine."

He slid a finger slowly down her neck and towards her sternum. He lifted his hand back up to her cheek and examined her eyes. "Who hurt you, Erin?"

How can he tell?

"I have just been overwhelmed."

He moved his hand to the back of her head while threading his fingers through her hair.

"I can make you forget."

Those words caused shivers down her spine.

"Please." She pulled down her dress and let it fall to the floor.

His eyes burned with hunger.

I need him. She knew she wouldn't hold onto the anger for long as she began to lose control. His hand steadied on the back of her neck as he pressed his tongue into her mouth and kissed her like he hadn't seen her in months.

He was the flame that ignited her wick as she melted for him. He unsnapped her bra while revealing to him her breasts. Then he bent down while placing a finger on the outline of her pink laced underwear. His dark eyes compelled her arousal to strengthen.

He pulled her lace panties down gently while remaining eye contact with her through the movement. She closed her eyes as a pulsating beat played a rhythm between her legs. A wet and warm invasion caused her to cry from pleasure as he slid his tongue against her clit. As he applied just the right amount of pressure she could hardly stand still. "Sin," escaped her mouth.

She dug her nails into his shoulders as she fell into a sanctuary that reminded her of what it felt like to be underneath water. Everything was silent. Her mind, soul and body were at peace as it drifted into a form of release. Her consciousness found a way back to her when Sin stood up and unbuttoned his shirt. She moved his hand and finished the task.

When he pulled down his pants and revealed to her his cock she admired its beauty. She wrapped her hand around the thickness as he closed his eyes briefly from the touch. Her stomach tightened at the thought of it inside of her, filling her whole. She needed it, but was this the right time? "What if…?"

Sin pressed her against the wall while diving his tongue into her mouth and kissing her tenderly. She moaned as his hands massaged her breasts and teased the buds of her nipples. This had to stop, or else, but who cares? She wanted to shove her consciousness down the drain.

She stopped while thinking of her selfish acts.

"We have to save Flora."

"She is already free. I went to the dungeon, and the bars had been broken apart."

He tipped her chin up and kissed her while pulling the bottom lip slowly with the tease of his teeth. Sin continued like an animal that wouldn't deny the instinct to devour its prey. "Damn, I missed you, little jackrabbit." Then without warning he filled her with all his cock.

A yelp tore from her mouth and then a rush of euphoria came over her.

"Are you okay," he asked.

She nodded her head, "Better than okay."

His smile was devious as he began to rock his hips back and forth. He grasped the back of her hair and devoured her lips. As he thrusted in and out, she squeezed her legs tighter around his waist and he held onto her ass and yanked her body closer to his. He slid his finger against her clit while working her arousal.

As he held onto her tightly, they both began to reach a climax. She almost closed her eyes until he grabbed her chin and forced her to look him in his eyes. Her orgasm sent thrills through her body as she became a puddle. He kept her mouth closed with his hand.

"You are a goddess," Sin told her as he held on to her tightly.

He lowered her legs, "Can you stand?"

There was a trembling sensation that caused her to feel unsteady as she held onto his arms for support.

"Yes, I just need a moment."

Then she stared into his eyes and realized the warm feeling of home. She envisioned cuddling up to his chest while reading her favorite book by a fire. "I love you, Sin."

"I love you too, Erin."

#

Unwanted memories of what happened between her and Zach flooded her mind— a reminder that she betrayed Sin.

Sin grabbed her hand and led her down the hall. "There isn't anybody here. I rounded this whole place, and this was the last area I covered."

She furrowed her brows and tightened her fists.

"Of course, just when I gather a plan, Kayleon flees."

"We will punish him for what he has done," Sin said while squeezing her hand.

Erin sighted a bathroom down the hall and ran toward it happily, but then a force brought her to a stop. Zach stared down at her, smiling. As he looked behind her, his smile quickly faded, and his eyes grew into storm clouds.

"Weren't you supposed to stay back? Of course, you can't follow rules to save your life," Zach complained.

Sin glared at Zach.

"I'm not letting my woman walk into trouble alone."

"Too bad she's not yours," Zach yelled and held onto her arm. Erin could feel the tension as she stood there afraid to intervene. A tight squeeze in her lower abdominal muscles reminded her of what she had done with Sin as her lips tingled from Zach's last kiss. This is not going to end well.

"Oh, trust me, she has been claimed, and I will never let you lay a finger on her again," Sin snapped while pulling her body against his and jerking Zach's hand away from her.

Erin's heart pulled apart, and she didn't know what else to do. He was heartbroken, and Erin could see the pain in his eyes as she forced her head away from his direction.

"I'm not backing down. She was mine first," Zach said.

Zach's glacier eyes bore into her.

"Erin, you still have time to decide on who to marry. I enjoyed that kiss in the woods, and I know you felt something too."

Then he opened the door to the chambers and slammed it behind him. Her stomach twisted in knots.

Erin could feel the rage flaming from Sin's captivating caramel eyes. He looked at her with disappointment. "What the hell happened in the woods?"

She glanced down at her feet, ashamed of what would come out. Time to reveal the truth.

"Zach asked for a kiss due to an exchange of information. I wouldn't have, but he said he would stop trying if I proved that there was nothing between him and me."

He pulled away as the cold air crept upon her skin. Sins eyes lowered as he frowned.

She felt guilty for allowing it to happen.

"I don't know what to make of it because he was all I had known for years. I had feelings for him, but he lied to me for years."

She met his gaze with her own, "I love you, Sin."

He sighed. "Nothing else—he didn't touch you?"

"That was all."

"I can't be upset with you. Zach is persistent. I just ask that it doesn't happen again." As he grabbed her waist and pulled her into him, she felt a hint of relief. He held onto her while squeezing her tightly.

"I may just have to punish my little jackrabbit."

CHAPTER THIRTY-NINE

Erin noticed the dagger sticking out of Zach's back pocket as she ran toward him. "Hey, I was looking for that," she said while holding her hand out for him to return it. She had no idea the deal would work if someone else used it, but she wasn't willing to find out.

"Nah, I think I will hold on to it for a bit," Zach teased while turning around to walk away.

Irritation grasped her voice. "I don't think that's a good idea. I made a deal with that witch, remember?"

"Yeah, and if you haven't noticed, your veins have darkened since that little visit," he said firmly.

She lowered her gaze at her arm and then lifted it back up to catch Zach's concerned expression.

"You noticed?"

He placed a gentle hand underneath her arm and traced the veins with his finger.

"I pay attention to you, especially when I notice something is off."

A laugh escaped from her mouth.

His face twisted deviously as his eyes caught ahold of hers.

She cut her eyes. Don't even think about it.

He dove his hand towards her side as she took off running. "Zach, this is not the time."

He chased her around the room until they fell onto the floor laughing.

This is what she missed, friendship.

He placed his hand on top of hers. "I will protect you. Don't worry. Whatever this is, we will figure it out together."

"You two are awfully close." Sin's shadow covered Erin's light.

Her body froze at the thought of her acting nonchalant about everything. She had been letting Zach off the hook, but she missed the laughter.

Sin pulled out his arm to help Erin off the floor.

"We we're talking," Zach stated.

"And now you're done," Sin smirked.

Zach lunged toward Sin until a roar of thunder hit. Power seized in the building, causing the room to become eerily quiet. Sin grabbed Erin's hand and pulled her away.

He guided her into a dark room and lied her down gently onto a soft mattress.

"Do I have to mark you to prove that no man shall touch you?"

"No, and we shouldn't be doing this. We need to investigate before it gets too late."

"Baby, I can be quick," he whispered in her ear. Jolts ran down her body as she remembered their fun from earlier. As a knock on the door stole their attention, they froze in place.

"I will rip your throat out if Erin is in there with you," Zach growled.

Erin jumped up quickly and ran toward what appeared to be a closet.

"Where are you going?" Sin said.

"Away from you two—you're both suffocating," she said and shut the closet doors behind her.

"There you go running again," he said as the door busted open. Erin caught a glimpse of Zach's angry eyes from the lightening flickering through the windows as his fists bawled. She winced. Sorry, Sin.

As she shuffled through clothing, she noticed a small door hidden behind some boxes. She shoved them aside and bent down to crawl through it. Once she was on the other side, she was surprised to find a light-blue room with the stardust of neon-green stars painted on the walls. Then the power cut back on, blinding her vision.

The room almost felt familiar as she walked over to a full-sized bed that was decorated with stuffed animals and small pillows. She picked up a stuffed wolf and brushed her fingers along the soft fabric. It reminded her of Zach's wolf form with white fur and baby blue eyes.

As she rummaged through the rest of the room, she found pictures in a box of Zach and Kayleon standing beside each other. Her eyebrows furrowed.

She was sent to that home with Kayleon and Zach, but why? Her parents couldn't have trusted their daughter's life in that man's hands. I don't understand.

Once she crawled back through the closet, she pushed the door open. To her surprise, the room was empty. She could imagine ghosts from the past haunting the rooms and halls of the castle as a chill tickled across her shoulders. When she left the room, she saw Zach sitting on a red velvet couch by the fireplace.

He turned his head toward her.

"I think you were conned, princess."

"Why do you say that?"

"Flora checked your dagger for power—and the books about it—and found nothing. It's just a normal dagger." Her expression fell. She was ashamed for trusting that witch.

Zach grabbed her arm and glided his finger across it. "Your arms are radiating with heat. What have you gotten yourself into?" He slid closer to her. The warmth of his body made her cheeks flush.

"I don't want Sin to find out," Erin said as she watched the fire. "He will get himself killed trying to protect me from this. Besides, I am the owner of the mess I created.

"We must return to that cave. I need answers."

"On our way back, we will make a pit stop," Zach replied.

What do you think would've happened if I'd never been sent away?" Zach glanced back at the fire. "Enemies would have hunted you. A princess born in power is resourceful to individuals with desperate desires."

Then she thought of what her mother must have lived through.

Her eyes glanced toward the fireplace. Living a life in fear sounded awful.

"Don't let that fool you. Your bloodline comes with power that could force someone to their knees. Women are meant to be fighters just as much as the men here," Zach said while lifting Erin's face with his hand. "A rose is soft and gentle at first glance until someone tries to pluck it from its home. Words spoken from your mother."

She leaned into him with wide curious eyes. "She fought off multiple men from trying to steal you as a baby, but there were smart people who would sneak beyond the barriers and kill innocent people. I remember her walking past me with a sword covered in crimson. She had curly dark-brown hair and a white long-sleeved lace blouse with black leather pants and laced-up boots.

"When I witnessed the fierceness in her eyes, I knew you would become the spitting image of her someday. I smiled at the thought and protected you ever since while falling madly in love with you. She also broke many hearts—that woman had a trail of men that would kiss her feet if she let them." He laughed.

"We must find her. I need her," Erin pleaded.

"We will. I know it's hard, but it will get better." He wrapped his arms around her as if they were a security blanket. It truly felt comforting as she leaned into him and closed her eyes.

#

Erin felt a pull on her body as she was lifted from the chair and into Sin's arms. He carried her back to the room to lay her down on the bed.

Her senses awakened as he slid his tongue from her ankle toward her upper thigh.

He bit down into her flesh and pulled back her skin with his teeth while forming little bruises on both of her thighs. She winced from a mixture of pleasure and pain.

"Sin." She groaned.

"Are you going to be a good girl?" he asked deeply.

"I'm sorry. We were talking, and I passed out—that's all that happened," she said as if she were about to receive the worst punishment for her crimes.

"I believe you, but your carelessness is causing me to see red like a raged bull." He slid up and brushed his lips across hers. Then he pulled the covers taunt while holding her down.

"What are you doing?"

"I want you to feel the pressure I feel when I can't control your actions," he said. She tried to wriggle free but couldn't budge.

Her breathing slowed, and she realized the more she fought, the tighter he would hold—

like a snake when it's wrapped around its prey. The more the mouse struggles, the more the snake crushes it before it devours it whole. In her case, death would not be her ending. She hated being held down, that feeling of vulnerability.

"I will stay away from Zach. You don't have to worry," she squeaked.

"Good, because next time I catch you in his arms, I will kill him, brother or not." He pressed his lips into hers and squeezed her cheeks with his hand. He loosened his grip on her body and ran his hands down to her lower parts.

She placed her hand on his chest. "Maybe we should wait," she pleaded.

"You wanted to be forgiven, don't you?"

A flame of desire reminded her of how much she wanted him, again.

"Yes, but…"

He rolled his tongue around her areolas to tease until her nipples hardened. Then he sucked and teased each nipple. A shock of pleasure rolled down to her pussy. Once he slid his hand down, he slipped it between her thighs and pressed his fingers onto her clit while working up a slow and steady pace.

Before she reached the top, he held back while resting his hand on the back of her neck and pulling her into him. "Whose are you, little jackrabbit?"

"Sin, please," she whimpered.

He placed his palm on top of her lips.

"You can say my name when I am inside you." He silenced her with a gentle kiss. "Now don't make me ask again," he growled.

"I am yours."

The edging had her begging for his mercy. I think that I can get used to this.

Just like a push of a button, he sped the pace back up with the right pressure to send her into a dizzy haze. She desired to scream so loud, but she didn't want anyone to hear so she grabbed the pillow from beneath her head and released her orgasm with muffled breaths in between.

He grasped her hand and lowered it down to allow her to feel his length.

"You will be my weakness forever." Sin moaned.

"Good," Erin said as she flipped him over and guided him inside her. He held onto her hips as she rolled them back and forth, enjoying the ripples of pleasure. Sin grew impatient as his cock lengthened inside her while flipping her back over and filling her deeper.

"Mine," he whispered.

"I love you too," Sin said.

He kissed her as she collapsed onto his chest.

"I need to tell Zach that I am in love with you."

"That's fine. Do you need my assistance in case he decides to be an ass?" Sin laughed.

"No, that would cause more harm than good, I'll tell him when we're back at the palace."

"Yeah, especially since we can only turn into wolves together," Sin admitted.

Erin glanced at him with shock in her eyes. "Yeah, our brother bond is what allows us to become the wolves that tear and shred people apart. It's passed down to each of the sons in the bloodline, and if one brother is not connected to the other, then their powers are useless. That's why your father had swords built for us, as well as powers embedded in the stones—to allow us to find one another if necessary."

"Sin, you can't be apart from your brother. You're stronger together."

"It's too late. That's why our father split us apart—he knew we'd kill each other for you."

"That's toxic, which means—"

Sin grabbed her face and pinched her cheeks together.

"I won't allow the devil himself to take you away from me. You're mine, till death do us part." He smiled, releasing her face and kissing her.

Erin stuck out her tongue.

"Not yet."

She laughed and jumped off the bed, then ran to the door as he ran after her and tried to tackle her. He wrapped his strong arms around her waist, and she fell back onto him.

"Try to run all you want, but wherever your rose petals lead, I will follow."

"To the bathroom?"

"Anywhere, baby."

CHAPTER FORTY

A weightlessness shifted in Erin's body as she awoke next to Sin. She placed her hand on his shoulder while yearning to simply stay in place. As Sin squinted, she caught sight of his golden eyes, irises reminding her of the golden rays of a sunrise.

He placed a gentle kiss on the top of her head.

"I believe we should wake like this more often."

She leaned in for a kiss and then twirled off the bed. "Good morning, handsome," she said and smiled while stretching. Then she peaked out the door, checking that the coast was clear to tiptoe to the bathroom.

Hearing water rushing, she assumed it was probably Flora as she grabbed her essentials and a dress. This one was a deep rouge with a velvet feel, sheer sleeves that cuffed at her elbows, and a sweetheart neckline. She stripped her clothes off and set her towel down next to her, then turned on the water.

As she stood underneath the hot water it trickled down her body. She closed her eyes and relaxed her muscles, remembering her night with Sin. She lowered her hands to her breasts while remembering the tease of his teeth and tongue on her nipples.

"Just keep doing that for me, princess."

Erin flashed her eyes open as her jaw dropped in shock.

Zach stood there running his fingers through his blond hair, water falling down his muscles. She saw what was lower and widened her eyes, then covered her bits as if that would do anything. He already saw you, stupid.

"Zach, you could have told me you were in here!"

"Why would I stop a free show?" he grinned.

"Whatever," she yelled aloud while continuing her shower. At this point, they had seen each other, and she didn't care to hide. Although if Sin found out, it wouldn't be good.

She cut her eyes at him while grabbing her clothing.

"Don't tell Sin,"

"Princess, you're keeping a lot of secrets from the man you claim to choose." He snorted. As he finished his shower, he wrapped a towel around his lower half while walking closer to her.

"Zach, back up. I don't need Sin walking into this. I was already in trouble last night." She gasped while smacking her mouth shut. Damn, I shouldn't have said that.

"Oh, is that right?" He walked toward her, closing her in on a wall.

"Don't tell me he was jealous of you falling asleep in my arms."

He is way to close, not to mention I am still wrapped in only a towel.

She watched as the steam rolled around the room. Her breath hitched when he pressed himself into her. He made it known that he wanted her just by the hardness of his cock when he dropped the towel. If her mind were strong enough, she'd have pushed him away, but her body was just too damn weak. Pushing her hand onto his chest, she felt the warmth from the water on his muscles.

"Please," she begged. That was all she could say without trembling to the floor.

"I can feel how bad your body wants me, Erin. You can't deny that." His eyes had her in a lock, and she felt as though he had some kind of paralyzing spell on her. He placed his hand on her cheek and slid down to her neck while closing in her space. "It's only a matter of time before I reclaim you," he whispered in her ear while gently brushing his lips against her collarbone. Then he turned around and exited the bathroom.

Erin slid down the wall as her knees gave out from shaking. What the hell was she going to do? She grounded herself with a plan. Find the witch, kill Kayleon, and tell Zach it's never going to happen. What if the hot seductive beast—the one who's changed so much from her sweet Zach—manages to work his way into her heart? Her fantasies involved him before Sin. Was she a monster for wondering what it'd be like if she had chosen him instead?

Shaking her head, she stood up and calmed her breathing. It was time to stop thinking about them. The rival between these brothers and her heart could wait. She worked her magic as she put on makeup—something to make her face stand out from the bleak paleness, aside from a few freckles spread across the top layer of her nose and cheeks.

As she left the bathroom, she decided to speak to Flora and see if she knew anything. Sin was already arguing with Zach as she walked around the corner, so she walked the other way, not wanting to get in between the two. Searching through rooms, she couldn't find any trace of Flora.

Then she found the room Flora was staying in and knocked on the door. When there wasn't an answer, she cracked the door open, "Flora." Met with silence, she pushed it open and discovered it was empty. She must not be here.

On the mattress was a note and a bright orange and red bracelet. She picked it up and felt the weight of the glass beads cling to her skin. There was a charm of a fairy wing with red and orange patterns.

Dear Erin,

I'm so glad we were able to reconnect again. You have been a great friend, but I must depart to strengthen my abilities. I need to return to Owlery Falls where I can regain my voice and power. I also want to work on becoming stronger. I never want to be the damsel in distress—we hated that part in those stories, remember?

Erin, I know you'll be okay. You'll save Rosanafalls and find your parents. If you're anything like the girl I remember when we were little, you were the one telling me that you would be saving yourself, not the other way around. You know where to find me. See you again, my friend. Next time, stronger and wiser, the both of us.

Lastly, I found a bracelet in my belongings. It was a friendship bracelet that our mothers gave to each other when they were girls, then passed down to us. I remembered to wear mine, and this one is yours.

Love,

Flora

Warm tears ran down her cheek as memories of her childhood friend sent her back in time. She remembered running in the woods while laughing and pretending they were in a different world. Swimming in the waters and unafraid of what lurked underneath. Dancing by the fire at night, pretending to be the warriors that saved towns.

Her first girl best friend. No one could ever replace that, and she'd do anything for her. She wished she could've been with her as they grew older through time. She was stripped of it, and she thought that their bond shattered the moment they split apart.

Before she had any more time to reminisce, Sin busted in the room with wide eyes. "There you are." He let out a sigh of relief, then walked over to Erin as he saw her tears.

"What's wrong?" he asked while wiping them with his thumb.

"Flora left, and my mind was just wandering."

As he pulled her into his chest, she embraced him, sobbing for the past life that had been stolen from her. She'd never get that back, and she felt as though she were mourning it. He placed his hand on the back of her head to calm her down.

"You can give me all your pain, tears, fear—anything you want to—and just know I'll be here to listen if you ever need me too."

Sin was showing a new side she hadn't seen much of yet, and it was so damn appealing.

"These invading memories are bittersweet," she admitted.

Lifting her chin, he said, "As painful as they may be, understand they aren't your reality anymore, and you're here with me now, safe and sound." He placed a soft kiss on her lips, and she kissed him back. "And one more thing," he said while pulling her arms out to look at them. "No more keeping secrets from me."

Erin looked down, feeling a little ashamed.

"Zach told you!" she folded her arms into her chest.

"Never underestimate me. I pay close attention to what's mine," he whispered in her ear, causing warmth to appear in the lower part of her body. As he locked eyes with her, she felt his frustration. "What do we not do anymore?" he asked in a demanding tone.

"Lie to you," she said, a prisoner in her own body.

"Good girl." He slid his tongue into her mouth and kissed her, as though he intended to take her soul with him for the rest of their lives.

Flora, I'm so mad at you right now. I need my best friend and a distraction from these men. She took a final look at the castle, knowing she'd have to return to it for answers.

"I should've known you'd get her ass in deeper trouble," Sin glared at Zach.

Erin placed herself in between them, not ready for this walk. She'd rather be alone.

"Both of you behave, before I tape your mouths shut!"

CHAPTER FORTY-ONE

"Zach, what's going on? Are we lost?" Erin shifted her weight to the right side with a hand on her hip.

"It looks like the location was moved. Witches have a way of hiding."

"Great." Erin threw her hands up in frustration.

"I'm not bothering Flora, so let's head back to the palace and ask Sylvian for help,"

She glanced at Sin and then back at Zach.

"I am not staying in the woods till nighttime. Let's race," she winked. Time to toy with them. "Let's make it fun. First one who wins earns themselves a prize."

Sin's eyes revealed a flicker of irritation when he glanced at her way. The hair on the back of her neck spiked as she enjoyed pissing him off. Teasing him is becoming my new favorite habit.

A rumble in Sin's chest radiated as his eyes changed from brown to emerald. Zach's flashed a lightening blue. Then they were gone. She huffed, "That's cheating."

She threw her head back and laughed at them, then slowed down her pace and knew her fate before the race began.

"You're such a tease playing with those brainless wolves," a deep voice said. She tried to catch her breath as she looked around and caught sight of only the trees.

"Who's there?" she yelled into the woods. Although she was alone at this point, she was not defenseless. She still had her dagger.

"I am literally inside of you," the voice said again.

"Oh, I'm losing my mind," Erin said and dropped to the ground while holding her head.

"Remember when you offered your blood to that witch?"

"Yes."

"The universe decided to link us together as a punishment instead of allowing you to offer your gift."

"Okay, but why you and not her?"

"I don't have the answer to that. If I did, I would be back in my own body."

"So, you're alive?"

"Yes, I was in the middle of helping a friend right before my subconscious was pulled out. The name is Trace, and please, no more lovey-dovey stuff until we sort this out."

"That's going to be a problem," she winced. "None of this is going as planned."

"At least you still have your body. Who knows what's happening to me as we speak."

"Wait, when did you realize you were inside of mine?"

"Not until you were reading that note," he said. "I didn't want to ruin your moment—I do have a heart—well, not right now, but you know what I mean."

"Looks like we're going to have to speak to Sylvian and possibly go to the Owlery for information."

"I can also direct you to my home and maybe we can locate my body," Trace revealed.

"Yeah, that's fine."

"Erin," Sin shouted as he ran back toward her with a confused expression.

"Why are you sitting on the ground?" he asked while giving her a hand to help her up.

"Don't say anything until we know more about the situation," Trace said.

"Okay," she answered in her head, now feeling unattached to herself.

She directed her attention to Sin. "Sorry, I needed to catch my breath, who won?"

"I did. No way I was letting Zach win. And we should chat about you offering yourself as a prize."

Erin maintained eye contact. "I never said that I was the prize, you two just came up with that idea on your own." She began to walk away until he grabbed her arm and pulled her back into him.

Her heart sank into her chest as her stomach did back flips. "What did I say about running from me, little jack rabbit."

He held her down while holding her from moving.

"You're just going to let him handle you like that?" Trace spoke without hiding the sarcasm in his voice.

She rolled her eyes. "Sin, enough. Playtime is over," she demanded.

He tugged her hair back while leaning in, "Worried about your next punishment?" he teased.

She twisted her body around until he released her from his hold. Then she placed a kiss onto his lips, "Actually looking forward to it."

His eyes darkened.

"Time to run away, little rabbit," Trace joked.

Erin's shoulders tensed.

"You're forcing me to keep this a secret, and Sin is a possessive man."

"That's your problem; you made a deal with a devious witch," Trace said.

"Trace, you must have done something too or else you wouldn't be in this situation." Her brain was silent for a moment. "That's what I thought. Now stop talking before I say something aloud by accident."

Sin held Erin's hand as they walked along the forest. When they caught up to Zach at the palace, he was sitting on the ground still playing with the dagger.

"Oh shit, that's mine," Trace yelled, causing Erin to gain a splitting headache in the front of her head.

"Hey, princess, you didn't even put up a fight," Zach said as he rose from the ground.

"Wait, you're a princess?" Trace asked.

"Shut up," Erin yelled, and this time not in her head. Zach and Sin looked at her like she had gone mad.

"Umm, yeah, Zach—just hush your mouth," Erin said, walking past him as her cheeks flared.

"Let's go find Sylvian," she said while leaving Sin and Zach behind. "How did you know they were shifters?" Erin asked Trace.

"I can feel their energy. It's one of the first things a warlock learns at a young age—kind of like an instinct."

Erin nodded as she proceeded to the front door, Ron glanced anxiously at her while furrowing his brows. He leaned down close to her ear and whispered, "Kayleon is here."

When she pulled back a fire burned inside of her chest. He will pay for what he has done to Flora.

"You are to attend the masquerade ball tonight," he says.

Erin remains silent as she follows him inside the palace.

Ron opened the door to her room. Sin and Zach's shoulders tense as they squirmed uncomfortably. Neither of them wants to leave me alone after everything. I can understand their concern.

"I will meet you two back here," she says.

Sin kissed her on the cheek and Zach squeezed her shoulder. Then Ron forced them away and allowed her to be alone.

Her outfit was set out on the red comforter of the King-sized mattress. The walls were painted black with golden roses painted all over. Whose room is this?

"Shouldn't you know," Trace asked curiously.

"There is a lot that I do not know."

She walked towards the mattress. Red roses were stitched onto the shoulders of the silk red gown. A red-laced eye-mask was paired with it, and a golden crown with rubies were attached to each of the spikes that ran along the band. While standing in front of a mirror she gasped at her appearance.

I look like a Queen.

#

A knock interrupted the silence. When she opened the door, she found Sin and Zach dressed in suits. Sin wore a black eye-mask with a black suit. Zach wore a white mask with a white and black suit. Her stomach tightened in knots as they both stared at her like she was underneath a spotlight. Time to face Kayleon, again.

As both men stayed close to her, they walked toward the ballroom. Groups of people filled the room, this time wearing masks and dark gowns as if they had come for a Halloween ball. She took careful steps around the black-and-white scaled snakes that slithered onto the floors.

Her eyes cut across the room at Shane drinking wine, with a luminous bright-blue snake hanging around his neck. A tap on a glass interrupted her thoughts.

Kayleon requested silence from the ballroom. He wore a royal-blue suit, and a frost-blue mask as a man stood beside him. The man was tall with light-brown hair with a reddish tint, flawless curls at his neck, and emerald-green eyes. He wore a black suit with a bright-green mask. He had muscular arms and a jawline that worked with his stature.

"Holy shit, that's my body," Trace said, panicked.

"Looks like we didn't have to go too far." Erin announced to Trace.

Where are Sylvian and Benny? Her eyes wandered around for her friends.

"Welcome to the masquerade ball! Enjoy tonight along with a special announcement later. Now let's celebrate the present, and the plans for a luxurious future." Kayleon raised a glass to the man standing beside him. Once Kayleon finished his speech, everyone clinked their glasses and tilted their heads back to swallow the poison.

Kayleon's eyes snapped in Erin's direction.

Shivers danced across her shoulders while causing her to shake.

Her anger for him was unmatched compared to Trace's, for he was forced to live without his body and watch someone else partake in it.

"I'm going to kill him," Trace said, sending a cold chill down Erin's spine. As Kayleon was distracted by a couple of women, the person inhabiting Trace's body walked down the stairs and toward Erin.

Shane came up from behind and placed a blue viper onto her shoulders. Frozen in place, she looked to both sides and realized Zach and Sin had snakes hanging around their necks as well. Zach had a white one and Sin, a vibrant red one.

Shane walked behind Zach and Sin, "Hand me your weapons," he ordered.

Zach didn't hesitate to surrender his, but Sin stood still.

"Sin, if you do not cooperate then you will be forced to suffer consequences."

The snake began to slowly work its way around Sin's neck. Erin watched as his shoulders tensed at the movement as he pulled the sword from his back. His face scrunched with disgust as he threw it onto the floor.

Shane smirked and bent down to pick it up while handing it over to the guards standing against a wall. Shane glanced back at Zach, "All of your weapons." Zach hesitated as his snake began to move. He pulled the dagger from his back pocket and handed it over.

Spikes of tingles cut across Erin's skin as Shane walked towards her. It wasn't that she was afraid of him, she was more irritated. Not only that but surrounding eyes were on her like she was a villain when she was supposed to be the ruler of the palace.

She cut her eyes at Shane when he was near.

"You've been pulling strings this whole time."

Shane stretched his hand out towards her, but she smacked it away.

"Just what do you think that you're doing?" She snapped firmly.

"Lay a finger on me and I will not hesitate to kick you in the balls." She glared at him.

He maintained eye contact. His face didn't break. "Hand over your weapon."

She rooted herself in place. "What weapon?"

His lips thinned into a line. He closed in her space while inches away.

"Fucking touch, her, and I will kill you," Sin shouted.

Shane smiled. He kneeled in front of her. She gasped when glancing down at her feet and noticed snakes wrapped around her ankles. He reached his hand up through her dress while unsheathing the rose-handled dagger. She could feel the rage in both Zach's and Sin's eyes burning as Shane ran his hands through her dress and onto her body.

With each brush of his fingertips gliding against her skin she felt her stomach twist in knots. She felt violated and helpless. She sat in this feeling because she wanted to remember her reason to fight it ever happening again.

"I may not know how to use my powers now, but when I do you will regret this," she seethed.

He stood back up while using the blade of her dagger to glide it across her cheek, "Looking forward to it, little toxin."

Sin clawed at the snake as his eyes turned into an emerald green. "You're dead Shane."

"You should bite your tongue, I am the one in control," Shane spoke.

"May I ask for your hand," someone said, redirecting Erin's attention.

It was the tall man who was in Trace's body.

"Only if you unlock Sin's neck," she said.

The man glanced over to Shane and nodded his head. The snake had its body wrapped around Sin's neck tightly. His face began to redden as the veins in his arms became visible. Erin was afraid that he would die trying to escape. If only I knew how to control the snake. With a snap of his finger the snake loosened its grip on Sin's neck as he gasped for air.

CHAPTER FORTY-TWO

Erin reached out her hand and allowed the man to pull her onto the dance floor. He placed his right hand on her left and her right onto his shoulder as his free hand rested on her lower back. Thanks for those dance lessons in the living room, Zach. Nothing to it other than maintaining the rhythm, not stepping on your partner's feet, and allowing them to guide you.

"Who are you?" Erin asked softly.

"My dear, you should already know the answer to that question." He tightened his grip on her hand. The weight of the snake was more comforting than the awkward dance with a stranger.

"I am Viola."

"I have you to thank for my freedom," Viola smiled.

"Mother?" Trace said loudly, and Erin's body tensed.

"You're Trace's mom?"

"I am sorry son, but you will return to your body soon enough. Kayleon and I are planning a future together, and with your help we can become the new rulers of Rosanafalls."

Erin's body began to shake uncontrollably. Trace was taking over as her control began to slip away. "Trace," she fought.

They had already stopped dancing as Erin's fists were tightly balled against her sides.

"And how is that mother," Trace asked.

Viola's face twisted into an ugly grin, "Once I marry the two of you, I will be offered a gift from the royals to live the life that was taken from me."

You're the reason for that, or did you forget? You're mad if you think I am going to marry someone I don't even know," Trace stated.

Erin's arm flung back then smashed into Viola's face.

She stepped back with a look of disgust.

"Guards!" Viola shouted.

Men dressed in black gear, dark masks and gloves grabbed onto each side of her arm.

Erin began to squirm her arms as they tugged her back. She glared at Viola. "This is my palace, and my home. You will pay for this!"

The guards placed her hands behind her back and chained them together. As they dragged her away, she felt the pull from Zach and Sin's anger. Sin's eyes displayed a wild-green, and Zach's an icy blue.

They locked her arms up into chains and threw her into a dark dusty dungeon as the cold floor scraped underneath her forearms.

"Trace, what the hell!" Erin yelled.

Trace's voice calmed as his tone was apologetic. Its slow and steady drag reminded her of the man she had danced with and how handsome he had been.

"Sorry, my anger got the best of me. My mom is the devil's companion. She will do anything for someone if she benefits in return. This time, a chance at living on earth."

"What are we going to do?" Erin cried, placing her head onto her knees.

"I need to take you back to my family's house. My mom caused a lot of trouble when she was on this earth, and I doubt it will be any better if we don't figure out how to contain her powers," Trace said softly.

"What did you do last time?" she asked.

"We had to collect a piece of her hair, any form of DNA, and bind her soul to an object—my family knows the spell. I was just a kid when they performed it due to her almost killing my father."

"I can get us out of here." A familiar voice echoed through the darkness. Erin knew that voice. It was Sylvian!

"How?" she asked.

"I need the friend you're talking to inside your head to channel his powers through your body," he said. Erin assumed Sylvian figured the plans out when Kayleon threw him in the dungeon.

She straightened her back as the chains on her arms reminded her that she was stuck in place. One day I will be strong enough to break free on my own.

"Okay, tell me what to do."

"Just close your eyes and allow him to take over. Don't fight it, even if it hurts."

Closing her eyes, she took herself to a place where she felt calm and safe. She was lying down on the beach, the sunlight warm on her skin as the waves crashed in the background. As she imagined the sound, she could smell the salt in the air.

Then it was completely dark, and she became the outsider looking in her own body as Trace gained control.

"Alright stranger, what's your plan?" Trace asked.

Erin could hear his voice surrounding her. It was comforting and warm. Listening to it would put her asleep if she allowed it. Silence broke her chaotic thoughts. At times they controlled her more than she wanted. This time she felt at peace.

"Grab onto your chains and chant this with me," Sylvian said.

"Our power will connect with the energy and force the chains free. The force of energy lies within me. I command you to set me free from these chains that hold me down, use elements from the ground to intertwine in the metal fibers, and ignite with flames of a fire."

As they repeated the mantra the chains heated and then exploded along with the surrounding bars and chains.

Erin awoke with Sylvian picking her up from the ground.

"You, okay?" he asked.

Her body felt bruised and beaten as she grinned through the pain.

"Never better," she said.

"Thanks for the help, I don't know what I would have done without you."

"I am sure you would have figured something out. You're already becoming stronger and wiser than the first time I met you. You really did prove me wrong." He smiled while brushing her hair behind her ear.

Those words made her smile.

"It's nice to have you by my side, Sylvian. Remember I have your back so don't hesitate to ask for help."

"Thanks, Erin."

"Sylvian, do you know if Benny is safe?" she asked, concerned.

He shook his head. "I am not sure."

"We must be careful of Viola. She is dangerous, and she was going to take over Flora's body but decided not to when she learned of her being a witch."

That explains why they left her to die. "Well, we're going to have to escape this place, but I need to get Zach and Sin."

Sylvian placed a hand on top of her arm.

"Leave that to me and just let Trace take you to his home so that you can get the resources to take Viola down."

"Okay, just be safe," she said while giving him a quick hug.

"Erin, one more thing. She glanced back at him. His golden eyes darkened.

"Don't trust Ron; he isn't on our side anymore.

She sucked in her breath and nodded. "Good to know." Don't trust Ron.

When she escaped the dungeon, she was careful to watch out for guards. She snuck up the stairs and opened the door that led to the hallways. Then she tiptoed her way to the front door and slipped out.

She wanted to stay and find Zach and Sin, but she trusted that Sylvian would find them.

If I don't gain confidence in them then how could I ask them to do the same for me?

"Alright, Trace. Lead the way." Her chest fluttered at the thought of never seeing her friends again.

"See you soon," she whispered then shut the door.

CHAPTER FORTY-THREE

"As we take a stroll through my town, we'll find a horse for transportation. I'm not counting on your legs to get us there fast enough," Trace said.

"I've never ridden a horse, but I guess there's a first time for everything," Erin announced.

"I can guide you through the steps."

She nodded her head as if he could see her, "Sounds good, teacher."

He lowered his voice, "I can teach you whatever you like."

"I will keep that in mind," she grinned.

"On another note, Dad is going to be pissed when he finds out about Viola," Trace laughed. "Good ole family reunion was needed, I guess."

"At least you know where yours are. She slapped her mouth shut, "That was insensitive."

"When all this is over, I will help you find your family. I know you have a dozen people already helping, but maybe my family can pull some strings."

"Thanks, that would be helpful."

"When you arrive in town, we need to grab a disguise. Kayleon is going to have his men looking for you," Trace said.

"I don't have any money." Erin groaned.

"Oh, you won't have to worry about that. Money isn't involved in town; we all work together to help each other out."

"That sounds like a dream. Nothing like the outside world."

"We take care of our own. I can't wait for you to see it for yourself."

The sun glowed behind the trees, its orange light radiating throughout the forest. Erin sat against a tree, watching the birds pass through the clay-colored sky.

"Wings would be so helpful right now." She mumbled.

"Erin!" shouted voices from behind. Her eyes lit up as Zach, Sin, and Sylvian caught up to her.

As she pushed herself from the tree and waved her hand in the air excitedly,

Sin ran toward her at the speed of a jaguar. She jumped into his arms, and he spun her around before squeezing and planting a kiss on her lips.

Tonight, she'd have to keep her distance from Sin.

"Too bad we don't have any tents or food." Zach coughed.

"Maybe we should just continue on foot through the night," Erin said.

"Yeah, sounds good. At least we have each other." Sin winked at Erin.

Trace made vomiting noises as Erin rolled her eyes.

#

Sin grabbed Erin and pulled her behind a tree, then grasped her face, ready to pull her into him. Before Sin could continue, Erin placed her hand on his chest and pushed him back. "Let's slow down a bit," she said softly. He placed his fingers on her wrists gently and locked his eyes with hers.

"Everything okay?" he asked her, as if he knew she was hiding something.

"Trace, now that I think about it, we're going to your family's house."

"Good point. I guess we have nothing to lose now. Best you share the news," Trace said.

"Sin, do you remember that new guy we saw at the palace? The one that made me dance with him?"

"Don't tell me you have fallen for another man," Sin teased.

Erin couldn't contain her laughter. "Hell no!" Both Erin and Trace yelled at the same time.

"So basically, that guy is trapped in my body, while his evil witch mother is living in his," she blurted out.

Sin backed up as if trying to process the information. "That's a big fucking problem," he stated with anger.

"Yeah, so we have to go to his family's house and figure out how to extract her soul from his body and place Trace's back in there."

"He's lucky it was his mother dancing with you and not him," Sin said.

"He is lucky that I am not in my body right now." Trace snorted.

"I guess I'm going to have to keep my hands to myself until we figure this out," Sin said while running his fingers through his dark luscious hair.

"Just until then." She placed a kiss on his cheek.

#

The next morning, they arrived in a little town called Jinx. Erin stepped out of the way as multiple horses and carriages traveled down the dirt road. The horses were a variety of breeds and colors from charcoal to mud brown, and the one that caught her eye was the color of the clouds, with a beautiful long silver mane.

"They're so gorgeous." She gasped. Sin grasped her hand and pulled her along the sideline while admiring the town's charm.

Multiple stands with fresh fruit such as apples and pears reminded her of a farmer's market. There were wooden houses, and everyone was dressed as if they were living in Salem, MA, a place Erin wanted to visit someday. The unique orange and red trees made the town vibrant with color.

166

"Up ahead, you will enter that black building. It contains a stable with multiple horses," Trace said. Erin did as she was told when the smell of hay and dirt filled her senses.

Horses were lined up behind stables, seeming to enjoy their comfortable and quiet atmosphere. The stables weren't locked, and they were free to roam if they desired. Erin found one that had caught her eye. It was a caramel color and had a white stripe down its nose, as well as a charcoal black mane. She gently placed her hand up toward the horse's nose for it to become familiar with her scent. The horse took a minute and then bowed down as it allowed her to pet it.

"Ah, you would find my favorite," Trace said. "His name is Rustic, and he is strong and fast, but gentle with the ladies." Trace laughed.

The horse sniffed and shook its head as if he could hear what Trace had been saying. "He knows I'm in your body. You're safe to ride him."

"Okay." Erin didn't argue as Sin brought her a satchel and helped her up onto the horse.

Sin jumped on a black horse that had silver tufts of hair along its body. Sylvian rode the light-golden horse, and Zach the white horse with cream-colored hair.

"Alright, are you ready?" Trace asked.

"Yes." Erin grabbed the satchel.

Rustic lifted off and galloped out of the stables, leading the other horses his way.

"He already knows where to go. Hold on tight." Trace said.

Erin's hair blew through the wind as the Rustic galloped down a trail through the forest. The others were falling behind, as Rustic was obviously the fastest. The breeze and the sun's warmth caressed Erin's skin.

They passed fields of land, leafy green trees, and wide fields. The horse led her into a corn field, and she laid down her head while dodging the whips from the leaves. "We go this way all the time," Trace said, "our shortcut." As they cleared out of the field, there rested a body of water that was wrapped around the most beautiful home Erin had seen. It was a five-story home with a bright-red farmhouse style, as well as white porches wrapped around each floor. The horses all slowed down to climb the hill toward it.

Once they arrived at the front of the house, Erin noticed baskets of hay, apples, and carrots alongside the home as well as fountains of fresh spring water. Erin flipped one leg over and slid herself carefully down from the horse. She turned to Rustic and patted his side gently.

"Good work. Thank you, Rustic" she said as the horse nodded and blew air through his nose. She walked up the white stairs and toward the door. It displayed rainbow glass doors with a green vine that was wrapped around each side.

"You can just walk in," Trace said. "They know you're here; they have protection placed upon these lands, and only those welcomed can enter."

"Nice to know," Erin said as she placed her hand onto the door handle while pulling it open. As she stepped inside, the entryway was massive. The floors were made of a dark cherry red wood, and a chandelier with colorful crystals hung from above their heads. A staircase with naturistic animals such as bears, wolves, and hawks were carved onto the railings. Erin felt instant comfort as she walked down the hallway that led into a living area with a room full of people.

The room was filled with music from a piano nearby with laughter. Upon tables were vibrant foods and wine bottles next to wine glasses. The scent of sweet cashmere flooded the halls. No one batted an eye at them as they walked into the room.

A man with similar features to Trace appeared. He had dark-brown eyes, medium-length light-brown hair with white streaks running through his short curls, and a white button-down shirt with a red jacket and black slacks.

Jasper!" Erin slapped her mouth shut with her hand.

"Trace, calm the taking over would you!"

He laughed, "My apologies. I haven't seen him in a while, he's normally gone."

Jasper's eyes locked in on hers. He furrowed his brows as they widened and then he smiled.

"I knew your energy was familiar. Where is my brother?" Jasper asked.

"Don't tell me he found himself a woman, finally."

"Ugh, still the arrogant prick as always," Trace huffed. "Tell him to take you out of this room so that we can have a private chat. I wouldn't want to worry our people," Trace ordered.

"Maybe we can go to a quieter place?" she asked.

"Sure, my lady." He offered his arm for her to take, and then snapped his fingers, locking Sylvian, Zach, and Sin in the room before they could leave.

"Sin is going to be so pissed." She winced.

He led her to the stairs, then leaned against the railing.

"What's the problem?" Jasper asked while crossing his arms.

Erin reported the news to him while watching his face twist from emotions.

"Oh dear, mother loves to stir quite the witch pot." He laughed while rubbing his forehead. "Father is going to love this. Okay, let me relay the information to him, and we'll come up with a plan to report back to you tonight. He's out, so I'm going to have to hunt him down. For now, make yourselves comfortable, wash up, and pick a room."

He then bowed down to her. "It's an honor to be in the presence of the princess of Rosanafalls. I hope this mishap doesn't sour your impression of our family."

"Your hospitality has shown me enough. I would never let one person influence my opinion on the entirety of a family," she reassured.

His expression softened as he rose back up to her, "You're going to be a great Queen."

"How are you sure of that?"

"I just know," he winked.

#

Erin found her way back to the party while lost in her thoughts. Her attention gravitated towards a group of giggling girls. The girls wore dresses with a mixture of white and black with bows tied to the back of their necks and gloves running up their arms. She noticed Zach and Sylvian had been caught in the middle of them. One of them pulled on Zach's arm, "Dance with me please," she begged.

Erin began to giggle at how cute Zach looked while at the mercy of all the girls. He was always kind natured towards kids. It must be that blonde hair and those crystal blue eyes. When he smiled his face softened as his eyes lit up. Then he looked up at her. A sensation rolled up her spine, then she was pulled back and away from the party, along with Zach's gaze.

CHAPTER FORTY-FOUR

Sin pushed Erin lightly against the wall, and before she could speak, he pressed his lips into hers.

"I asked a friend for a favor, and they were able to silence Trace for the night."

"Oh, and how did you manage that?"

"Let's just say I owe a favor now."

Sin bent down and whispered in her ear as he took ahold of her hand. "Come with me." They entered a room with a glass ceiling that revealed the night sky. The light shone down into a pool of steaming water. She stepped closer while feeling the heat from Sin's eyes burn into her.

She slipped from her restrictive clothing and stepped into the heated water. It was just the right temperature as it hugged each inch of her skin. Turning around, she caught a glimpse of his dark eyes. He's so handsome, she thought as she took a breath and dived into the water.

Floating on her back, she felt weightless and at peace as she watched the sky above her. She could feel the ripples from the water moving as Sin broke through the barriers. Her heart shuddered as she felt him move through the water, gliding like a water moccasin. Inhaling deeply, she closed her eyes, allowing the water to maintain its stillness around her own body.

"I can't wait to tear open each layer, one by one," he said while gliding his tongue up her neck.

Feeling powerless, she fell back down into the water, then interlocked her tongue with his. He is the weapon that breaks into my barrier as I watch the walls shatter. Then it's just me and him. We are vulnerable to each other's weakness in being consumed by our desires.

"Sin, I just realized I don't truly know much about you, other than pieces of my childhood memories."

He slowly pulled away from her and held her face in his hands.

"I'm an open book, shoot," he whispered. "What's your favorite color?"

His eyebrows furrowed as if she insulted him. "That's what you ask?" Sin laughed. "Yellow. It reminds me of my mother. She was fond of the color and would go on about how it could change a person's mood." Erin studied his features and felt just a little closer to the man who held her captive in love.

"That's sweet," she said. "For me, it's silver because of its uniform and sleek ability to represent strength. I used to love silver bows."

Sin smiled as he caressed her cheek. "You're an interesting woman. Now no more questions. We don't have much time, and I want to take you in until I can't anymore."

She became breathless as he pulled her in, and their mouths collided. Sin pushed her toward the wall, and she could feel jets pushing through underneath her legs. He slid his fingers down her body—slowly from her jawline, then down her arms and breasts, circling each nipple thoroughly with his tongue. Finally, he inserted his fingers inside her until she whimpered, and he covered her mouth with kisses.

As he worked his way further in, she lost sight of everything else, clouding her mind. He continued harder and faster, and then she lost herself in the euphoria of the orgasm while riding his finger in the water. As their mouths collided, she ran her fingers through his hair, held on tight, and let her worries drift away.

"I love—"

"I want to hear it when I am inside of you, little jackrabbit."

The throb between her legs encouraged her to reach down in the water to feel for him. Kissing her again, he sucked on her lips, leaving small bite marks down her neck. She felt for his cock while grasping around it, playing with him as he forced her legs around his hips and led her hands to thrust him inside.

"You are mine. Do I make myself clear?" His voice rumbled in her ear before he pushed in, just past the tip, pleasuring her just enough to make her yearn for him. "Now, promise me."

"I promise," she moaned as the need for him to fill her was rising.

"What was that?" he asked.

"I promise, I am yours, and you're mine until the day we take our last breath, please," she begged.

"That's my good girl," he growled.

Then he pulled her chin up to gaze into her eyes. Her stomach tightened as her pussy throbbed for him. His eyes darkened, "I wouldn't even let you go then," he said while shoving his hard cock fully inside her as she forced her head back, surrendering. Erin held onto his back as he pulled in and out with slow and steady strokes.

She pressed her heels into his back as he sped up and played with her sensitive spot. As both panted and melted into each other, she whispered, "I love you, Sin," and they both began to climax together.

Sin wrapped his arms around her body and held onto her tightly. He kissed her lips, "I love you too my seductive rose."

#

Erin slipped back into a white gown that Sin had found for her. It was made of silk as the sleeves fell to her wrists. It reminded her of a Greek styled dress as the design was ethereal. "Let's find something to eat and then rest." Sin opened the door, blinding them from the bright light. They went toward the party room and realized that the lights were off and that it was empty.

"I guess we missed the party," Erin teased.

As Sylvian walked around the corner, his expression fell. "Where the hell have you two been?"

Erin glanced at Sin while feeling a pinch of guilt.

"Never mind, don't answer that," he said while pinching in between his eyes.

"Zach left when he realized you two were missing."

"Where did he go?" Erin asked, feeling the guilt in her chest.

"I don't know, but he was not happy. He took one of the horses and left."

"Alright, well nothing we can do about it now. We need to rest and plan for the morning." Sin placed a hand on Sylvian's shoulder.

"I know my brother, and he's just blowing off some steam. He'll be back, eventually."

"Let's hope. We need all the help we can get." Sylvian shook his head and walked past the two.

As everyone calmed down and claimed a room, Erin sprawled out onto the king-sized mattress and opened her mom's book of poems. Once she flipped past the last page, she found an envelope taped to the back with a red wax-pressed stamp in the shape of a rose.

She flipped it open and pulled out a card. An invitation to a Halloween ball, along with a letter behind it.

You're invited to the Halloween festivities.

Wear a costume and enjoy the fun! It's not the masks that ensure fear, but the monsters that lurk in the shadows.

Dear Amaryllis,

I hope you won't miss it. I'm counting on your presence.

Yours truly,
Prince Thorn

Hmm, I wonder why she saved this. The door flung open as Sin walked over with a grin. He gently pulled her from the bed and wrapped a silky white ribbon around her eyes, tying it behind her head. She allowed him to pull her out of the room, a little uneasy, but safe with him. "Where are you taking me?" she giggled.

Her senses were flooded with garlic and herb spices. She inhaled deeply and her stomach rumbled. He pulled the ribbon off her face, and her eyes lit up at the breathtaking view in front of her. The lights were dim, with a couple of lit candles placed in the center of the table, two wine glasses, water, and two appetizing plates with steaks, potatoes, and vegetables. He pulled out the chair as she sat down, and he pushed it in. There were rolls in a basket, along with butter next to it.

Sin took a sip of wine and leaned in for a kiss. She rolled her tongue inside of his mouth as she tasted the sweet and tart mixture from the wine. "I'll continue to fill you with anything you desire," he said, and her cheeks flushed.

When Sin captured her with his honey-colored eyes, she felt safe. "You know, just looking at you is dangerous," Sin said as he threw back the rest of his wine into his mouth and licked his lips. She smiled as she sipped her drink. "Is that so?"

As he rubbed her leg with his, she felt the tickling sensations in her lower abdomen. The flickering of the candles lit half his face while leaving the other side in the darkness, one eye lighter than the other. She felt warm and calm as the alcohol spread through her body.

He could take her as much as he wanted, and she would release herself to him. She felt as though she were under his seductive spell, and she would never be able to fully come out of it. Pushing herself from the chair, she walked on over to him and bent down to lock her lips to his. The smells of lavender and sandalwood filled her senses as her hair fell into his face.

Once she came up for air, she whispered in his ear. "I will bend to your will and please you for the rest of our days." As he forced her to sit down on his lap she could feel the hard bulge in his pants. He pulled her in tightly, kissing her as though she were going to be pulled away by some imaginary force. Before she knew it, the candles were blown out, along with everything knocked off the table. Sin didn't hold back as he thrust her on the table.

He slid his tongue down her neck and to her breasts slowly, tracing her as though she was a puzzle that only he knew the answer to. As she ran her fingers into his dark, soft hair, she held on to the pleasure while edging herself from the orgasm.

For the first time in years, she was choosing herself. Nobody would steal this from her, and she would eternally choose her happiness and desires. She would never feel guilty for choosing this as she moaned and screamed his name.

He climbed on top of her body as they kissed harder as she wrapped her legs around him, feeling hot, wet, and weak. Sin flipped her around and pulled her into him, digging himself more into her as she moaned even louder.

He pressed his hand on top of her mouth, silencing her while playing with her clit with the other. Right before they climaxed, he flipped her back around and kissed her hard. Then they fell into each other's arms.

"I can never get enough of you," Sin revealed.

Erin's heart fluttered as she wiggled free from his grasp and jumped from the table while grabbing her clothing.

"Go wash up. I'll worry about cleanup duty," he offered.

She did as he said, mostly because she was tired and sure that it had to be past midnight by now. Her mind was only hers momentarily, for Trace would be back in the morning along with the plan they had to come up with to defeat Kayleon and Viola.

When Sin climbed into bed, he pulled her into him while wrapping his arms securely around her waist. "Remember, you weren't born to please the world. You must learn to take care of yourself to become powerful." She knew that, yet knowing and acting were simply two opposing factors.

CHAPTER FORTY-FIVE

"I hope you enjoyed your night because mine was welcomed with recurring dreams of what my life would be like if I were in my body," Trace said.

Erin rubbed her eyelids and yawned while realizing that Sin was missing from her side. A letter fell from the pillow.

Come to the party room once you have eaten, and we will discuss a plan for today. I didn't want you to lose your beauty sleep.

Love,
Sin

"Oh, how sweet," Trace said.

Erin glanced at the bedside and noticed a table with a hot plate and a cup of orange juice next to it. As she lifted it open, her eyes grew wide at the sight of blueberry pancakes, eggs, and bacon.

"This man is determined to fatten me up," she said aloud.

"Yep, he wants to make it to where you won't leave him. If you are too fast, you won't be able to outrun him."

"I liked it when you were quiet. Besides, he's a wolf. I'm sure he can outrun just about anybody in that form."

"Good point."

When she finished eating, she placed on the outfit that Sin laid out for her. It was a silver dress that elegantly flowed down past her knees. It had a sweetheart neckline and tied around the neck with a bow on the back. She slipped on her silver heels and laced them up. Then she brushed out her long brown waves. Once she was finished, she took a quick look in the mirror.

"Too bad you're taken," Trace cursed.

"What was that?"

"Oh, nothing."

"I can't wait to get your voice out of my head," she admitted.

"Likewise, little Sterling."

"Oh great, now we're giving each other nicknames?" she teased.

"Time to go talk to your family, Sparky," she smiled.

"Mine's better," he argued.

#

Erin walked into the party room that smelled of warm amber and bergamot. Her stomach felt tight with knots as everyone's attention gravitated towards her. She held her head high and straightened her posture to maintain the image of confidence.

"Look what the cat dragged in," said a girl with long black curly hair and a cutthroat expression while blocking Erin's path. She wore a dark-green dress that reminded Erin of a siren as it clung against her body, drawing attention to her curves.

"Being born into royalty does not allow you princess treatment, you must earn that title."

"Don't go scaring away our guest, Victoria."

A tall, slightly muscular man with broad shoulders and arms appeared. He wore a black suit and tie and had a tamed black-and-gray beard, hazel eyes with yellow outlines around the irises, and a black leather top hat with golden stitches around the ends and an embroidered image of the letter J.

"Her claws are dangerous, but she means well."

Erin dropped her tense shoulders and extended her hand. "I'll take your word for it. I'm Erin."

He grasped the tip of her hand. "Tyrant, and I'm the head of the Jinx lineage. We take pride in helping each other in this village. Welcome to our home. I appreciate your help with taking down my ex-wife."

She left out the part where it was all her doing and nodded. "Yes, that is the plan."

"I fear that Viola will cause damage to Rosanafalls. But remember only you can give them what they want. And that is power."

"I will do my best to keep that from that happening," Erin assured. This time, I have learned from my mistakes.

Tyrant smiled, "I will hold you to that. Now, I want you to meet your people. We will stand by your side when you are ready to take the throne as Queen."

Those words reminded her that she needed to learn more about them. It is the best way to become familiar with this place.

Tyrant rose is hand up in the air and then made a quick snap with his fingers as the people in the room formed a circle around them. The group was split between men and woman that wore a uniformed black and white tuxedo. Each of their faces were blank as they held their heads high. They revealed courage and confidence through their assertive eyes.

They remind me of assassins and Dalmatians.

"The women will be hiding in the darkest corners of the palace. They are trained to take out targets swiftly and silently, and they will make sure the guards are put down first. The men will be your bodyguards. They don't hide or run away but fight like the decoys. I'm assigning Victoria to be by your side as you search for Trace's dagger. Viola was tied to it once before, and we can do it again. Once you have that in your possession, we will need blood from each of you to bind her soul to the dagger.

"Then we'll place Trace back into his own body. I can't be there, as Victoria will know my presence, for it is the strongest among the family. Remember, she is one of the most powerful witches. But you are destined to rise as Queen, and that makes you the most powerful royal of Rosanafalls. Just like how you play a part in protecting Rosanafalls, we play a role in protecting you."

"Long ago when the world was threatened by power hungry men, a witch and a royal came together to solve the problem. They were able to fill the land with magic and protection by collaboration. The main waterfall is provided with magic to assist the royal with healing when necessary. The witch is allowed freedom from becoming bound to being used for their power."

"Kayleon and Viola are trying to break the peace and take over the power for themselves. We must stop them from ruining what our ancestors have worked so hard for and set the world right before it is destroyed. I know this is a lot of weight to bear, but I believe in you, Erin. And you have our people to back you up."

Tyrant placed a hand on her shoulder.

Erin bowed her head.

"I will do what it takes to save our home."

He lifted her head with his hand underneath her chin.

"You need to raise your head like the future queen-to-be. No woman from the Rosana bloodline ever bows down to a man."

There was a lot to learn. She was no longer the girl who grew up watching scary movies and reading fairytale books. This was the real world, and she had to strengthen her power if she wanted to survive. She did not want to give up on finding her parents. I will become stronger and wiser. My friends and my people are counting on me.

#

As everyone gathered supplies and food, they mounted onto their horses. Sylvian stood on one side of Erin and Sin on the other. "We have plenty of backup, so let's just hope that this goes well," Erin said, looking at Sylvian and then Sin as they strutted forward toward the palace.

Once they were there, Tyrant's crew became no more than shadows, except Victoria. She was forced to help Erin find the dagger and the other hidden weapons.

Victoria cut her eyes towards Erin.

"Once I help you find the dagger, you're on your own."

Erin nodded. Why is she so angry with me?

She followed Victoria's path through the trees while leaving Sylvian and Sin behind. Erin knew Sin was probably furious, but there was a plan to follow, especially if they wanted things to go smoothly.

Victoria had her dark hair smoothed in a slick ponytail and wore a tight black outfit and a belt full of multiple throw knives. She was everything Erin wished she could be—swift on her feet while prepared for battle, and a striking beauty. Her lips were a deep red, and she had on smoky eye makeup to match her dark spirit.

"She was betrayed by someone she trusted. Don't let her get to you," Trace said.

"Yeah, I believe you, but I am not trying to get burned in the crossfire, so I will watch myself around her."

"It takes time. She's going to test you and figure you out before she lets you in."

Victoria shoved Erin down quickly as she noticed Shane walking out of a side door from the palace. He had a snake around his neck and one on each arm as he walked in another direction, lost in thought. Victoria's body shook with disgust.

"Here I am thinking nothing could scare you." Erin teased.

Victoria snapped her head back at Erin.

"There's a difference between fear and being creeped the hell out. I'll take out every one of those god-awful creatures." She shivered.

"Come on," she said, pushing Erin over the walls.

Erin tumbled down as Victoria swiftly landed on her feet like a cat.

"Alright, I need you to teach me how to be a badass like you," Erin said.

Victoria rolled her eyes as they snuck through the door and locked it behind them.

It was dark with soft lighting and warmth in the enclosure as they slowly crept down the hallway. When they rounded a corner, there were wooden stairs that led to a ceiling door. Victoria slowly pushed it open while studying the surroundings, and when the coast was clear, she flipped the door open as Erin followed.

The room was huge and was filled with surrounding glass, like a terrarium with dozens of snakes slithering through the dirt and rocks. "This must be where he keeps his snakes," Erin said while slowly walking around and looking for a door, or some clue to tell where the weapons could be.

There were branches and green plants brushed along the walls, and buckets filled with water in designated locations. Tan-colored rocks and small trees were placed in corners for the snakes to hide behind. At least he takes care of them. She watched as Victoria stepped to avoid them while shivering.

She could tell that this was one of Victoria's fears, even though she was too stubborn to admit it. Fears can feel a bit like loss of control and with the way Victoria is I can understand why she may hide it. Erin placed a comforting hand on her shoulder.

"If you need to leave, I'll understand."

Victoria's expression hardened as she stepped back.

"I follow direct orders from my father, so I'm not leaving your side."

Victoria is a person that I could learn from, I admire her ability to follow through with orders even if she is scared. She proves her loyalty well.

Erin nodded.

"Let's find these weapons. Hopefully they're not in the snake pit itself."

Erin caught a glimpse of Victoria's body twitching from the thought.

CHAPTER FORTY-SIX

"This place is disgusting, let's hur . . ." Victoria fell silent.

"Looking for this?" Zach appeared from the shadows with both the daggers in his hands. Erin ran straight to him and hugged him, practically falling onto him with excitement. He wrapped his arms around her, inhaled her scent, and squeezed her tightly.

Before she could pull away, a loud thud hit the floor. Erin gasped at the sight of Victoria's body lying down in the dirt as two snakes pierced their fangs into her skin.

"Victoria!" Erin screamed.

"Let go. I need to save her."

He only tightened his hold.

"For too long I have been the good guy for you, and it made me a fool. You see, all these years, I thought you were mine, Erin. But it turns out you were doomed to fall into my brother's arms, and like a tangled web, the more you moved, the more you became stuck. I'm done playing the nice guy. I know what I want, and this time I am not asking."

His deep blue eyes, which used to be a haven for her, became a dark pool of water, and nothing more than a stranger was left in them.

"Get over yourself. I don't love you," she screamed as she tried to free herself, but he strengthened his grip. "No matter what you try to do, I will love Sin. Just let me go," she screamed as warm salty tears flooded her cheeks.

"I can't," he whispered in her ear.

"Only by choice!" she seethed.

"Zach, just let me save her. Please, I'm at your mercy." Erin watched as redness and swelling enlarged around the bite mark. Victoria held onto it as blood drooled through the cracks of her hand. Sweat beaded from her forehead as her face paled. Hold on just a little longer Victoria.

"Fucking bastard!" Trace roared. "Erin, distract him. I'm going to help you."

"Zach, maybe I was wrong all this time. I do love you, especially because you took care of me all these years."

She was telling the truth and trying to calm him down as Trace used his powers to pull the daggers from Zach's back pockets.

"Once this is all over, I will choose you," she said as she leaned herself into him and his lips.

He pushed her up against the wall and crushed his lips onto hers. Then he wrapped his hand around her throat while placing pressure on it as he felt for her breasts. She tried to gasp for air, but he buried himself in her. It hurt, and she wanted to cry, to punch him for being so forceful and mean.

He really would take her, right now, as Victoria lay there dying helplessly. That disgusted her. As he snapped his pants down something broke inside of her. It set off a spark of anger as her mind silenced from all thoughts.

"You forget how observant that I am." His face twisted with a smile as he pushed Erin to the ground, and the daggers fell next to them. Pinning her down with his legs, he grabbed one of the daggers and forced it against her throat. "Tell your witch friend to back off before I decide to cut him out," Zach said, holding her own blade against her throat.

Erin felt a desperate need to let him cut her and end her life, to live in the misery of killing the one girl he supposedly loved. She pushed herself toward the blade, feeling the sharp fresh cut as a trickle of blood ran down the edge. "Go ahead, take my life then."

She grimaced in discomfort, and he pulled his hand away. "What's the matter, Zach?" she said as he pulled his shirt off to soak the blood that dripped from her neck. She glanced over and saw that Victoria's lips were a hint of blue. I am running out of time.

Closing her eyes, she tried to feel the power that was given to her at birth. Surely, it couldn't have just been her extracting poison from victims. As she lay there by Victoria she tried to reach out, she hoped that something would just give, but Zach pressed his lips onto her again, and again, until she couldn't feel anything. She just became numb, and hopeless, like a doll. She fell into a deep sleep, and instead of the real world she was back in that dream with her grandmother.

CHAPTER FORTY-SEVEN

SIN'S POV

Tyrant's crew snuck into the palace while disappearing into the shadows.
I place my hand out to halt my friend from following me into danger, "Sylvian, stay put until it is safe."

He nods and allows me to investigate the grounds.

The palace is quiet, but I don't take silence lightly. Anyone could be hiding behind the walls. As I glance up at the balcony, I notice behind the bars glow deep seafoam eyes. When I focus on the body behind them, I realize it's a large muscular sized creature with short hair and rounded ears. I take a step back and admire their ability to camouflage.

"I'll be damned," I whisper.

"They shift into panthers," Sylvian says as he sneaks up behind me.

"Did you know?"

"I had a feeling." He smiled.

As we continue to walk through the hall a faint beeping alerts me.

I turn to Sylvian, and I shout "Bomb!"

The panthers move into action. Luckily, they're able to speed away from the trap. I shift into my wolf form to take the blow and shelter Sylvian. The heat from the explosion burns my fur and there's a sharp ringing in my ears as the force pushes us across the floor.

I fight the pain, as it feels like I have just been tossed off the fastest rollercoaster and thrown into concrete. Men scream in the distance as I force myself up off the floor. Sylvian stands as he holds the back of his head.

"You, okay?" I ask while trying not to wince from the pain inflicted from cuts and bruises.

"I've been better, but I'm alive."

I nod, "Alive sounds good to me."

Screams echo through the room, and when I glance down, I notice a trail of crimson blood splattered across the floor. Massive panthers sneak out from the fire and smoke as they pounce on their victims.

Tyrant's men are tearing apart Kayleon's.

"Of course, the sick bastard would allow his men to sacrifice their lives for him."

A guard wearing black metal and holding a sword runs behind Sylvian as he realizes it by the widening in my eyes. Sylvian acts as though he already saw it coming as he flips around and dodges the sword. A sharp crack strikes my jaw. When I gain my balance, I glance up to find Shane with a smirk on his face.

I straighten my posture and tighten my fists.

"You will pay for that!"

Shane glares at me, "You have something that I want."

A nauseated feeling sets inside my stomach. "And what is that? Dare I even ask?"

"Erin," he says as he swings a sword in my direction.

I jump back in enough time as the tip of the blade rips part of my shirt. "Why?"

"You don't need the reason; I just need her."

My anger takes control, and I can feel myself shift. My voice deepens.

"Over my dead body."

Then I feel a block and realize that I'm unable to shift into my wolf form. "Sin!"

I turned my head back as Sylvian handed me my sword.

"Thanks, I tell him before turning back around to face Shane."

There is a vibration of power that runs through the sword from the emerald jewel inside. I grasp the handle firmly and wait for Shane's next move. He raises the sword up and clashes it down as I catch it with my own.

"Where is Kayleon?"

"He's already gone," Shane says.

My eyes widen, and I almost lose my concentration as he tries to knock my sword out of my hand.

"His motive was never to harm Erin."

"So, you're telling me that we're fighting his men for no reason right now?"

"Why don't you just give up already? I hold a peace to her heart that you'll never have, Sin."

My body heats with fury as I tighten my grip on the hilt of the sword.

"You will never have her," I yell as a volt of energy shocks through my sword and down at the floor. I look at the destruction it has caused and glance back at Shane. Then there is a subtle tapping noise that distracts us. Tyrant's panthers appear as if they were called. Dark shadows with glowing seafoam eyes circle around Shane.

"You're going to lose her to your brother anyway. He's a threat to us all and has been since he took her," Shane says.

"I already know," I say as he finds a way through the snarling panthers.

Sylvian grabs my shoulder. "Sin, something's wrong!"

When I turn around, his eyes are filled with panic.

"What's wrong?"

The realization kicks me in the side, "Let's go!"

I follow him through the hall while jumping over lifeless bodies and puddles of blood underfoot. Everything smells of iron, and it makes my head spin.

When I see Erin lying on the floor next to Victoria, I almost lose it. I bend down and pull her body into my arms. I see the slight rise and fall of her chest, then dried blood trailing from her neck down to her chest. Tightening my arms, I feel a burning sensation in my soul.

CHAPTER FORTY-EIGHT

"I'm helpless. I didn't gather the tools necessary to survive," Erin cried.
"Child, that's just what they want you to think. Flowers are all unique and delicate in their own way, their beauty and gentleness threatened by possessiveness for eternity. Toxins aren't visible. They come from our blood, which is our most powerful weapon." She smiled as she pushed Erin back into reality.

#

Erin opened her eyes while feeling a tug and pulling at her dress and a heavy weight lying on her body. Then she understood what her grandmother had been trying to say all along as she closed her eyes and pictured the sticky black venom inside her bloodstream.

She felt connected to anything that possessed poison such as the snakes that slithered on the floor beneath her. Her bond with poisonous creatures and plants was her magnetic force, connecting her to nature like the power of a tornado ripping through buildings. She was the new threat, the force to be reckoned with.

Zach's eyes locked in on her legs as he slowly began to slide her dress up. He trailed his fingers up her leg as she trembled from the sensation. When she realized that his guard was down, Erin pulled the dagger from his grasp and slashed open her skin. She proceeded to force-feed the blood into his mouth as he pulled back and watched his throat move from swallowing her venomous blood.

The snakes in the room wrapped themselves around Zach's limbs and held a tight grip. She pushed herself up while pulling her dress back down and shot a death glare towards him.

His veins darkened, and he vomited. She didn't have time to worry about him as she knelt to Victoria, holding her cold clammy hand in hers.

Closing her eyes, Erin used as much energy as she could to extract the poison from Victoria's body. Once it was all out, she began to feel weak. She fell next to Victoria while holding her hand, losing consciousness.

#

Erin awoke to a gentle hand caressing her temples, and she could feel warmth from the touch. She glanced up, and she felt relieved as Sin peered back at her with sadness in his eyes.

"You're awake," he whispered, hugging her tightly. Erin looked over to her side and saw that Victoria was gone, and so was Zach's body. She jumped up quickly, but before she could move too fast, she became lightheaded, and Sin caught her fall. "You must have had a lot of excitement. I hate to ask what the hell happened," he continued. "Oh, and Victoria is fine. Sylvian brought her home to take care of her, but she did mention being in debt to you."

Erin held Sin's body and buried her face in his chest, but instead of crying, she felt nothing but rage. Tired of being a pushover, she wanted revenge for everything. More than anything, she wanted to stay in Sin's arms, kiss him, and let him take all the pain away, but she couldn't give in to her desires right now. Slowly, she pushed herself from him while holding onto his hands for stability and dissolving herself into his caramel-brown eyes. She only managed to allow the name to escape her mouth. "Zach."

Sin observed the fresh wounds on her body. The cuts, bruises, and blood caused his eyes to darken. "I'm going to kill him," he said, not looking at Erin, but more toward the direction of the chaos.

She grabbed his hand. "Let's go." Once they walked through the entrance, the world grew silent as they studied the bodies lying on the ground.

The smell of iron from all the blood filled the halls, and most of Kayleon's men were dead. Erin didn't catch sight of Tyrant's people; she wondered if they retreated until Tyrant himself came up behind her.

"The damn fools fled," Tyrant yelled from across the way as she and Sin stood in the middle of dead bodies.

Erin's heart sank to the floor, knowing that this was becoming more frustrating, but she realized her head was silent. "Trace," she said. Nothing, just silence.

A hand slid onto her shoulder as she jerked her body from the touch. When she turned around her eyes widened. The man before her had soft curly hair and leafy-green eyes, along with a grin that showed off his dimples.

"Trace," she screamed while attacking him with a hug. He squeezed her back and let go as Sin pierced him with a death glare. "Viola must have transferred herself into someone else's body," Trace said. "I'm happy to be back." He laughed while combing his hair back with his hand.

"I don't know. I'm going to miss sharing headspace with you, Sparky." She winked at him as he flashed her with a handsome smile.

Trace stopped and gently hugged her again. "I can't say the same. Nothing beats freedom, Sterling."

"For what it's worth, Erin, you held your own back there. It takes strength to overcome your fears and find your power from within. I'm thankful that you saved my sister, and for that, you have earned my respect. I'll be here for you whenever you need me. Don't be afraid to visit. You still have a journey ahead, but you're not alone."

Erin held back the tears welling up in her eyes. "Thank you for your kind words. I may take you up on that offer someday but also know the same goes for you."

"Come on, son, we have a lot of catching up to do," Tyrant called. "We have to figure out a plan to take down your mother."

"Words I never wanted to hear." Trace laughed.

"Your mother is going to be the death of me," Tyrant said.

Tyrant held Erin's gaze, "We will keep in touch."

"Till next time." She nodded then waved them off.

When she looked around, her stomach twisted in disgust. She was surrounded by death.

Sin lightly touched Erin's wrist. "I will take care of this. You just go get cleaned up and breathe."

CHAPTER FORTY-NINE

Although the dead bodies were disturbing, what happened between her and Zach caused bile to rise in her throat. That wasn't Zach, was it? The Zach I know would never hurt me; he was my protector. He loved me. But love can lead to an unhealthy obsession. She would need to learn to control her powers. She never wanted to feel helpless again.

I wonder if Victoria would teach me to fight.

Opening the door, she walked in to find something easy to wear—at this point, she would settle for one of Sin's shirts again.

She found a unique, knee-length black dress with long sleeves and green thorns that were wrapped around the arms. It had a cinched waist and flared out at the bottom. The middle had red amaryllis flowers wrapped around the waistline. "This dress is immaculate."

She allowed the heat to wash her skin from the shower. She wished it were easy to do the same for her recent memories. I will visit Flora and see what she can do to help me out with recovering my memories. Unless I can find my parents.

The water flushed through the cuts on her skin and brought back the nightmares from earlier. After turning the shower off, she climbed into her new dress. I look so tired, she thought, noticing her eyes were more of a bright green from all the crying.

The silver dress that Sin had gifted her was covered in dirt and blood. She clenched the fabric in her hands. Tears stained her cheeks. Being pushed past my breaking point revealed the strength I had all along.

After laying her dress down, she walked toward the door and placed her hand on the knob. A force pulled her hair back, spun her around, and slammed her against the wall and shut her mouth closed. Her heart ached as she realized the trouble she was in.

"Zach?" she tried to mumble, but he pushed harder. "If I let go and you scream, I'll knock you out. You're going to be a good girl and listen," he whispered close to her face. Erin nodded, though she was still going to put up a fight at an opportune time.

"I thought you were smarter," he said. "Ron used his magic, and you killed him." He gave a dangerous laugh.

Erin's chest twisted into knots. "What the hell!" she yelled.

"I ordered him, and damn did he do an excellent job. Luckily you killed him before I could sink my claws into him for trying to hurt you. I am not that low, and the fact that you believed I would do such a thing . . ." He shook his head in disgust.

"But you're not going to like what I planned for us." He gave an even wider grin than before. Unable to move, she stood still as the crippling anxiety took over her body.

"I made a deal with Kayleon." He rolled a strand of her wet hair in his fingers.

She waited as he took his slow sweet time to torture her.

"You will be my wife." He smiled while caressing her cheek with his thumb.

Backing up against the door, she turned her face away. "The hell I am," she yelled.

"And if you don't . . ." He pulled out a phone to show her a man with a silver beard and blond hair who was shackled in chains in a dark room. Her brows furrowed from confusion.

 It can't be.

"Kayleon has your father, and if you follow my rules then he will be freed."

A threatening pain cut through her side. Warm tears rolled down her cheeks. Zach softened his hand against her mouth and sharpened his gaze.

"You marry me, and he is set free."

"I thought you were my friend, Zach! You'll never come back from this."

She meant every word while hoping he would have a change of heart.

"It's already too late for that. If you believed there would be one big happy ending, then you're just as delusional as your mother!"

Erin's eyes widened at the mention of her mom. "Your mother already lost, Erin. I know exactly where she is too. I can help you with that as well."

He dropped his hand from her mouth and lowered it underneath her chin.

"I need you to disappear from Sin. Vanish like a ghost."

There was a sharp stabbing sensation in her heart, but she'd have to separate her feelings. If only she could leave him a note, assure him she'd be okay. I'll be back for you, Sin.

Inhaling deeply, she already regretted her next words.

"I will marry you only when my parents are set free, I will sacrifice my freedom for theirs."

Zach's eyes softened. "You have my word. We free them, and you become my wife."

She hated hearing that. Each time felt like another stab in the middle of her back, a force field that would separate her and Sin even more. Looking back at him, she studied his face, wondering how she could let a man bend her will for his desires.

But she swallowed her hatred down with her pride. Things would be set right again. She had to believe that, or else she wouldn't manage to continue.

He will not win. I'll play his game for now.

"Deal."

"I'll work hard to please you, fiancé," he whispered and reached inside his pocket. Then he pulled out a diamond ring and slipped it onto her finger.

Erin studied the ring. It had a wolf-shaped diamond along with small paw prints wrapping around the band. If this weren't forced, she would melt at how cute it was, but this wasn't what her heart wanted.

She frowned as he leaned in for a kiss. She let him lock his tongue with hers while thinking of Sin, how it felt when he kissed her.

Once he pulled free, her lungs expanded as she gasped for air. Her emotions tried to control her, but she knew that she had to remain calm. Falling apart wasn't optional.

It will be okay.

"Now we have a queen to save, my princess."

He winked at her as though he weren't the demon who had revealed himself to her all along.

SNEAK PEEK

AMARYLLIS

I tiptoe to the waterfall and watch as my mother stares down at a red rose. Guilt stirs in the pit of my stomach, as I know I can't escape the role I was born into.

But I must try.

As I turn around and begin to take my leave, a warm sensation covers my arm. I glance up at the offender and realize an attractive man is there peering down at me. His hair is the color of sand, his eyes a swirl of green and blue, like the color couldn't make up its mind. Not much older than I, around eighteen or nineteen.

He wears a deep-red collared button-down shirt with gold buttons and tan pants. I have never seen such a beautiful man with flawless skin, a muscular build, and a charming way about him.

However, nobody touches me without permission. With that, I yank my arm from his hold and walk in the other direction without a word. I count in my head because normal men can't handle rejection, but to my surprise, when I turn back, he is gone. I won't be here for much longer, so it doesn't matter.

"Mari," my mother calls from above the waterfall. I walk in her direction with a smile on my face to conceal the fear of her discovering my plan.

"How are you doing, mom?" She has hazel eyes and bright blonde hair, and she wears a black dress stitched with red roses, one of her favorite flowers.

Roses are the most common flowers.

I'd rather have something unique like a stargazer lily. She smiles down at me as I come in for a hug. Her soft floral perfume never seems to leave her skin and has become her permanent scent. I instantly feel comfort in her arms.

"I'll forever be grateful for having you as my daughter." She squeezes me slightly.

I want to say, "Mother, must I marry?"

191

But she continues. "Mari, I'm proud of the woman that you've grown into, and I know that your strength and courage will provide a sense of safety and security in Rosanafalls. You will continue to protect our home with the nature of your power, and that will strengthen your bond. Prince Alabaster can manipulate one's power by simply turning them against the host. Wouldn't you find that helpful in case someone turns against you?"

My mother is a smart woman, but her ideas on love don't align with mine. She sees a partner as an opportunity for gain, whereas I could never desire someone simply for their abilities. Falling in love with someone for their personality feels much more meaningful.

"Besides, you have to admit that he's easy on the eyes." She winked and pushed me to the side. "Now, run along and enjoy being a single maiden."

I rolled my eyes and swatted my hand at her. "Yes, mother, I shall."

Too bad I won't be marrying Prince Alabaster. If his name weren't as awful as his attitude, I may have reconsidered. Smiling, I walk off from her side. Before I run home, I catch sight of a familiar gold-haired man who disappears into the forest.

"What are you up to?" I whisper to myself while I follow the mysterious man from earlier. After I throw my long ash brown braid onto my left shoulder, I pull my green dress up, so it won't snag on a twig.

The sun begins to set as I disappear into the forest. Even though I know this is a bad idea, something pulls me further in his direction. Then I see a silver dagger sticking out of his back pocket. As he turns his head at the slight shift of my feet, I quickly dart behind a tree.

A lock of my hair falls into my face as I stand still. I slightly glance around the tree and then continue to follow him as he walks. Why am I following him? This is a bad idea.

"Why haven't I seen you before?" I whisper.

Then he reaches for his dagger, and I begin to panic that he is on to me.

But then there's a shuffle in the leaves ahead, and I witness a small white fawn lying on the ground in front of him. Instantly, I wonder if he means to kill it, and my actions work faster than my logic as I run toward him.

"Wait, don't hurt it!"

Then I forget to watch my step as a stump causes me to fall forward. I brace myself for the fall until I'm caught in the arms of the golden-haired mystery man instead.

Pine and the sweet subtle smell of berries flood my senses. It feels warm and inviting, and I almost do not feel the need to pull away from his arms now that he holds my body securely. When I ground myself and look up at his eyes, I feel as though they have already swept me away into a far-off land where only he and I exist.

Why does my body feel connected to him? As we pull apart there is an ache in my chest.

He turns back to the fawn, and I follow his moves as we both lean down to examine it. Its black beady eyes stare at us helplessly as I see its foot stuck in a thorn bush. The man uses his dagger to cut through the bush carefully and pull the fawn's leg out. Once free, it shakes its leg for mobility and then stills itself. It stares into his eyes with soft wet eyes and then runs off into the forest.

He turns to me while still bent down.

"Not everyone in your world is a monster."

I take a step back and glare at him.

"Not everyone in yours is a saint."

Then his mouth twists upward into a charming smile, and I know that I'm in a ton of trouble because he looks even more attractive. I blush, although it's unlike me to do so.

He stands up to face me, "If I'm not mistaken, for someone who believes the world is full of harm, you have chosen isolation in the woods with a stranger."

I roll my eyes and place my hands on my hips.

"I know how to protect myself from men." I begin to walk in the direction I had traveled down because I can feel the flames in my skin grow higher. Then, an arm wraps around my torso and pulls me up like I'm a doll.

"Men are not the only harmful creatures, little vixen," he whispers into my ear.

My spine tingles as I glance down at a snake slithering down where I had almost stepped. Once it clears, he sets me back down on my feet, and I feel a sudden weakness draw in my knees.

"I'll escort you out of the woods." He wraps his arm around mine and pulls me against him.

"It's quite alright. I can handle my own." I try to wriggle free from his hold. Then a sudden rumble in the sky interrupts my thoughts.

He holds my gaze.

"Are you a fast runner?"

I shrug my shoulders, "Maybe."

I can already feel the shift in the temperature and smell the scent of rain approaching. He grabs my hand and pulls me forward, and I allow him as the rain begins to fall. It splashes onto the earth while replenishing the plants.

I don't realize how free a person can feel in one moment compared to a lifetime. I feel free as I run and laugh at how silly we must look from becoming drenched from head to toe. My body is cold, yet warm from his touch. We take shelter in a cave underneath a waterfall. I glance down at his face, and my eyes falter to his lips.

They are enticing, and the electricity in my body is lit up from a fire that I never knew existed. We waste no time as our lips meet. Thunder shatters and lightning flashes through the cave, and I'm just a woman.

I'm not a princess to be married off to a man for financial or physical gains. I'm not someone who has to have the world piled onto her shoulders. In this moment, I'm like the clouds freed from the rain because they couldn't handle the pressure.

#

When I'm at the top of the stairs to my palace, the golden-haired man holds onto my hand before I can continue further inside.

I soften my face with a smile.

"What's your name?"

Before he can answer the sound of a door opening causes my shoulders to tense.

"Amaryllis!" I freeze and slowly turn around to face the voice.

The man's eyes—one a dark brown and the other a muddy green—look furious.

He wears a long black coat with silver buttons and black slacks. His black hair rests on his shoulders, and there's a shadow from his stubble along his sharp jawline. Although he's an attractive man, his personality doesn't match it. Standing in the doorway is Alabaster, my nightmare.

I furrow my brows. "What are you doing here?"

"Your mother requested that I move into the palace," he said.

He removed his gaze from me.

"Must I ask why my wife is holding another man's hand?"

I was shocked to realize that I was still holding onto his hand. "I am not your wife!"

"Not yet." He smiles.

Slowly turning back around, I hope that this man doesn't judge me too harshly. When I catch his eyes, a flood of guilt glazes through my soul. Disappointment and sadness rests behind them. All I can do is apologize because I can't reveal my plan with the Ala-disaster ruining it. I turn back around and whisper, "I don't wish to marry this man. I hope that you understand."

He slips something into my hand, then gives me a wink and smile.

"I'm Sebastian. See you again, little vixen."

Then he disappears into the night as I hide the note before Ala-disaster catches sight of it. When I turn around, he's right on my heel glaring down at me.

"What is the meaning of this?"

"I forbid you to ever see that man again." Once he clutches onto my wrist, he pulls me inside the palace. His boots are loud, and I feel like a prisoner. I yank my hand from his and quickly run off to my room when he releases me. I read the letter Sebastian slipped into my hand.

It's an invitation to a masquerade ball. I smile. It's tomorrow night, the day before the wedding.

SEBASTIAN

"For you to protect our home, you will need to bond with the princess of Rosanafalls. She possesses abilities that can ignite your own. Then we shall gain the advantage over the court that is threatening us," my mother says to me as we walk down the halls of the palace. The large windows are open, allowing plenty of sunshine to stream through the stained glass. I glance her way and watch as the sun shines onto her silver and blonde curls.

Gifted with natural beauty, she walks through the halls with no makeup on her face and wears a soft, cream-colored gown. She strides in confidence with her head raised. Father suffered from an illness that caused him to pass on early in their years, which left her alone to rule over our court of sunshine. She loved him, yet not in the way that took her breath away. It was more of a companionship. When I was young, she taught me that the heart can learn to love someone, even in the absence of passion.

She turns and stops. "You should venture out and learn more about Amaryllis. From what I hear, she has turned down a handful of potential husbands. She has never seen you around, so you could use that to your advantage. New can be mysterious and inviting." She smiles.

"Mother, I am here to protect you. You shouldn't worry yourself with matchmaking."

"I don't need anyone; we can do this on our own without bringing in outsiders."

As we arrive in the kitchen, she hands me a rose. My brow furrows.

"I also hear that Queen Jenevia is fond of roses." She then hands me an invitation to the ball she has hosted to pull in potential suitors.

"Fine, but no promises." I wrap my arm around her as I intake a mixture of vanilla and amber spice. "See you soon," I say and walk out into the sunlight.

#

Luckily, I can travel through portals to access Rosanafalls, which thrives because it draws power from a waterfall. One that has been a mystery and the main objective of hunters who seek power. If I were to marry the princess, then we would accumulate further protection against the opposite courts. I'd simply defend our home by myself if I had to, but I can understand Mother's point.

When I reach the waterfall, the scent of floral musk hits me. I hear rushing water and then see a woman standing at the top of it. Before I head up, she catches my eye as she paces back and forth, playing with the tailpiece of her hair that rests on her left shoulder. The gown that covers her body is a darker shade of green, much like the mountains.

I'm struck by the gentleness in her eyes way yet moves as she seems to have a war inside of her head. I watch as she paces and throws her hands midair while talking to herself. I can't help but smile. Slowly, I walk toward her, careful not to scare her while reminding myself that she isn't a fox but somehow reminds me of one. When I see that she's about to step on a frog, I grab her arm.

She turns around and freezes. Up close, I can see the silver in her eyes, and I adore them. I feel drawn to her, but I can't understand why. Something within her shifts, and she pulls away, then walks off from me. I feel torn between holding her in my arms and letting her go because she deserves to have free will.

I pull back and walk in the other direction into the forest. It seems I might've messed up my chances with her, but I'm not giving up that easily. A shuffle in the woods catches my attention. I noticed something white and then a cry from an animal nearby. I follow the sounds and kneel to find a fawn's leg stuck in a thorn bush. "Hello, there," I whisper.

It stares at me with helpless eyes.

"I will help you. Just give me a second," I say as though it can understand me.

I shift my focus on the energy it takes to create a portal back home. A ball of fire appears within my palm as it glows brightly as the sun. Then I tossed it in front of me as it stretched into a large black hole with flames surrounding it. As I step through it, I find my way to my room and find the rose jeweled dagger. I stuck it in my back pocket and walked through the portal to find myself in front of the waterfall. Why did it bring me back here?

I glanced up to find the woman that captured my eye from earlier as she spoke with an older woman. When I study the older woman, I realize it is the Queen as she wears a golden rose crown on top of her short blonde hair. I can hear bits of their conversation, and before I leave, the words "marry" and "Alabaster" burn through my mind.

When they seem to be wrapping up, I walk back to the forest to rescue my little friend. Frustration builds through my body as I realize I'll have to work harder at winning Amaryllis's hand. Then I hear leaves rustle behind me. Slightly looking back, I see the tail end of a braid hiding behind a tree. She must be curious about the mystery man. I laugh and allow her to follow me.

As I slide my dagger from the back of my pocket, I hear a scream from behind and see her foot catch onto a stump. I speed toward her just in time while laughing at how clumsy a princess could be. Then I made the mistake of looking down at her lips, so I placed her back down and shifted my attention to the fawn in need of my help.

She follows my move and kneels beside me. I carefully cut the fawn free, and it jumps from the bush, then stares carefully at the two of us. Its eyes soften and find their way to mine, then it runs off into the woods.

As we walk through the woods, I realize that I'm alone with the princess. I didn't expect her to follow me, the sneaky little vixen. My eyes peer down at her feet as I catch sight of a snake wrapped in her path. What is it with creatures beneath her? As she takes a step, I quickly lift her off her feet before she is bitten.

That might have been a mistake because holding her in my arms caused a feeling of never wanting to let go. The snake glides through the leaves and dirt from the scene as a flash of lightning sparks in the sky. I ask how fast she can run and thread my fingers into hers, deciding to take her to one of my favorite hideouts for shelter—a cave just beneath a waterfall.

We're soaked, and she shivers from the temperature drop. Her hair sticks against her skin, and her braid has already loosened to reveal her waves. She takes my breath away, and I can't contain my hunger for her lips and the touch her skin. I want to take her to my home that is full of sunshine and rainbows beyond the rain.

There is desire in her eyes, so I make a decision that hasn't been properly thought out. I place a hand on the side of her face and lower my head down to kiss her lips.

#

When the storm calms, we find our way back to her palace. She asks my name, and then the sound of a door opening distracts us. A man appears in the doorway, his manner egotistical as he held his head high and glared at Amaryllis as if she were a peasant in his presence.

He seems to claim ownership of her, yet she proves him wrong as she clutches my hand firmly. When he calls her "wife," I imagine ripping out his vocal cords. Over my dead body. When she turns around, I can see in her eyes that she wants to be saved. I slipped the invitation my mother had given me in her hands and told her my name.

"Don't worry, little vixen. You will be set free."

MASQUERADE BALL

AMARYLLIS

A bird on the top of the windowsill whistles its song, its feathers blue like the sky. There's a white and dark blue pattern on its wings, as well as a black line around its neck. Birds are unique in their colors and abilities to fly and communicate through whistles and songs. To possess such an ability would be phenomenal.

"If only I could fly away from this place and never look back," I whisper. I open the window to allow the breeze to enter the room. I flinch as the sound of fluttering wings pass my face and fly inside. I place my hands on my hips and examine my room.

"Now, where did you go?" I whisper.

"I apologize for the intrusion," a voice says, breaking the silence. I spin around and see a tall and slender woman. Her beauty is celestial. Her silver hair falls to her waist, and her eyes are partly violet and ice blue. She wears a navy-blue dress with the lace of the stars and moons printed onto her chest. Her dress flows down to her legs with waves as blue as the ocean.

"How did you get in here?"

"You opened the window," she says, as though that's a simple enough answer.

"How?" I ask.

She maintains eye contact with her posture upright.

"I'm a shapeshifter," her voice soft and slow like a melody.

My brow furrows. I've heard of them before, but my mother said they were extinct. "I was unaware of any shapeshifters nearby."

She curved her mouth into a smile. "Humans can become oblivious to secrets that surround them. We have been around, but only in secrecy. I show myself to you because I respect your recent actions. I have come to thank you for rescuing my daughter."

I cock my head to the side, and she continues. "The fawn. She has not fully understood how to use her abilities. I had paid the prince of sunshine a visit first, and he has led me to you."

I can't help the grin that spreads across my face at the new topic among us. She takes a step closer.

"He wants me to bring you to him. If that is what you desire, of course.

I am silent because—well, as much as I would like the easy way out—I know my mother would lose her mind. But do I really want to spend my life with Alabaster without at least pursuing another option? I think about it for a moment while staring at the ceiling and hoping for the right answer to come along.

I raise my head back up into her direction.

Would you be able to take me to the ball?"

She bows her head. "Of course. I shall return." Then she transforms back into a bluebird and flies out into the sky.

My eyes widened at the shock of the magic and how quickly it had been done. It was as if I had blinked my eyes and she was the blue jay that had been resting on my window seal.

How strange, yet extraordinary.

A sudden knock at the door attracts my attention. I rush to pull it open. Alabaster is waiting on the other side, and my smile drops instantly.

He leans into my space, and I hesitate with the thought of wanting to push him away.

"I have cleared my day to spend time with you."

I roll my eyes because I am not interested in spending time with this man. "Actually—"

"Amaryllis. I didn't ask. You are ordered." My brows crease as I feel lightheaded from his response.

Today will be the last day that I must deal with this man. I refuse to marry someone who orders me around. I cross my arms and stare at his soulless eyes. He grins and walks toward me, then places one hand on my waistline and the other underneath my chin. "Or we could simply just stay here."

He pulls my chin up and begins to lean in, but I back away from his hold.

"Give me a minute." I push him back and slam the door shut. I simply cannot marry this man.

Tears of frustration begin to fall. The light reflects something in my eyes, and as I glance up, I notice something on my bed. I pick it up and feel its lightweight fabric from the inside and a gold-plated outer piece. It's a vibrant collage of red and orange painted onto a gold fox mask, for the masquerade ball. Then I remember his words: little vixen.

#

Sabbath gallops along our usual path. I admire the shine on his charcoal black fur and thank him for knowing me so well. Then I glance back at Alabaster, a distance away on his white horse. "Amaryllis, slow down."

But instead, I giggle and pat Sabbath on the side, "Let's ditch Ala-disaster."

When we arrive at my favorite spot, I look out at the mountain view. I realize the beauty the world has to offer as the tension in my shoulders release. After

I climb down carefully, I hand Sabbath an apple and pet his nose.

"I will miss you. I wish I could take you with me," I whisper. A twinge of guilt causes my stomach to turn into knots. The sounds of hoofs clacking against the dirt grow closer as Alabaster jumps from his horse in anger. He paces in my direction, but Sabbath becomes overprotective and blocks me from his view. A gun resounds through the air, causing my balance to falter as I peek around the corner at Alabaster.

My body straightens as I set my eyes on him. "Don't even think about hurting my horse."

His eyes darken. "Obey me, and he will remain unharmed."

"Shh, it's alright, let me handle this," I whisper to my horse. I pat Sabbath on the head to calm him down and walk toward Alabaster.

"I will kill you if you ever hurt him."

He pushes me down onto the grass and covers my mouth.

"You're a helpless princess. Your threats mean nothing."

I slap him, and he forces my wrist back onto the ground. I can feel a twinge of pain from the tight hold he has on me.

"I can take you right now, and there's nothing you can do about it." He laughs. Energy forms in the pit of my lower stomach as I feel the need to hurt him. Then Sabbath kicks his feet into the air and pounds them next to us.

Alabaster loosens his hold as I roll out from his grasp and onto my feet. I am close to the edge of the cliff when he stands up.

Alabaster grinds his teeth while glaring down at me.

"I am done playing games with you. Once we're married, you will listen to me."

"I am never marrying you!" I scream as his back is turned while he examines his horse. He stands still, and then before I can react, there's a bang. The noise sends a sharp pain through my ears and echoes through the air as Sabbath thuds against the ground.

I hear nothing but the ringing in my ears, and I feel like my heart has been ripped apart. He mounts onto his horse. "Let this be a warning. If you choose to disobey me, you'll lose everything that you care about. Find your way back," he says and leaves.

I cling to Sabbath as tears soak my face. Red crimson blood and the smell of iron fill my nostrils as I tear off a piece of my dress to apply pressure to the wound. I placed a hand on his chest to feel his pulse still beating. My heart is shattered; this horse has been in my life for years. He will not die today. "Please hold on. Please," I beg.

"Please, somebody!" I scream as loud as I can until my throat becomes dry and irritated from the crying.

Yet I feel all alone and helpless at this moment. I almost give up hope until I hear a voice from behind.

"Amaryllis, what has happened here?" Her soothing voice finds me as I slowly raise my head up from my horse.

She kneels in front of him, and her hand hovers above his wound. A blue color forms around her body as the bullet flies into her hand. Then the hole begins to cover up and heal. It's like watching a magic trick. I can't believe what I'm seeing.

Sabbath slowly shakes his head and then pulls himself up from the ground. Feeling ecstatic, I ran to his side and squeezed him tightly. "You're not leaving my sight again," I promise as tears stain my cheeks. The pain in my chest in my chest softens from relief.

I turn to the woman. "Thank you."

She nods with a gentle smile. "Let's get you cleaned up and ready for the prince." "What's your name?" I ask before placing my hand into hers.

Her smile is radiant and soft.

"Elmina."

#

The sun has set, and I'm wearing a floor-length, sleeveless dress with a sweetheart neckline that matches the color of my mask. My hair is braided as it falls to my back while small strands of hair fall on each side of my face.

Elmina's eyes sparkle when I put on my mask. "How do I look?"

She walks over toward me and says, "Like you're the Queen of Sunshine herself."

My heart skips a beat at the sound of that. But I am meant to be Queen over Rosanafalls, not the Sunshine court.

#

The sky isn't dark enough as a swirl of purple and pink appears beyond the trees. A subtle breeze reminds me of the sea as I glance at the mansion before Elmina and me. It's bright and luminous with multiple windows displaying painted humans worshiping the sun. The gate opens for us as a spotlight illuminates the walkway toward the entrance. Birds chirp from a distance as we walk to the stairs.

Once I have worked up the courage to climb them, I realize that Elmina has vanished.

I sigh. Why did she disappear?

Once I step inside the mansion, I'm greeted by a tall man dressed in a black-and-white tailored suit. He leads me into the ballroom where the lights are dimmed as the music from a harp plays. I'm then surrounded by people wearing masks and long exquisite ball gowns.

Then my arm is pulled in a direction, and I'm no longer surrounded by people. A man with blue and green eyes stares down at me from a fiery red mask and gold suit with a red tie. As he pulls me into his chest, I inhale his scent of pine and berries. I feel calm and steady and like I don't want to move.

"It's nice to see you, little vixen."

I smile. "Likewise." We spin around the room, and although I know my feet touch the ground, it feels as though they don't. He pulls me tight around my waist, and his touch is all that matters. My fears are silenced because right now all I can imagine is the possibility of a future with this man.

A loud clapping noise echoes through the room and brings me back to reality. My breath hitches when I hear his boots. I turn slowly and witness Alabaster and his men staring at us. Then I remember his threat and feel a strike of panic rise in my pulse. Sebastian has already moved his body in front of mine.

"You are not welcome in my home," Sebastian says. His body is firm, and he looks as though he is prepared for a fight. I can't allow him to be in the middle of my mess. If he were hurt because of me, I couldn't forgive myself. I feel the warmth from his body as I look down and see small flames rise from his fingers.

Alabaster's face twists in anger as he points in my direction.

"Amaryllis, come here," he demands.

Sebastian tightens his hand into a fist as smoke slides through the cracks of his fingers. "She is not yours!"

Alabaster walks closer and finds his way to me. My heart races as breathing becomes heavier and harder. My eyes welp with tears, but I keep them from falling. He will not have that satisfaction. He only peers into my eyes. I am waiting for the leverage that he will have to trap me.

"If she wants her mother alive and well, she should choose wisely."

There it is the one threat he could use to bend my will.

"Where is she?" I push my way past Sebastian. Alabaster grins, and I feel disgusted that he thinks this is all just a joke.

"Safe, for now. But you might want to hurry if you'd like a cure for the poison that's currently settling in her system." I clutch my chest from the pain I feel from those words.

Freedom is unattainable when you are a bird or a flower that can be kept. Why allow something so precious to be free when you can capture it for your selfish desire? My options are limited. I must save my mother and marry this awful man. It's only a matter of time before reality sets in. I can't pretend to live freely anymore. He won't let me be free.

Turning to Sebastian, I pull my mask off to hand it back to him. I can't think of what to say as I see the pain reflected in his eyes. The colors that keep me guessing are green or blue. As he grabs my hand, I feel a rush of heat. He pulls me into him and whispers into my ear. "This isn't over. I will find you."

I wipe a tear that falls from my eye because I can't contain the overwhelming sadness in my own heart. I separate from him and find my way beside Alabaster.

A flashback floods my mind as I remember my mother's words:

"I didn't just name you after some pretty flower. Amaryllis survives through the winter while disregarding the rules of nature. Resilience is a woman's greatest weapon in becoming a powerful queen."

TILL NEXT TIME

I think we can all agree that Sin isn't just letting his little jackrabbit disappear that easily. Prepare for the next book, which will reveal more truth, heartaches, spice, and romance. Remember, through every storm there is a rainbow waiting on the other side. We may not make it out without scars and bruises, but we can always change our perspective to enjoy the beauty in life. There will be many reveals, new journeys, and points of view in the next narrative.

ACKNOWLEDGMENTS

"A writer falls in love with their story, because it is their vision and creation that collaborated into a reality.

When I realized my passion for writing at a young age, I felt like it became the antidote that I needed for healing. Writing distracted me from the trauma I had endured as a child. I became fascinated with how any world and situation could be made into a story. It became an escape from my reality, and it saved my life. It is a part of me that I could never throw to the side because I truly love it. I've fallen in love with this story and the characters, and I hope that you have as well.

I'm thankful to you, readers, for taking the time to fall into my story, one that I had been working on for what feels like an eternity. Readers and writers are just alike as we both crave the same thing, escape. We want a story that places us into a world full of mystery, magic, romance and wonder. Without books I would be distraught. And I have learned that each voice is unique, so if you have a story to share, please don't hesitate because I would love to read it.

As for Rosanafalls, there will be more answers revealed in the next book, and I'm thrilled that you've joined this journey. Just hold on tight, and I promise we will resume to our next destination. The characters' terrain will be a little rocky but remember you're safe with me.

I want to start by first thanking my editor, Shaina Clingempeel. I admire your professional and altruistic demeanor. Your advice and information has challenged me to become a better writer. I have learned so much from the edits you provided for me. I've smiled about how uplifting you are about my work. Because of you my dreams are becoming a reality as Rosanafalls will be revealed to the world.

John, I'm so happy I've had you by my side through these years. Thank you for being my anchor through it all. You've been supportive of my dreams and allowing me to spend multiple nights locked up in the room as I worked on this story. I love you.

To my family and friends, thank you for your support and encouraging me to follow my dreams. I love you very much, and yes, you will all have signed copies of my book first.

All my writer and friends on socials, I am grateful for your kind words and support. Because of you I could share my journey and pieces of me that I had never thought of revealing. I realized that there is a community full of people who will work together in promoting success for one another. I will always be here to support my Queens and Kings. You mean the world to me.

To each of my brothers, I hope you all realize that your life is what you decide. I want each of you to be happy, no matter what it takes. Everyone's dreams and lives look different, and that is the beauty in it all. We are all unique. I will always be here for you and protect you in any way I can, just as you have for me. Love, your sister.

Allison, you're such a sweetheart, and I'm thankful for your feedback. I will always be here for you, and I want you to become successful in what makes you happy. Just remember, that's the only thing that matters. Choose what you enjoy and remember you're the only one who can dictate the outcome of your future and happiness.

Laura, we've had our ups and downs, but I'll tell you what—our friendship will last till the end of time. Thank you for being my rock, listening to my cries, and spending much-needed time with me. I love you so much.

Tiffany, I will always hold you dear to my heart. Life has thrown us both some curveballs, but we are survivors. I'm just thankful that you've made it through and were able to turn your life around. I love you. Thank you for cheering me on.

Grandmother Jenny, I know you're not with us today, but I will cherish my childhood memories of you. You were my person; I gravitated toward you like a sunflower to the sun, and I'll always think of you as time passes. Some of the material I've written in this novel comes from memories we shared. The ocean will forever bring me back to the day we walked on the sand while searching for sand dollars together.

Grammy Donna, you are a beautiful soul, and I am lucky to be your granddaughter because I feel how much you love me and your other grandchildren. You never forget us and are always a call away when we need you. A grandchild can rarely share that experience with their grandparents, and I am just so happy that you have supported me through this journey. I will continue to be thankful for your presence in my life. I love you so very much.

I would like to thank my creative writing, journalism, and professional writing skills, as well as my English teachers who encouraged me to keep writing. You all made me realize that I was good enough through my essays, poems, and assignments. I enjoyed every class and will always uplift teachers because they mold us into intelligent beings.

Again, reader, please continue with the next chapter in this series, as there is more to be revealed. Don't jump off the bandwagon just yet or you may miss the fireworks.

Yours truly,

Erica Rogulski

ABOUT THE AUTHOR

Erica Rogulski lives in South Carolina with her two dogs, Gracie and Tigger. When she is not writing, she enjoys reading a variety of genres including the spicy, and unhinged ones. She is a video gamer, Tomb Raider and Resident Evil being her favorite. Her preferred holiday is Halloween as she enjoys rewatching the classic shows Casper and Halloweentown, along with attending spooky events such a fright night.

Visit her on Socials:

@ericarogulski
Bookish-Fantasy on Tik-Tok
Erica Rogulski fantasy/romance writer on FB
@ericarogulski on Instagram